and
BENEATH THE ASHES

E
tel
S

ple   cal

"   gh

"   you
V   ers
(ing

s."

Books by Sue Henry

MURDER ON THE IDITAROD TRAIL
TERMINATION DUST
SLEEPING LADY
DEATH TAKES PASSAGE
DEADFALL
MURDER ON THE YUKON QUEST
BENEATH THE ASHES
DEAD NORTH

And in Hardcover

COLD COMPANY

SUE HENRY

BENEATH THE ASHES

AN ALASKA MYSTERY

AVON BOOKS
An Imprint of HarperCollinsPublishers

AVON BOOKS
An Imprint of HarperCollins *Publishers*
10 East 53rd Street
New York, New York 10022-5299

Copyright © 2000 by Sue Henry
Excerpt from *Dead North* copyright © 2001 by Sue Henry
ISBN: 0-380-79892-1
www.avonbooks.com

First Avon Books paperback printing: June 2001
First William Morrow hardcover printing: August 2000

Avon Trademark Reg. U.S. Pat. Off. and in Other Countries, Marca Registrada, Hecho en U.S.A.
HarperCollins® is a trademark of HarperCollins Publishers Inc.

Printed in the U.S.A.

10 9 8 7 6 5 4 3

This one's for my sons, Bruce and Eric,
protagonists of my favorite,
most gratifying, intriguing,
and continuing
suspense stories

The fire which seems extinguished often slumbers beneath the ashes.

—Pierre Corneille, *Rodogune*

BENEATH
THE ASHES

Prologue

IT ISN'T DYING THAT FRIGHTENS MOST OF US, BUT THE IDEA of an agonizing death can give us shuddering cold sweats in the dark. Awareness of our vulnerability makes us gawk and wince at flaming pileups on the freeway, prompts us to entreat our gods for a painless departure in the ignorance of our beds. It is the nightmare notions that break us. And, of all fearsome concepts, the dread of fire is appalling in its ability to reduce us to gasping, gibbering, herky-jerky puppets.

If Joan the Maid had been nothing but a mad peasant girl who heard voices, she might have passed unremarked into the mists. It was the way of her dying that secured her a bright spark in the memory of man, for we remember fire. We may not instantly recall the names of our high school teachers, the current crop of politicians, or what we last watched on television, but we know the significance of Nero's fiddle, the MGM Grand, and Mrs. O'Leary's cow.

As necessary as it is to our daily well-being, fire is

1

never to be trusted, for it lives. It moves, speaks, breathes, consumes, stalks, and inspires in us a plea to drown, freeze, or even bleed.

Anything but burn.

1

———◈◈◈———

ON AN EARLY EVENING IN MID-MARCH, JESSIE ARNOLD was sitting on the floor by her huge sofa, surrounded by a gang of half-grown pups from two different litters that she had brought into the house so they could become accustomed to handling and interaction with a human, as well as to the other dogs. The seven pups tumbled happily on and around her, staging mock battles, chewing each other's tails and ears, crawling onto her lap for rations of the affection she was happy to give them. They were still cute and babyish at this age, falling over the big feet they were quickly growing into, curious about everything, full of life, and beginning to display individual characteristics that she was assessing closely, looking for traits that would make them good working sled dogs later on.

Her racing lead dog, Tank, the long-suffering father of four of them, had been trying to take a nap near the wood-burning stove, but he found it impossible, as some of the pups that couldn't crowd onto Jessie's lap turned their focus on him. Jeep and his

smaller sister, Daisy, were being especially attentive
to their dad. When they had run around and over him
several times, faking attacks to encourage him to join
their exuberant games, he finally grew tired of their
nonsense and growled a warning in Jeep's direction.
Jeep stopped in his tracks and growled back, which
amused and interested Jessie. The young dog was
showing independence and assertiveness, qualities
that could indicate a possible leader in the making for
a future racing team.

Socialization with humans early in the life of sled
dogs was important. It established relationships while
the pups were still imprintable and became a positive,
normal part of their lives, making training easier and
helping them develop skills for working with people
and other dogs. She sincerely hoped Jeep had inherited
the attitudes and abilities that made Tank the best
leader she had ever had.

Jessie had been trying to read an article she had
found in the latest *Mushing Magazine* on summer
training for sled dogs. She tossed it onto the sofa when
the adolescent gang of pups made it impossible to concentrate. Now, over their yips and immature growls,
she glanced at the magazine longingly, then suddenly
hesitated, looked toward the window across the room,
and held her breath for a few seconds to listen intently.
It had grown very quiet outside. The faint repetitious
murmur of rain that had been a background for the last
two days had stopped.

Shoving two pups from her lap in order to get up,
she walked across to the window that overlooked her
dog yard.

Snow. It was finally snowing again. Big white feathery flakes were falling thickly through the air, melting as they hit the wet ground. But here and there they were beginning to stick. The roof and hood of Jessie's pickup truck were already turning white. It would be wet, heavy snow, but at least it was not the unseasonable rain that had been turning the trails she used for training to slush.

Glancing at the large thermometer mounted outside facing the window, she saw the temperature had dropped from well above freezing to twenty-eight degrees. As she watched, it moved to twenty-seven. Still falling. No wonder the rain had turned to snow, and how welcome. Since it had started this late in the day, she thought it would probably continue into the night, replacing some of the old snow the rain had melted and, possibly, allowing her to take out a team or two tomorrow.

Finished with the Yukon Quest, the last race she would run this season, she and Billy Steward, the young musher who helped her at the kennel, had been working hard with mixed teams, one- and two-year-old dogs harnessed together with experienced ones. The days of rain had put a halt to that. Jessie, pleased with the progress they were making, was frustrated at being housebound. Running sled dogs in the rain was a miserable business that she and other mushers avoided when they could. It took all her attention to train inexperienced dogs without adding bad weather to the equation. Untangling the snarls they managed to get themselves into several times a day was work enough. It was fun to play inside with the pups who were not yet close to real training age, but it was more challenging to be out on the trails.

Two of the pups had quietly followed her to the window, and she almost tripped over them as she turned back into the room but managed to step wide, missing both. Crossing to the phone on her desk, she dialed Billy's number. The pups trotted along behind her, not giving up their attempt to reclaim her attention, but they were quickly sidetracked by a patchwork pillow that had fallen from the sofa. With a long reach she snatched it away, knowing how soon its feathers would be floating around the room like the snowflakes outside if she left it to their sharp teeth.

"Have you looked out?" she asked Billy. "The snow's coming down like crazy. If it keeps up we can run tomorrow. Right—about seven. Yes. Okay."

Dropping the phone back in its cradle, she returned to the window to watch the falling flakes with satisfaction, unwilling to sit back down. She wished she could go out now but knew there wouldn't be enough new snow until morning, and the plastic runners on her sled would grind themselves to tatters on the rocks and bare ground the rain had uncovered.

Flopping down on the sofa, she ignored the pups for a minute and picked up the magazine again. When she realized she had reread a page for the third time and had no idea what it contained, she tossed it to the opposite end of the large sofa and stood up again.

"That's it," she declared. "Time for all you guys to go back to the puppy pens with your moms."

Tank raised his head, ears pricked, alert to the possibility of activity in the offing. The pups, as usual, ignored her. Jeep and Daisy had settled into a semi-snooze, curled up next to Tank near the warm stove, but they scrambled up as he moved.

"Enough sloth. I'm going to Oscar's for a beer and a game of pool."

Tank was on his feet in a bound, tail wagging enthusiastically, recognizing the words *going* and *Oscar's*.

"Okay," Jessie told him, giving in with a grin. "You can come."

A significant number of other mushers, who had also been unable to take their dog teams out, would probably drop into their favorite pub this evening to commiserate with each other at the rain-enforced intermission in their training runs. Some human company will do me good, she thought, gathering up the puppies, which she transported back to their pens in squirming, protesting armfuls.

Before leaving, she added a log to the stove and turned off all the lights but one in the kitchen. Standing for a moment in the driveway, she raised her face to let the snowflakes fall on it, stuck out her tongue, and tasted one. Delightful.

With Tank sitting beside her in the truck, she negotiated the potholes of the long drive to the highway and headed for Oscar's, her mood lifting with the thought of going somewhere.

A little over five miles down the road she swung the pickup into the wide parking lot in front of Oscar's Other Place, which she was pleased to find was full of vehicles as she had anticipated.

When he had built the semi-isolated rural pub a few

years earlier, Oscar Lee had called it the Double
Dozen, for it was twelve miles from the main highway
and just over twelve from where he lived, farther along
Knik Road. The name, however, had never worked for
the simple reason that most of his customers were already familiar with Oscar's first bar in the nearby community of Wasilla. With the possessiveness of regulars,
they had referred to the new pub as Oscar's Other
Place, ignoring anything to do with double pubs or
dozens of miles. So it wasn't long until he bowed to the
inevitable, replaced the sign out front, and made it official. "Oscar's Other Place" it became and remained.

From the day it opened, located in the middle of an
area popular with racing aficionados where there were
more sled dogs per square mile than people, Oscar's
had quickly become a haunt for local mushers, han-
dlers, and their followers. So many of them stopped by
to warm up during training runs that Oscar kept a per-
petual kettle of chili or stew steaming fragrantly in a
huge slow cooker, and provided straw for their dogs to
curl up on in back of the pub.

Year-round, something was always happening at the
bar. Dart and pool tournaments were popular. Three or
four tables of bridge players usually collected on Sunday afternoons. A large television set above the bar
featured regular sports in their seasons, accompanied
by potluck dinners and many friendly wagers. A pig
roast became traditional on Super Bowl Sunday. Every
summer the Other Place sponsored a softball team that
carefully kept its error count just high enough to remain solidly in the B league, where the game was less
intense and more fun.

The battered jukebox was packed with an astonishing collection of much loved easy listening and country-western oldies. When an unwitting serviceman delivered a new machine full of current hits—and the result was a unanimous insurrection of patrons who threatened to toss it and him into the nearby creek—the antique player and its old tunes were quickly restored.

The walls had gradually been covered with an enviable collection of mushing photographs and memorabilia donated by mushers and their followers—a fascinating history of the wide variety of modern races across the state, mixed with reprints of early twentieth century heroes of the sport.

Coming through the second door of the pub's Arctic entry, and shaking the snow from the blond curls above her gray eyes, Jessie was brought face-to-face with an image of herself on the opposite wall. It portrayed her now-legendary run down Front Street in Nome the year that she had finished the Iditarod in second place. Tall and slim, she smiled for the camera, her lead dog, Tank, beside her. Though the photo had always pleased her it now precipitated a slight frown at a figure on a snowmachine in the background.

Alex Jensen was the Alaska state trooper she had met during that race and with whom she'd shared a relationship until a month ago. The disappointment they had both experienced at the separation was a still-tender emotional bruise she consciously refrained from fingering.

She moved on into the warm, crowded interior of the Other Place, Tank walking politely beside her. The large room smelled of rain-damp parkas, wool hats, and mittens; and it was noisily cheerful with conversation, laughter, the crack of pool balls sent flying around on two tables, and the thump of darts hitting a board in an out-of-the-way corner in the back.

The interior was decidedly informal, with little of what could actually be termed decor. The walls were concrete blocks painted a bright terra-cotta, the floor a worn gray-green commercial vinyl tile. About a dozen square pedestal tables sat among a functional assortment of plain metal chairs with padded plastic seats. The bar stools were of two different types, with and without backs.

Like many rural Alaskan pubs and roadhouses, the appeal of the Other Place had little to do with interior decor. It was a casual place where mushers could drop by in their working clothes—often grubby but warm parkas repaired with duct tape to retain their down—track snow or mud onto the floor without concern, and not worry about offending anyone with the smell of the dogs they drove and fires they built and hovered over.

"Hey, Jessie. Wondered if you'd show tonight. Pretty sad out there, isn't it?" A friend put out a hand.

"It *was* sad, Hank—now it's *snowing*. We can run tomorrow. *Yes!* Wanna play some pool?"

"Sure! Your turn to put up a quarter."

Tank sat down beside her and looked around carefully for Oscar as Jessie paused next to the blond, bearded man who had swiveled on his bar stool to greet her, exhibiting the front of a dark blue sweatshirt that bore a Crabb's Corner logo, one of the stops on the annual Yukon Quest, a race between Whitehorse and

Fairbanks. A well-mannered dog was as welcome as its driver in the Other Place, and, though his dignity would never have allowed him to beg, Tank was not unaware that Oscar kept a large jar of homemade moose jerky behind the bar for his four-legged friends.

"There's my buddy," Oscar said, coming around the end of the bar that ran along one side of the big room and leaning down to give Tank a few friendly pats and a sizable chunk of jerky. "Such a gentleman. No sleds today—right, Jessie? How're you keeping?"

"Bored stupid, or I'd have been here earlier." She grinned in response. "You?"

"Oh, tolerable. What'll you have?"

"A Killian's, thanks, and Tank thanks you, too."

His broad answering smile included a glance at the husky, who now lay on the floor, gnawing contentedly on his treat.

As the bottle of lager was efficiently set in front of her, along with a frosty mug, an arm waving on the other side of the room and a call from a woman seated at one of the small tables attracted Jessie's attention.

"Hey, Jessie, you ran the Quest this year. Come settle an argument."

"Sure. Let me know when we're up, Hank."

"Yup."

Pouring the contents of the bottle into the mug, Jessie sipped it and wiped a bit of foam from her upper lip. She laid a quarter on the edge of the nearest pool table as she carried her mug across the room, then pulled an empty chair to the table where three mushers were closely examining a map. Questions met her before she could sit down.

"The trail still goes across Lake Laberge before the Chain of Lakes, doesn't it?"

"No, they changed it last year. Now you go up the Tahini River, north to Braeburn, then east to the chain. It skips Lake Laberge completely."

"After that it's the same?"

"Except for the new run into Pelly Crossing."

"Trail any good?"

"Depends. Pelly's great—best of the race. Between Braeburn and Carmacks it's a nightmare—real pinball alley of turns and trees. There were a lot of broken sleds this year."

"You got through okay."

"Yeah, but I had to take it real slow. One rookie got to Carmacks, built a fire with the splinters of his sled, and went home."

The four mushers fell quickly into a detailed discussion of the international distance race and its difficulties that lasted until the game at one of the pool tables ended.

"Hey, Jessie, we're up."

For the next hour she and Hank successfully met all challenges, defended their claim to the table, and won the beer they drank. Finally running out of opponents, they played each other till Jessie won two out of three games and quit, returning the cue she had used to its rack on the wall.

"Come on, Shark"—Hank tried to coerce her with a wolfish grin. "Let's make it three out of five."

"Push my luck? I don't think so. Next time you put up the quarter."

"Aw . . . well . . . But I'll be practicing."

"Like you *really* need it. Dropping the eight ball was a mistake you never make. I'd be an idiot not to take what I can get."

Collecting her raincoat from a hook on the wall by the door, Jessie looked across the room at Tank, who had been resting cozily under a table, muzzle on paws. With a jerk of her head toward the exit, she let him know it was time to leave. He got up, stretched, and wound his way between the tables to her side.

"Hold up a minute," Oscar called, wiped his hands free of soapy dishwater, and emerged from behind the bar with another piece of jerky.

"One for the road, buddy," he said, giving it to Tank.

"Thanks, Oscar," Jessie said, keeping a straight face at the sight of a lock of thinning hair that stood straight out from one side of his head. "This place is a port in a storm."

"Sure busy tonight," he said. "You guys don't like being cooped up by bad weather."

She glanced around at the chairs and bar stools that had gradually emptied. It was late and only a few people were left, finishing their drinks and a last round of darts. At a table in one corner near the stove, a man in a blue plaid shirt slept with his head on his arms, face turned away toward the wall.

"Who's that? Tom?"

"Nope. Not a regular—Bob something—friend of Warner's. Getting over a bad cold, so it probably got to him, because he only had a couple of beers. I'll let him sleep while I swamp out—wake him up when I'm ready to leave."

It was like Oscar to let the guy get his rest, and

Jessie smiled to herself. No wonder he was so well liked and his pub so popular. Everyone felt welcome and at home here, because, unless they seriously abused his hospitality, they were like family. Like family, they were also protective of their own and respectful of Oscar's. Outsiders were carefully evaluated with watchful politeness, obnoxious behavior was never tolerated, car keys were requested and usually cheerfully relinquished by anyone whose alcohol intake was such that they shouldn't be driving, disputes were swiftly broken up or contained. Only once had Jessie seen a fight threaten to develop, and the half-in-the-bag visitor was immediately and firmly made aware that he should forget the Other Place existed and "don't let the door hit you on the way out!"

"See you soon." Oscar waved at Jessie, as she left, calling good night over her shoulder.

The drive home was short, but Jessie was yawning by the time she had pulled up in front of her cabin and clipped Tank back onto the line by his box in the yard. The snow was still falling, if anything, more heavily than before. Each box in the dog yard now had an inch-deep layer of white on its roof.

"Oscar's pretty good to you," she told Tank as she rubbed his ears and scratched his back fondly. "Good night, good fella."

When she came through the front door across the room on her big desk, the answering machine was blinking, and, removing coat and boots, she padded across in her wool socks to play back the tape, which contained no messages, only two hang-ups. Clearing it, she was turning toward the bedroom with another yawn when the phone rang again.

"Arnold Kennels."

There was only the sentient silence of an open line.

"Hello. Anyone there?"

"Jessie?" a hesitant voice queried.

"Yes, this is Jessie. Who's this?"

"It's Anne, Jessie."

"Anne?"

"Anne Holman. Don't you . . . remember me?"

"*Anne Holman?* My God, I don't believe it. It's been years. How are you? *Where* are you?"

In a part of her mind, Jessie was suddenly ten years younger, spending the winter in a borrowed cabin far from road or highway, just getting started in the sled dog racing game, and relishing miles of wilderness in which to train her dogs. A mile away on the wilderness trail that ran past her cabin, Anne Holman had lived in a similar log structure with her husband, Greg. With only each other for female company, she and Jessie had grown to be good, casual friends, encouragement for each other through a long cold winter, support in time of need or trouble.

"I'm in . . . ah . . . in Seattle."

Jessie's surprised response was a tumble of questions. "Seattle? Are you living there? What—"

Anne interrupted. "No . . . No, Jessie, I just flew in from Denver—a couple of hours ago. Jessie, I'm sorry, but—I'm in trouble."

"What kind of trouble?" Alert now, her attention was caught and she focused on the words and the stress-filled tone of the voice in her ear.

"Ah—well, I'd—ah—rather tell you when I get there. Sorry."

"You're coming? When?"

"If you'll have me for a few days. I already have a ticket. Is it okay?"

"Of course it is. You know that. But can't you tell me—*something*?"

"I'd rather wait till I see you." The voice on the line was momentarily stronger, but it held a note of unsteadiness, hurt, and—something else. It faded back to a soft monotone, "Sorry. I just . . ."

"Hey, don't worry about it. Come on ahead and we'll talk when you get here. When do you get in? I'll pick you up."

"I can leave here at six-fifteen tomorrow morning on Alaska Airlines flight number eighty-one. It gets into Anchorage at nine-twenty. Got that? Nine-twenty."

"Yes, I've got it. I'll be there waiting. Anne? Are you okay?"

"Ah . . . I think—hope—I will be. I'll explain when I see you tomorrow. Sorry. Nine-twenty. Right?"

"Right."

"Thanks, Jessie. Just—thanks. Bye."

There was a click on the line, and she was gone before Jessie could respond. She stood holding the receiver for a long minute before laying it back in the cradle, thinking hard.

Anne Holman, of all people. I haven't heard from her, haven't even thought of her in a long, long time. Trouble? What could *that* mean? She sounded so strange—broken—kept saying she was *sorry*. What could be the matter? And why would she be coming to Alaska so unexpectedly?

Well, tomorrow would answer the questions. But the odd, impulsive nature of the call made Jessie decidedly uneasy.

Out of the dark between birch and spruce trees, an almost invisible shadow slipped swiftly through the falling snow, along a packed trail used by many mushers, across the open space behind Oscar's Other Place, now closed and still, to a window near the back door. The distinct sound of glass breaking was followed by a listening silence. When the noise elicited no response, there were some sharp snaps and the tinkle of a few shards falling, before the figure easily hoisted itself up to slide through the empty window frame.

In a moment the door was unlocked from the inside and opened. The figure returned quickly to the trees and soon reappeared, pulling a child's sled upon which the limp body of a man lay curled in a fetal position. The dark figure dumped the body from the sled, dragged it through the door and out of sight into the building.

For a few minutes there was only the almost-inaudible sound of snowflakes hitting snow, ice, and ground, a continuous whisper in the night. The faint crash of more breaking glass disturbed it, soon followed by the small snick of a lock clicking closed, and a muffled thump as the shadow slid back through the paneless window and dropped into the snow on the ground. Had anyone been there to see, the figure would have been easier to distinguish on its way out the window, for a slight glow within the building now caught its agile motion in silhouette.

In seconds, the figure was once again only a shadow among shadows as it vanished into the white of the storm between the dark spruce and pale birch trunks, pausing only once to look back and allow a shrill scrap of vindictive laughter to float away through the falling snow. A few minutes later, somewhere far away, a vehicle engine purred to life. The muffled rumble faded quickly and was gone.

But the glow in the window of the Other Place remained—flickered and grew stronger. A thin thread of smoke found its way to the broken window and escaped into the night, drawing more smoke after it. Quickly it increased to fill the opening, pouring out in billows from under the edges of the roof as well, as the fire burned through part of the ceiling. Tongues of flame leaped and danced, following the draft, licking, then devouring the paneling of the interior walls. The blaze spoke in cracks and pops, sucking oxygen into its fiery maw until its voice gradually became a ravenous, insatiable roar.

Part of the ceiling fell with a crash, giving the fire access to the roof, which scorched through in minutes, allowing sparks to swirl upward in the cloud of blackening smoke, the bellow of the fire overwhelming the tiny hisses of snowflakes landing on hot surfaces.

The rear half of the building was an inferno before the driver of a truck passing on the road caught sight of the unmistakable glow and thick haze above it. Snatching up a cellular phone from the seat beside him, he punched in 911 as he turned into the parking *lot, simultaneously applied brake and gas to swing the truck around in a spray of wet snow and gravel, aimed the still-rocking vehicle onto the road, and headed back the way he had come.*

"Fire," he yelled frantically to the dispatcher who responded. "Oscar's Other Place is on fire. Twelve miles out of Wasilla on Knik Road. Hurry!"

2

▰⟨⟨⟨⟩⟩⟩▰

A FRANTIC POUNDING ON THE FRONT DOOR OF HER CABIN
and someone shouting her name rudely yanked Jessie
from sleep. She could hear the yard outside resound
with the familiar barking of her dogs.

Sitting up in bed she struggled to clear her head. It
had been long after Anne Holman's phone call before
she had been able to fall asleep, consumed with worried curiosity at the trouble to which her friend had
alluded, mixed with memories of their wilderness
days.

Now she could feel the vibrations of the desperate
door pounding.

"Hold on. I'm coming," she called, struggling to
wrap a robe around her as she padded barefoot to the
door. "Who is it?"

"It's me—Hank," his excited voice told her. "Open up."

She unlocked the door and he almost knocked her
over, barreling through when it was half open.

"Gotta have your pump and generator—fast. Oscar's
is on fire."

She handed him a key that hung on a hook beside the door.

"In the storage shed behind the house. Get it open while I put something on."

Jessie raced back to the bedroom and threw on the clothes she had been wearing the evening before. Stomping her boots on and grabbing her parka, she followed Hank around the side of her cabin to the shed. Together, through the snow that was still falling heavily, they wrestled the heavy generator, then the pump, into the back of the pickup he had backed close to the door.

"What happened?" Jessie panted as they worked.

"Don't know."

"How'd it start?"

"No idea. Looked like it started in the back room after Oscar was gone. I left Bill Thomas and Ned trying to break in through the front to get some water on it with a couple of buckets. There's enough overflow rainwater running in the creek to use your pump, I think."

"Fire department?"

"On their way. Called them on my cell phone—and five or six other people who live close."

"I thought you went home."

"I was going, but Willy's car wouldn't start, so I took him into town. Lucky, because I saw the smoke when I came back by. It could have burned down before anyone else noticed at this time of night."

"What time *is* it?"

"Almost two-thirty." He slammed the tailgate.

Jessie hesitated. "Do we need anything else? My truck?"

"No. Just get in and let's go."

"Sorry, Tank. Not this time," she told her alert lead dog as she sprinted past him to the passenger side.

As they sped down her drive toward Knik Road, rocking through new snow and muddy potholes, a fire truck raced past, siren screaming, followed by the vehicles of several volunteer firemen, emergency lights flashing from their dashboards. Turning in behind them, Hank drove fast enough to keep pace, allowing them to clear the way for him as well, though there was not much traffic at this hour. His windshield wipers beat time, regularly sweeping wet, sticky snow off the glass.

They were almost to the pub before Jessie could see the red glow of fire reflected from the trees around Oscar's and the huge column of smoke that rose into the snowy dark. As they pulled into the parking lot behind the firefighters, she could see bright sparks being sucked aloft and thought it was a good thing that the surrounding forest and fields were too wet to burn.

"Too late, dammit," Hank swore, seeing that the building was more than half engulfed in flames that were spreading fast. They jumped from the cab into a confusion of people in motion and a tangle of vehicles hastily parked to leave room between for the fire equipment.

The firefighters went immediately to work to contain the blaze. Dark shapes against the red-orange rage of fire, they moved swiftly, unrolling hoses, directing streams of water from a pumper truck onto the angry, roaring inferno the building had become.

"*Now* the rain stops," Jessie growled in frustration. "This afternoon it could have put this out."

"Would have gone anyway," a musher she had earlier seen at the dartboard told her. "By the time it burned through the roof, even a hard rain wouldn't have done much good."

The roar and crackle of the fire drowned out all but the shouts of the firefighters, professional and volunteer, as they threw their efforts into moving equipment and training water on the flames. Hank had headed off at a run to join them, but Jessie stayed by the truck, shocked and incredulous. Several neighbors and dog drivers were already assisting where they could, but many others simply stood as she did, watching in disbelief and dismay. She knew without being told that it would be better to stay out of the way since she could see nothing that would benefit from her effort. With the arrival of the firemen, the need for her equipment had disappeared as well. There was no room to move Hank's truck close enough to use the generator and pump. The inactivity made her frustrated and impatient.

A gust of wind caught a large part of the smoke and sent it billowing through the parking lot, smelling acridly strong of scorched wood and chemicals. The momentary suffocating nastiness made the bystanders cough and rub their tearing eyes, reminding Jessie of all the flammable petroleum products that were used in modern buildings. The Other Place had been full of them—plastic chair seats, vinyl flooring, plastic shades over the lights above the pool tables, unseen PVC pipe in the plumbing, and coating on the electrical wiring inside the walls. All released gases to poison the smoke and those who inhaled it.

She heard the sharp report of glass breaking inside the building.

"Bottles," someone behind her muttered.

"Lot of good booze going to waste," another observed. "Hope he had insurance."

A front window exploded in the heat, scattering shards into the parking lot, and, after a long, agonizing complaint of twisting timbers, half the roof collapsed in slow motion. A wall quickly followed, falling with a crash, creating a giant fountain of sparks that reminded Jessie of Fourth of July fireworks.

It was now possible to see the once-familiar room glowing like a furnace, white hot in spots, almost unrecognizable. The falling wall had missed a small group of chairs that stood in one corner around a table with a flaming top. They looked untouched in the inferno of shimmering heat, but Jessie realized it was their metal frames she was seeing, padded seats long gone.

Her stomach lurched with nausea. She wondered if she had breathed too much of the smoke that had now swirled away in another direction, but knew that the knot in her stomach had more than a chemical trigger. It was also the result of apprehension and helpless anger. She was furious that it was too late to do anything but watch while the remainder of the Other Place burned.

It took quite a while, but when the firefighters finally had almost contained the blaze and were pouring water on defiant hot spots, Hank returned, soaked, covered with soot and grime, and smelling as evil as a demon out of nightmares. He stood slump shouldered and coughing, but he retrieved a crushed package from one pocket, dug out a bent cigarette, and lit it with a kitchen match. When a woman standing nearby cast a startled glance at the small flame, he chuckled humorlessly and wound up coughing again.

"Guess we're all gonna be spooked after this."

"What started it?" Jessie questioned. "Electrical? Something Oscar forgot to turn off?"

Hank frowned and shook his head. "No way. Oscar always checks everything—twice. I've helped him close up, and he never leaves until he's sure it's all off." He lowered his voice. "Not sure yet, but I heard one of the Wasilla guys say that it didn't look like an accident."

"Oscar—where *is* Oscar?" She turned to scan the yard full of people. Another truck pulled off the road into the crowded parking lot. The telephone system had evidently been used effectively.

"Don't know."

"Did you call?"

"Tried," Hank said. "His line was busy, so I figured someone else got him."

"I haven't seen him."

As Jessie carefully searched the faces of the crowd, a car with state trooper markings pulled into the lot, drove through a narrow space in the sizable collection of cars and pickups to park behind the fire truck. A uniformed figure stepped out and moved to join the firefighter who was directing the efforts to extinguish the last flames in the smoking ruin. For a few minutes they conversed, then walked together and disappeared behind the blackened remains of the Other Place. She knew him. Phil Becker was a trooper who had often worked homicide with Jensen. Why was he here?

The fire was now under control, reluctantly it seemed, as greedy fingers of flame flared up momentarily and were knocked down by water. The glare became a black, charred heap of rubble, still glowing here and there and putting out clouds of wicked-looking and -smelling smoke.

A tall man, looking as exhausted and filthy as Hank, strode across to the woman who had flinched at the lighted match, and stood frowning tiredly down at her.

"There's a body," he said, "behind the bar. Somebody died in there."

"*Jesus.*"

"Behind the bar? Oh, God," Jessie blurted, without thinking. "It's Oscar."

Heads turned in astonishment, eyes widened, and no one moved or spoke for a couple of shallow breaths as the appalling idea sank in. The silence was broken only by the sound of two late-arriving vehicles pulling off the highway.

A hand was laid on Jessie's arm and she turned to find a frowning Phil Becker standing next to her.

"Are you sure, Jessie?"

So it was true. Someone really had died in the fire.

"No, Phil. It just makes sense."

"Why?"

"When Oscar's tending bar, he's always the last to leave—he locks up."

"He was behind the bar tonight?"

"Yes—and—"

The group of people, crowded around them to listen, suddenly parted, and there were gasps of recognition as a figure pushed its way through.

"Whoever it is, it's not me," Oscar informed them, reaching Jessie. "What the hell happened? Someone's dead in there? Good God. Who?"

"You're the owner?" Becker asked.

"*Was*. The operative word seems to be *was*. Yeah, I'm Oscar Lee and this *was* my Other Place."

"What took you so long?" Hank Peterson asked. "I tried to call you at home, but the line was busy."

"I wasn't there. We almost ran out of Budweiser tonight, so I went to town for another keg."

"And you were headed back here?" Becker questioned.

"No, I was headed *home*. It didn't seem cold enough to freeze a keg in the truck tonight, so I was going to bring it over in the morning."

"Took you a long time after closing."

"Damned incompetent bartender left without restocking. I had to clean up there, too. There'll be somebody else behind that bar tomorrow. You can bet on it."

"Anyone with you there?"

"No. Why?"

"Just checking, Mr. Lee. Someone died in this fire. We're going to have to check a lot of things."

"Do you know who?"

"Not yet."

"What happened? Everything was fine—everybody had gone—when I left."

"We don't know, but an investigator will be here soon. I called dispatch in Anchorage and he's on his way."

"What kind of investigator?"

"An arson investigator. It looks like this fire might have been set, Mr. Lee."

"Dammit. You mean somebody burned my place *on purpose?*"

"It's possible, but that's not my call. You'll have to wait for the results of the investigation. Right now we're concerned with the identity of the body. You have any ideas at all?"

"God, no. Everyone was gone when I locked up. My truck was the last one in the lot, except for one that wouldn't start and was left."

"Anyone leave angry?"

"No, and I think I'd know."

"Anyone got a mad on in your direction?"

Oscar shook his head slowly.

To Jessie it was clear that he was having trouble taking it all in—the fire, the death. She empathized with his obvious feeling of unreality. His attention kept wandering away from Becker's questions and toward the charred, smoking ruin of the Other Place, his face a moving record of his loss, anger, and concern.

"You got insurance, Oscar?" Hank asked.

"Sure—sure." He waved a dismissive hand. "But I can't think who'd want to do this to me—and to have somebody *die*—that's just . . ." He swallowed hard and stopped. "I locked up like always. How'd someone get back in?"

"You're sure it was empty?"

"I check to be sure—the johns, the back room. I don't see how—unless . . ."

"The investigator may be able to tell you how, Mr. Lee," Becker told him, "but not until he finishes his job; and that's going to take till sometime tomorrow, I think. Why don't you wait and talk to him when he gets here, then you might as well go on home. There's nothing you can do here tonight. He'll want to talk to you again in the morning—and the rest of this crowd."

He raised his voice to speak to the spectators. "Will you all please leave your names and where to get in touch with you? Thanks."

Turning back to Jessie, Hank, and Oscar, his next words did not carry so far. "We'll need to know who was here tonight before the bar closed. You three were here. Can you work that out?"

Oscar frowned and shifted uneasily. Jessie stared at Becker, dismay rising.

"You *really* think someone who was here did this, Phil? One of our regulars?"

"I didn't say that, Jessie. It could be anybody—someone with a grudge, a disguised robbery. We just need all the names we can get."

"But why would someone . . . ?"

"No way to know yet. If you can think of anything—any hint—put that on the list, too."

Hank was shaking his head, and Jessie shared his repugnance at naming friends and acquaintances.

Suddenly, she felt exhausted—rain soaked and cold. There was nothing she could do here. It was time to go home.

3

UP EARLY TO START FOR THE AIRPORT, JESSIE WAS DE-
lighted to see that four or five inches of new snow covered the ground. It lifted her spirits and helped her
forget that her usual eight hours of rest had been reduced by half, though she was still discouraged and
concerned about the fire at Oscar's. The unexpected
warm spell and ceaseless drizzle of the preceding two
days had melted the icicles from the edges of the cabin
roof and dissolved much of the packed snow from the
ground, turning parts of her dog yard to a quagmire
and her long driveway to muddy ponds. Now, the mud
and standing water had frozen and been covered in the
night, and her world was once again a bright clean
white. She resented having to call Billy and postpone
the training runs she had planned, feeling that she
should be taking advantage of every opportunity. The
early thaw had been a warning that winter would soon
be over, and the new snow was merely a suspension of
the fast-approaching spring.

Breakup was her least favorite time of year and having it come early, when she wanted training time on snowy trails, made it worse. It seemed that all the grime that accumulated during the winter washed out and floated to the surface, leaving dirty ridges on the snow, creating gluey mud that clung to the knee-high rubber boots she wore into the yard to feed and care for her dogs. Even the mutts grew muddy. Handling them transferred the unpleasant muck to her raincoat, gloves, and jeans. The dogs slept away most of the rainy hours in their individual boxes, staying as dry and warm as possible, though the inactivity made them restless enough to exhibit their boredom in ill-tempered snaps and growls at each other.

As Jessie looked out into the yard this morning, she could tell that their mood had also lifted with the return of snow. They were all out of their shelters and moving around energetically. Putting coffee on to brew, she went to shower and dress, so she could feed and water them before starting the long drive to Anchorage to pick up Anne Holman. She would much rather have gone back to bed or, better, out to slide quickly away into wilderness on a sled behind a dog team, leaving all the trouble behind. Maybe this afternoon, she had told Billy. Maybe . . .

It was twenty-five after nine when she parked her pickup in the multilevel airport garage and hurried through the underground passage toward the terminal, a few minutes later than she had planned. The strong coffee in her thermos hadn't been a complete cure for too little sleep and had done nothing to diminish her continuing anger and regret over the destruction of the

Other Place or her discomfort over having to make a
list of all the pub's customers. She felt slightly out of
sync with everything around her as she stepped off an
escalator and headed toward the security checkpoint
for Concourse B, wishing she felt more capable of
handling whatever new trouble the arrival of Anne
Holman was about to add to her growing list.

The plane had evidently already arrived. Passengers
were streaming down the hallway toward her from the
Alaska Airlines gates, crowding one another, glad to
have escaped their three-hour Seattle-to-Anchorage
confinement.

Might as well wait where I am, she decided, skip the
security hassle and catch Anne as she comes along.
Leaning against a pillar, she yawned and watched people go by.

Two gray-flannel-suited men with briefcases strode
purposefully, one already muttering into a cell phone,
"No, the senator wants . . ." Scowling, a young mother
with a fretful two-year-old halted abruptly to unfold the
stroller she was carrying, blocking the flow of passengers and prompting an impatient young man in wire-
rimmed glasses to make an abrupt detour in his rush to
embrace a girl who flew into his arms with a welcoming, "Tim!" Jessie's attention was caught by a cautiously moving fellow in a neck brace as he stumbled
against a wheeled carry-on towed by an anxious-looking
middle-aged woman and was deftly rebalanced by a
flight attendant. A father herding twin boys in matching
jackets and Seattle Mariners caps was followed by a
grossly obese woman anxiously searching the concourse for someone she clearly expected to meet.

Anne? Could she have changed so much? No—too tall. But the one just behind her . . . ?

"Jessie?"

The middle-aged woman with the carry-on had stopped beside her and half raised a hand. Probably a fan who had recognized Jessie from media photos. Be nice, she told her tired, less-than-usually-tolerant self, and forced a pleasant, if somewhat distant, smile.

The woman's expression was slightly asymmetrical, the right side of her face not quite moving with the left, pulling her hesitant half smile a little crooked. Jessie looked back toward the gate, afraid she would miss Anne as she responded to this unfamiliar person.

"Yes."

At Jessie's lack of complete attention, the woman's brows drew together. She glanced down and released the handle of the carry-on. When she looked back her smile had vanished. Startled, Jessie suddenly recognized the shape of her brows and the soft gray-green of her eyes, a tiny spot of darker color near the iris in the left.

"Anne?"

"Yeah. Look, I—ah—know I've changed, but . . ."

Except for her familiar eyes, she was so different that Jessie could only stare, speechless and unable to mask surprise. She had not known—would never have known this woman as her friend from a decade earlier.

Back then, Anne had been a bright bird, with a lively face and agile body. Though her delicate features and slim stature had invited the assumption of fragility, she had actually been a tough bundle of muscle with the energy and graceful strength of an athlete.

Jessie saw little of this now. Anne was so thin she looked anorexic, the jeans and sweater she wore hanging on her like clothes she had borrowed from someone several sizes larger. The luxuriant, dark hair that Jessie remembered escaping in wisps and tendrils from Anne's heavy braid now hung limp and lifeless, cut severely straight at the level of her jaw, and it could have used a wash as well as a good combing. But most of Jessie's dismay resulted from the odd appearance of the face turned questioningly toward her with a guarded look. The once attractive features were slightly blunted and coarsened—nose a touch off center, lips uneven, jawline a little blurred. The dark circles beneath the eyes were not smudged makeup, and the pale line of an old scar caused the left lid to droop just a little.

Anne had entered the terminal with none of the animation and easy, eager stride Jessie had expected. She had looked like an older person and moved with instinctive caution, shoulders slumped, chin down, arms defensively close to her body.

How could I have known her? Jessie wondered, appalled and embarrassed at the transparency of her own reaction.

"You haven't changed much," she prevaricated. "I'm just not tracking too well—didn't get enough sleep last night—there was a—"

"Don't, Jessie," Anne interrupted sharply with a hint of exasperation. "I look in the mirror every morning. Pretending just makes it worse."

"Okay." Jessie gave in. "What *happened* to you?"

Tears welled and ran down the coarsened cheeks and mouth that was now twisted with resentment.

"Greg happened," Anne said, bitterness spilling over with her tears. "My husband—may he fry in the flames of hell—is what *happened* to me. Can we just get out of here?"

When the two women reached the baggage pick-up area on the lower level of the airport, the carousel was crowded with people waiting to claim their luggage. But it was another ten minutes before suitcases and bags began to make their appearance through an opening in the wall. One after another they moved on an endless track that snaked through the large room in two large loops. People began to grab their luggage from the moving display and Jessie noticed that, as usual, no airline official was bothering to check claim tickets. Many of the cases were very similar in size and color, which led to a few inevitable confusions. Across the room she saw a large man shake his head and set a suitcase that apparently belonged to someone else back on the track.

Anne, now full of nervous energy, barely stood still, moving close to see what was coming next, pushing people until Jessie finally stopped apologizing for her and took firm hold of her arm.

"You won't make it show up any faster by climbing on the carousel. What does it look like?"

"It looks like—that." She shoved between a young couple, who gave her disgusted looks, and leaned to reach a large suitcase that matched her carry-on bag. As she yanked it off and swung it around, directly into the shins of another passenger, Jessie once again caught sight of the large man who had returned a suitcase to the track. He was moving quickly away through the crowd, but as she thought for an instant that she recognized him she was distracted by a cry for help from Anne and the grumbling of a man who was rubbing his shin.

"Watch it," he growled. "What's the big rush?"

Anne ignored him. "Let's go," she demanded, practically running for an elevator.

When Jessie glanced over her shoulder to look for the man she had seen, he had disappeared.

All the way to Jessie's truck, Anne cast nervous glances behind her and suspiciously examined everyone they passed.

"You expecting somebody else?"

"I hope not. I'll tell you later."

When they were finally on the Glenn Highway, leaving Anchorage, she leaned back against the seat, took several deep breaths, and seemed to relax a little. But even then, she wouldn't explain why she had come or what she was afraid of but insisted on waiting till they got *home*. For most of the hour's drive she kept up a stream of bright, artificial chatter about the winter they had spent as neighbors. "Remember that time we took your dogs and camped overnight in the snow? That was great, wasn't it? And all those silver origami birds we made for our Christmas trees out of candy wrappers? Did you ever get another dog as good as Pete? You still have him? Great! I want to see him. Do you remember . . ."

Jessie drove and listened, feeling more than a little overwhelmed and confused.

Reaching home, Jessie made a fresh pot of coffee and puttered in the kitchen for a few minutes, trying to let go of the tension that was beginning to give her a headache and allowing her unexpected guest to wander around and become familiar with the cabin.

"Nice place," Anne commented, returning from the bedroom, where she had put her luggage. She had a bottle of Jessie's favorite Crabtree & Evelyn freesia body lotion in her hand. "Mind if I use some of this? I'd forgotten how dry it is up here in the cold—turns my skin to flakes."

Jessie nodded. "Sure, but there's some Vaseline Intensive Care that works better, if you want it."

"Naw, this'll do fine. You built this cabin yourself? I'm impressed." She rubbed lotion into her hands and left the bottle on the desk Jessie used to keep records for her kennel.

"Well, I had a lot of help."

Jessie frowned. Anne, in constant motion, was beginning to get on her nerves, restlessly moving through the rooms, picking things up, putting them down, examining everything that attracted her attention as if it wasn't real to her until she laid hands on it.

"I really like your chairs," she said, running her fingers over the back of one of the mismatched dining chairs Jessie had picked up one by one at yard sales and painted assorted bright colors.

"Thanks, I . . ."

But Anne was already across the room, pressing the buttons on the CD player. Finally she settled on the sofa near the stove and Jessie, relieved, handed her a large, steaming mug and curled up against the pillows on the other end with one of her own.

"Now," she demanded, "what's the problem?"

Anne sipped, took a deep breath and sighed, looked up, cocked a dramatic eyebrow as if deciding where to start, and then words flooded out so fast she stammered.

"Well—you've guessed from what I said that I've—ah—left Greg? Right? And you've probably figured—correctly, by the way—that he's responsible for the ugly way I look—the changes."

Jessie nodded and waited for Anne to continue her account any way she liked. "Okay. And . . . ?" she said, to prime the pump.

Anne clearly took the *okay* as acceptance and agreement, for she sat up straighter.

"So—I'm really—ah—*terrified* that he'll come after me—that he'll do what he said—find out where I am and . . ." She hesitated, glancing up through her eyelashes to watch closely for a reaction, "And hurt, or . . . *kill me*."

She paused, waiting.

Jessie scowled and shook her head at this exaggerated bit of drama. "*Greg?* Oh, Anne—*really?* That doesn't sound like . . ." She looked up to see that her friend was clenching her teeth so tightly that a muscle worked in her jaw below the ear. "You aren't really *serious?*"

"He swore—lots of times—that if I *ever* left he'd find me no matter where I went."

"But why?"

It was unbelievable. Dumbfounded and incredulous, Jessie had trouble accepting the idea, particularly since Anne's presentation seemed overstated. The woman she remembered had not been above spicing up a narrative with a few histrionics. This went beyond exaggeration for effect, but there was still something theatrical about it.

"It's a long, depressing story," Anne said, shrugging off the question. "Nothing much different than lots of others. But I *desperately* need your help, Jessie. I've got to do something I can't do *alone*."

"What?"

"Go back out to the cabin where we lived that year. And I need you to go with me—to take me out there. Will you?"

Not without knowing one hell of a lot more, Jessie thought to herself.

"Why do you need to go?" she questioned.

"To dig up something I left. It's important."

"What?"

"Ah . . . money—some money that I . . . buried and couldn't get back then. Now I've got to have it."

"It's a long way out there, Anne—a major trip. The ground's still frozen and there's deep snow—more new snow, now. We'd have to shovel down, then thaw the dirt before you could dig anything up. It may be almost breakup here, but out there it'll be at least another month."

"But we could do that—right? Thaw it, I mean."

"Well—yeah, we *could,* but it'd be a lot of work."

"That's okay. I'll do it—all of it—if you'll just take me."

Jessie sat staring at her without speaking for a long minute, trying to get her thoughts together.

"Look," she said finally, getting up from the sofa, "I've got to take care of my mutts. There's soup and stuff for sandwiches in the kitchen. Why don't you make us some lunch while I do it? Then we'll talk some more."

"Okay. But can we go really soon—like today or to-morrow?"

Doesn't she realize that I have a life with other plans? Jessie wondered. Where does she get off, as-suming I sit around waiting to be asked for stuff like this—that I can just drop everything and take off? A working kennel is not easy to leave on a whim.

"Anne," she snapped impatiently, hopping by the door with one boot half on. "I have a training schedule that has already been interrupted by two days of rain. This time before breakup is really busy. I can't just take off at a moment's notice, and this doesn't sound so immediately important or necessary to me."

"Oh, Jessie. I'm sorry to get in the way. But it *is*—it *really is*. Honest. I've got to get out there—just *got* to. I wouldn't ask if it wasn't *really* important."

So rent a snowmachine, Jessie thought angrily, and leave me alone.

"We'll talk when I come back," she told Anne shortly and went out. She shut the door behind her and leaned against it for a few seconds in relief at having escaped from the woman's demanding presence. Her own cabin had almost seemed to close in claustropho-bically.

As she went to get water that her dogs didn't really need this time of day, she tried to assess the situation and decide what to do. The whole thing seemed unreal. But I'm tired, she reminded herself, and not thinking straight.

Not being very patient or generous either.

She's asking—demanding—an awful lot from me.

Is she? If it hadn't rained for two days—if Oscar's hadn't burned last night—if you'd gotten lots of sleep—would you feel this way?

Yes—well, maybe not. But that's not all of it.

She paused in the process of pouring water into individual aluminum dog pans, considering. Anne clearly wanted her to understand and believe—to be on her side. But something about her old acquaintance's watchful demeanor rang a tiny bell of discomfort and caution in the back of Jessie's mind. She couldn't tell if Anne's obvious desire for acceptance and help would account for it, or if embarrassment and nerves could explain her slightly self-conscious, wheedling tone. She had not seen this woman for ten years—long enough to make a significant change in her outlook and approach—long enough for Jessie to need to become reacquainted with her before making judgments or commitments.

Dammit, she thought. I don't want to take off on some nutty trip miles from anywhere. I want to get on with training my young guys. If I interrupt their schedule now, I'll have to do half of it over again, and long overnight runs are not part of the program yet.

Well, give it some more time. Get her to talk some more—listen to her till tomorrow. Then make up your mind.

But I just want to get rid of her, she realized.

Maybe giving in and taking her where she wants to go will be the best and quickest way to get rid of her. How long would it take—a couple of days, maybe three?

That's possible. I guess I can at least think about it, she

decided. Billy *could* stay with the dogs—make a couple of training runs a day till I get back, though that would cut what I wanted to do in half and they really need *me*. I could even go out this afternoon for at least one run.

She put the buckets away, then went back to the middle of the yard to spend a minute or two with a few of her dogs. Every day she made sure to take time with each dog, giving it lots of affection, watching it move, assessing its attitude. At least a couple of times a week she checked each of them over physically, alert to any developing problems. Only by being familiar with each one's normal condition could she detect any changes in their health and well-being.

Pete stood up from a nap and stretched as she stopped beside him, gave her a doggy grin, and leaned against her leg as she checked his teeth. Mitts and Sunny, housed next to each other, greeted her with wriggles and friendly licks as she knelt to scratch their ears and under their chins. Their tails wagged like metronomes, as if she had been absent a week.

"Good guys. You're such good dogs. Glad it snowed again, aren't you? Shall we just hook up a sled and take off—run away from home?"

The idea was tempting, if escapist and impractical.

Jessie's conscience got the better of her, she sighed, and went back toward the house, hoping Anne had lunch ready by now and fervently wishing she hadn't answered the phone the night before.

4

〜◆◇◆〜

IN HER STOCKING FEET, JESSIE QUIETLY PACED THE WIDTH of her cabin, restless and unable to settle into the nap she had intended to take on the sofa. Seemingly exhausted by her travels and relieved to have made her request, Anne had eaten lunch, taken a quick shower, and fallen asleep almost before she could curl up under the colorful quilt on Jessie's big brass bed. But before she slept, she had filled in some information about the ten years since they had seen each other.

What she had revealed was incomplete and not pleasant—a one-sided litany of physical and emotional abuse that disturbed and discouraged Jessie as much as Anne seemed reluctant and troubled to be telling it. According to her, Greg Holman had always beaten her.

"Not when we were first married—when we lived close to you. Oh, he smacked me once or twice, but only when I asked for it—and I really did, Jessie. You know me—I never could keep my mouth shut. I had it coming. It wasn't till later that he got really mean."

She said they had left Alaska about a year after

Jessie moved closer to town that spring—gone to Boulder, Colorado, where they rented a small house on the edge of town. Greg had found work as a carpenter, but, as Anne told it, he had refused to let her take a job—any job—though she had been offered one as a clerk in a bookstore.

"He was afraid I'd tell somebody that he was hitting me," she had told Jessie. "He refused to have a phone—afraid I'd use it to report him. He watched—wanted to know where I was all the time. We only had the truck and he always took it with him to work. He got more and more suspicious—like jealous of everyone: neighbors—though there weren't more than a few—the checker at the grocery store; the guy who read the electric meter, for God's sake. And he yelled at me. I never knew when he was going to hit me.

"We moved three times in those years—each time farther away from town. I worked really hard to be good, to do what he wanted, but he kept beating me up. I tried my best to do things right, to be whatever he wanted, but he blamed me for everything—and he imagined a lot. I never knew what would set him off next. It was like living in a shooting gallery—if I cooked the wrong thing, if anything wasn't clean or where he wanted it or put away right. Whatever I said—or didn't say—it was bad. He put me in the hospital twice—broke my nose and fractured this cheekbone."

She laid a finger on the right side of her face and Jessie understood the asymmetry and the crooked smile.

"But you saw people in the hospital. Why didn't you tell someone—get away from him?"

"—I didn't want them to know either—you know?

He promised we'd work it out—said it was our private business. He also said it was *my* fault, and if I told anyone he'd make me sorry. I was *afraid* of him, Jessie. Besides, it wasn't all his fault. If I'd been able to do things right—keep him happy—he wouldn't have hurt me, would he? He was always all torn up about hitting me—after. I felt like nothing—hated myself for making him mad. Why are men such children?"

Like the release of swift water when the key log in a jam is pulled, Anne's account of injury and hospitals, years of lies, constant fear, and finally escape and flight had poured out, accompanied by a flood of tears and caustic condemnation of both Greg and herself that had astonished and alarmed Jessie.

Now she restlessly walked the floor, trying to decide what to think—and to do. Pausing at the window that faced the dog yard, she looked out at the inviting snow. She still wanted to harness up a team and take off into the wilds, leaving behind all the confusion and trouble she seemed to have walked abruptly into. Frowning and biting her lip, she resented being forced to deal with the uninvited trouble and stress, still waffling about making the trip into the wilderness with Anne. But then she'll be gone—wherever—and I can get on with training, Jessie told herself.

She would have liked to talk to Greg Holman, hear his side of the story, for her memories of him did not fit the pictures Anne had painted. When Jessie had moved into the nearby borrowed cabin for that single winter, the Holmans had still acted like newlyweds— touching each other in passing, glancing affectionately, deferring endearingly to each other.

Greg Holman, a large bull of a man, had seemed an unusual dichotomy of efficient strength and a quiet sort of innocence; he was one of those people whose smooth skin never seems to age and gives them a child-like, ingenuous quality that suggests limited intelligence and prompts more-brawn-than-brain assumptions. A hardworking man, more comfortable outdoors than in, he had impressed Jessie as handy with his hands, capable of making or fixing almost anything. She had assumed he was completely, guilelessly in love with his spouse, and would not have suspected he was a wife beater.

Behind his stillness, however, she had slowly come to recognize a shrewd and discerning astuteness—a keen mind that saw much, missed little. He had old eyes in that calm, youthful face. There was nothing lacking in his thinking, nothing inarticulate when he had something to say. Questioned, he had spoken briefly of his upbringing as an only child in a remote location where he had learned wilderness craft through years of experience. His home schooling had ended at fourteen when his mother had died, but she had evidently succeeded in creating in him an eclectic love of reading. His self-education sometimes took off in unexpected directions—archaeology, electronics, the English Romantic poets, hydrology and the art of dousing, meteorology.

As a couple, the Holmans had demonstrated the attraction of opposites: He was disinclined to small talk and what he considered unnecessary expenditures of energy; she tumbled, burbling, through life like a stream in spring thaw. Jessie had felt an amused connection with his quiet appreciation of Anne's cheerful, sometimes theatrical verbalizations. But there had been a dark side, too, she recalled—remembering things that might help reconcile the contradictions now bothering her.

Holman's temper, though infrequent, had not flamed and died, but often smoldered and threatened to flare up long after others had forgotten what ignited it. He had nurtured, and sometimes exaggerated, grudges. He expounded on the crass stupidity of city dwellers and politicians that he insisted were maliciously intent upon restricting the traditionally free Alaskan lifestyle and turning the state into some law-infested supermarket. Jessie recollected coffee cups rattling as he pounded his angry frustration on the tabletop. She had avoided similar subjects thereafter.

He had had no patience for procrastination, and halfhearted efforts offended him. To him, there was no excuse for not doing a thing as soon and as well as possible *the first time*. "Your life may depend on it," she remembered his saying, and she agreed. More than once in a long-distance race she had been relieved that good preparation had kept her from trouble, even disaster, and had thought of Greg. But hadn't there been something obsessive about his pursuit of perfection and insistence on action without delay? Could he actually have pounded more than a tabletop with his hamlike fist?

There had been no obvious hint of the problems Anne had just described. Jessie recalled nothing more significant than a single visit when Anne had displayed a bruise on one cheekbone and a purpling eye. Asked about it, she had given a hoot of embarrassed laughter and said that you would think by now she would have learned to use an ax so it didn't send a stick of kindling flying back in her face. Had her injury been caused by something other than airborne firewood?

Jessie thought again of how different Anne had become. Her once-unsophisticated optimism had vanished. In its place was an angry, resentful, yet fearful and oddly apologetic person who reminded Jessie of a whipped dog she had once seen in the kennel of a poor excuse for a musher. When its master had come close, the animal had crouched, moving nothing but its terrified eyes, clearly hoping that total stillness would make it invisible.

From her looks, Anne had clearly been beaten—or injured somehow. And along with her anger, she exhibited a strong thread of guilt. At times she'd seemed convinced that the abuse had been all her fault, that she'd deserved—had earned—the punishment Greg had inflicted on her, and if she had only done things differently it wouldn't have happened. It made her assertions more disquieting and believable.

And Jessie couldn't shake the disturbing feeling that there was some calculation in Anne's telling, as if an artful child were watching carefully to see how Jessie would react before deciding whether to tell the truth next . . . or a lie. There was something about the dispassionate way Anne had told parts of the story that made Jessie's skin crawl, feeling she was being manipulated and disliking it. *Was* Greg responsible for Anne's state of mind? Her fear of him seemed real to Jessie, at least. If she was telling the truth, he might very well show up. Then what? Would he be dangerous to them both? Was there some way she could find out?

"If you think he might follow you, why come back here? Why not somewhere he'd never think of looking?" she had asked. "This place isn't hard to find."

"I have to go back to the cabin," Anne had answered. "Please, Jessie? I'll go—disappear—somewhere else right after that—okay? I promise I will."

"Let me think about it a little more, Anne," she had told her.

As Jessie slumped tiredly onto the sofa and finally lay down, she heard her dogs start to bark and beyond their unmistakable announcement of company, the sound of a vehicle coming up the driveway. Going to the window, she watched a car with a fire department logo on the door pull up beside her truck. State Trooper Phil Becker and a lean man she didn't recognize—both in civilian clothes—got out and came up the porch steps to the door. She opened it before their knock.

"Hi, Phil."

"Hey, Jessie. Glad you're home. This is Investigator Michael Tatum. Mike, Jessie Arnold."

"Nice to meet you, Ms. Arnold."

The hand he offered was strong but a little stiff, and, glancing down, Jessie saw that it bore the unmistakable, melted-looking scars that only fire and skin grafts create. Looking back to his face, she found no apology or defensiveness in his clear hazel eyes, but rather a wry cynicism, a hint of mocking watchfulness through which he assessed her reaction.

"I was on the line before I became an inspector," he offered in brief explanation.

"You must have had a lot of long hard work in therapy with that."

"I did." His nod and half smile seemed to include an approval of her response as well as agreement, but then he frowned suddenly and turned away, as if to avoid further discussion of his injury.

She swung the door wide, inviting them inside. "Can I talk you guys into some coffee?"

"Wouldn't turn it down," Becker accepted, leaving his boots at the door. "Haven't got any of that carrot cake Alex was always bragging about, have you? Oops. Sorry," he apologized as he saw her eyes narrow involuntarily at the familiar name.

"That's okay, Phil. No cake, but I've got oatmeal cookies—fresh yesterday."

"Great. If I recall, your cookies are way ahead of whatever's in second place anyway." He grinned, tossed his western hat on the sofa, and took a chair at the round oak dining table. Mike Tatum pulled out another and sat, laying down a notebook and pen.

Jessie crossed swiftly to close the door to the bedroom so their conversation wouldn't disturb Anne, then brought the coffeepot and a plastic container of cookies to the table and sat down across from them.

"We need to hear what you know about last night's fire, Jessie," Phil said, dunking a cookie in his coffee. "You were one of the last people to leave the bar before it closed, right?"

"Yes, but there were two or three people still playing darts and a guy asleep on one of the tables."

"Who was it?"

"I didn't know him. Oscar said it was a friend of someone's."

"Drunk?"

"No—nursing a cold, according to Oscar. Just tired, I think."

"Funny to be in a bar if he was that sick. What'd he look like?"

"I didn't see his face. Sorry. Is this an official interview, Phil?"

"Well, yeah, I guess so. But we're just collecting the usual kind of information—trying to get the people and timing straight."

"Did you find out who died?"

"Not yet—lab's working on it."

"I'll help if I can, but I don't know much. I didn't see it start—didn't get there until it was too late to put it out."

Tatum had been taking notes. Now he looked up and spoke in a quiet voice. "How long were you at the bar last night, Ms. Arnold?"

Becker snagged two more cookies, leaned back in his chair, and let the investigator take over.

"A couple of hours—maybe closer to three," she answered. "And it's just Jessie."

He smiled. "Okay—Jessie. And I'm just Mike. Can you tell me who else was there?"

"Better. I made a list of everyone I could remember."

She brought him the list she had made the night before. "It was crowded."

"You talk to anyone in particular?"

She related the racing conversation at the table and

the casual comments and teasing while shooting pool with Hank Peterson and the players they had defeated.

"Anybody get mad about losing?"

"Na-aw. We don't play serious pool at Oscar's."

"This list is everyone who was there while you were?"

"I might have missed a few. People were coming and going."

"Oscar?" Becker asked.

"Oh, right—Oscar, of course. He was the last person I spoke to."

"What about?"

"Oh, just good-bye—how busy he'd been. He gave Tank some more jerky."

"Tank?" Tatum asked.

"My lead dog. He and Oscar are tight." She smiled, recalling the jerky.

He frowned. "How well do you know Oscar Lee?"

"Pretty well, I guess—casual friend. I'm one of his nearest neighbors and a regular."

"Ever any hint of money trouble from him?"

"No." She grinned, suddenly remembering. "Unless you count accidents. Once—a year or so ago—he lost a whole night's cash and checks in a snowbank— didn't know he'd dropped the bag on his way out. It finally showed up in the spring melt, and somebody carted it in from the parking lot."

"So, Oscar's casual with his money. He's lucky it was found by an honest man."

"I wouldn't say *casual,*" Jessie told him, stung into defensiveness by his insinuation. "He's not care- less, if that's what you mean. It was a mistake anybody could have made. Besides, it's a good crowd of regulars—local people. They feel—*felt*—at home there. I can't think of anyone who would steal from Oscar."

"How about this Peterson person?"

"You're not serious."

"You say he came for your generator and pump."

"Yeah, he did. Pounded on the door till I thought he'd break it down, but the fire department got there before we could use them."

"He discovered the fire?"

"That's what he said. He was almost in a panic wanting to put it out."

"He lives farther on out the road? Why was he going past the bar?"

"He gave Willy Wilson a ride to town because his car wouldn't start, so he was on his way home."

"You see him going toward Wasilla?"

"No. I left before they did, so I was already home."

"So you just think that's true because—"

"I *know* it's true, because he *told* me. Ask Willy, if you don't believe me."

"We will."

She got no reassurance, and Becker gave Tatum an unhappy look.

"How and for how long have you known Hank Peterson, Jessie?" he broke in.

"Ever since I moved to Knik eight—almost ten—years now. He's a local musher who's been handler for me a couple of times—once for the Iditarod."

The inspector again: "He doesn't get paid for that. What's he do for a living?"

"He works construction in the summer. Odd jobs the rest of the year, I guess."

"He ever work for Lee?"

"As a matter of fact, I think he helped build the Other Place. Probably volunteered half his time. He's a nice, dependable guy."

"So he'd be familiar with the building," Tatum said, ignoring her endorsement.

"Yes—but so would a lot of other people." She hesitated, frowning. "You really think the fire was deliberately set?"

"Don't think so—we *know* so. The evidence is clear. Nothing but arson could have done it."

"How do you know that? Where did it—"

The beep of Becker's pager interrupted her question, and he took it from a pocket to read the number.

"The office. Use your phone, Jessie?"

"Sure."

He crossed the room to the desk and was soon deep in conversation.

"Comfortable place you have here," Mike Tatum commented, suspending his interrogation and looking around.

"It works for me. I built it several years ago with help from friends—lots of them regulars at Oscar's—including Hank Peterson," she told him pointedly.

"Good place to raise dogs?"

"It's far enough from town so that the neighbors aren't bothered by their noise. Easy connections to the trails I use for training, including the Iditarod Trail, and it goes all the way to Nome." She smiled at the thought.

"You've run some big races. And done pretty well, I hear."

"I've done okay. I'd like to win the Iditarod once, though."

"Running next year?"

"Hope so. I skipped it this year—did the Yukon Quest instead."

"Tough race?"

"Different. It's more rugged and has fewer checkpoints."

Becker hung up the phone and tossed a name to Tatum as he crossed the room.

"Robert Martin—the guy who died in the fire. Lab just finished and ID'd him from prints off the hand that was under him and didn't char. He'd spent some time inside for—guess what?—arson."

"Interesting," Tatum said. "Makes sense. Caught in his own game—maybe."

"Maybe you should say *flame*." Becker grinned, unable to resist the pun.

"Robert?" Jessie repeated. "Oscar said, 'Bob something.' Was it the same guy who was asleep on that table when I left?"

"Can't say for sure. Maybe. Oscar didn't know him?"

"No. First time he'd been there, I think. He came with a friend."

"We'll get someone to take a look at his file photo— Oscar, or . . . Do you know the name of his friend?"

"Chuck. Chuck Warner. But I didn't see him there last night. Wonder why he'd leave without someone he brought and who was—"

The bedroom door opened suddenly and Anne walked in stretching and yawning sleepily.

"I thought I heard voices."

"This is Anne Holman—old friend of mine who's visiting. Anne—Phil Becker and Mike Tatum. They're investigating a fire that burned down our local pub last night."

With only a glance at the two men, Anne made an abrupt right turn into the kitchen.

"Any coffee left?"

As she started to get up to show Anne where to find a mug, Jessie was caught by an unexpected expression on Tatum's face—a gleeful mixture of satisfaction and suspicion.

"Martha Anne *Gifford*. What a surprise," he said in a tone that made it clear his prior acquaintance with her had left no warmth in its wake. "Hey, Marty. Set any nice fires lately?"

5

━━◆◇◆━━

THE TWO MEN HAD GONE, TATUM GIVING BOTH WOMEN A
look of distrust and skepticism that left Jessie bewildered
and troubled and Anne angrily sobbing on the sofa.

"Can't you leave me alone?" she had wailed at Mike
Tatum.

"Not likely. Now that you're back in town, I'll be
keeping an eye on you, Marty," he warned sharply as
he went out the door. "Don't think you can get away
with it again."

"Don't *call* me that," she howled furiously back,
glaring at him. "My name is Anne."

"*Right.* And you had nothing to do with the Mulligan's garage fire."

"You know I didn't, you bastard. Get a life."

Tatum would have slammed the door on his way out
if Phil Becker, following close behind and looking as
perplexed as Jessie felt, hadn't caught it.

"What the hell was all that?" she demanded, as soon
as the two men had disappeared and she could hear the
car going away down the drive.

When all that came back was tears and swearing, Jessie lost what composure she had left.

"Dammit, Anne. I not only don't know what's going on—I'm beginning to overload on all this. You're telling me *part* of the story. There's a lot more, isn't there? Well, you'd better spit it out, because I'm not helping with anything I don't understand."

She stood glowering, fists on hips, waiting for an answer.

Anne reluctantly sat up and wiped at her face with the sleeve of her sweater, glanced at Jessie, then away, once again calculating a response.

Grabbing the box of tissues from the desk, Jessie shoved it at her.

"Grow up, blow your nose, and tell the truth."

Swiveling a straight chair, she sat astride, facing Anne, arms crossed over the back.

"Don't try to sort it out. Just *tell* me."

"Aw-w, Jessie. It's such a mess that—"

"It sure is. So get it straight. I'm not a total dummy."

"You don't understand."

"That's right, I don't. So you'd better make sure I do. What's the Mulligan garage fire? How does Tatum know you?"

"It was a long time ago—before I knew you or Greg even. There was this fire . . ."

"Where?"

"Not a house garage—a truck-repair place up the road from Wasilla. Somebody set it on fire and Tatum tried to pin it on me."

"Why?"

"Well, I was living out near Big Lake at the time and

I was—ah—friendly with the guy who owned it. The thing was—his two kids were asleep in the apartment upstairs. Tatum was one of the firefighters and he got burned trying to get them out, but he couldn't save them, and he let it get to him. Mr. Wonderful—what an ego. He wanted someone to blame and I was handy."

For a second or two, Jessie couldn't say anything as she absorbed this appalling information.

"His hand—right? In *that* fire?"

Anne nodded. "Yeah. His own dammed fault—and hers. Shana should have got those kids out, but she didn't. Just herself."

"The owner's wife, you mean? Oh, I get it—you were having an *affair* with her husband."

"Well, yeah—okay—I guess you could call it that."

"What else *would* you call it? What made Tatum decide it was you?"

Anne shifted uneasily on the sofa, pulled up her knees, and peered at Jessie over the arms she wrapped defensively around them.

"They found out from a guy who was working late in the shop that Cal had had a fight with Shana the night it happened. This guy, Buzz, heard them yelling at each other and saw him take off. Cal—you know, the owner—came by my place for a while before he went on to a bar in town."

Clearly uncomfortable that Jessie was so close, she got up abruptly and moved away from the sofa as she continued. "I was home all by myself, so I didn't have an alibi like he did. I couldn't prove I didn't go out and, since I'd been in the shop before, they found my fingerprints." Turning from the window, she flung out an arm in anger, fist clenched. "Cal—that son of a bitch—didn't back me up. He told them I was jealous of her—that I could have done it, damn him. He made like he was all broken up over losing the kids—hell, he hated those kids. And she told a bunch of lies about me—probably to keep from admitting she hadn't tried to get the kids out. Who knows? She was probably down in the shop doing Buzz."

"My God, Anne. That's too much. So what finally happened?"

"Oh, Tatum couldn't ever get enough evidence to prove I had anything to do with it, because I didn't. Honest, I didn't, Jessie. I don't know who did. Somebody with a grudge—her—Buzz, maybe. I really did think that maybe she and him were—you know—so it could have been her. But Tatum was—like—obsessed or something. He wanted someone to pay and I was an easy target, so he tried really hard to make sure it *was* me. Even after it was over, he followed me around. I'd see him watching me everywhere I went. Finally, when I married Greg and moved out to the cabin, he couldn't find me. But I still saw him a time or two in town. He's a real bastard. It was all so stupid—and scary."

She plopped back down on the sofa and sat still, looking at Jessie with her chin in the air defensively.

"Now. Let's go out to the cabin right now—this afternoon, okay? How do we know Greg isn't on his way here at this very minute?"

Jessie sat staring at her, astonished at the repeated demand and what she had walked into by agreeing to give Anne a place to stay and listening to her troubles. Could this possibly be the same person in whose company she had taken casual pleasure ten years before? How much worse was it going to get?

"No, Anne, we can't. This afternoon I'm running my dogs. But, if I can arrange for my handler to stay here and take care of them while I'm gone, we'll go tomorrow. There's stuff to do before we can take off, and you'll have to help."

"Oh, I *will*—anything you want. Thanks, Jessie. I knew you'd say yes. You won't regret it. I promise."

Jessie already regretted it, but she would just do it, get it over with, then, like it or not, Anne would have to leave.

On the road to Wasilla, as Tatum took a corner too fast in the fire department car, Phil Becker gave him an anxious, quizzical look, then covered it with his usual boyish grin.

"Hey, Mike. Never seen you treat a suspect quite like that before. I assume you don't think too much of Jessie's friend. What's the deal?"

Tatum eased his foot off the gas a little, shrugged in rueful apology, and frowned.

"Sorry about that. Marty Gifford is the last person I expected to see back in Alaska—and in Jessie Arnold's house, for Lord's sake."

"Who the hell *is* she?"

"Old news—*bad news*—is what she is."

Lifting his scarred right hand from the wheel, he held it up for Becker's attention.

"I can personally thank *her* for this, Phil. But worse—she should be locked up because two kids died in a fire over ten years ago—a fire she set."

"Why wasn't she?"

"There wasn't enough evidence to take it to trial. It didn't help that the police still tend to view fire as an occurrence, not a weapon—a circumstance surrounding a death—but the kids who died weren't the intended victim."

"Who was?"

"The owner's wife, Shana Mulligan. Gifford was having an affair with Mulligan—wanted his wife out of the way. How well do you know Ms. Arnold?"

"Very well," Becker informed him, irritated. "Don't get any dumb ideas about Jessie, Mike. She's the real thing—totally reliable. She was in a close relationship with one of the guys that was in our division until a month ago."

"Yeah? Smart. Maybe too smart. But Marty Gifford's another thing and the company you keep . . . you know. People cover things. She said Gifford was an *old friend.*"

"Jessie's friendly with a lot of people. She's okay. Believe me."

"I've learned the hard way to believe what I *know* and can prove, Phil. Sorry, if that crumbles your cookie, but it's the way I am."

"Well, you're wrong about this one, Mike. I don't know anything about Anne Gifford—Holman—whatever her name is. But I *do* know Jessie—who's no *cookie,* by the way—and you're *wrong.* You'll find out."

"We'll see."

They rode the rest of the way into town in silent disagreement, Becker thinking that perhaps he should have a private chat with Jessie about the situation and

Tatum's negative attitude. The next time he saw her, however, so many things had happened that he forgot.

By the middle of the afternoon, Jessie and Billy were several miles from her kennel, each gliding along a trail on the back runners of a sled behind their two teams of dogs. The new snow that covered everything looked like a soft fuzzy blanket and was not melting, for, though the temperature had risen a little, it was still below freezing. The sky was pale as milk with an even cloud cover that hinted at more snow on the way.

Though she'd been unable to locate her favorite blue knit training hat, Jessie's mood had grown lighter with every bend and turn they followed. She had determinedly left Anne's troubles and last night's fire behind her and was almost singing as they climbed a gentle hill and wound to the right around a small stand of birch. On the crest, she whistled to Billy, who was ahead of her, whoa'd her dogs to a halt, and paused to take an appreciative look at the tremendous landscape that flowed away to the west as far as Mount Susitna, the Sleeping Lady, that rose to dominate the horizon beyond the wide reach of the Susitna Flats.

Jimmy, a promising pup just over a year old, instantly, and not for the first time that day, sprang over the gang line to be next to his teammate, Tux, who finally lost patience with this misbehavior and nipped at the transgressor's closest ear with a warning snarl. The pup yipped and tried to move away; but, caught between Tux and the line, he couldn't get back to his place. The older dog ignored him and lay down to take advantage of a few minutes rest, leaving Jimmy to cast an apologetic and imploring look back at Jessie, the accepted alpha leader of this pack. She couldn't help being amused. Tux was easygoing but would tolerate only a limited amount of such nonsense. She managed to keep a straight face as she stomped in the snow hook and walked forward to assist the culprit.

"No, Jimmy," she told him, as she took him by the loose skin over his shoulders and rump and gave him a light shake as she lifted him back over the line. "*No jumping.* Sit down and stay on your own side."

He gave her a soulful, embarrassed glance, knowing he had been literally out of line, and sat down obediently. Before the rain interrupted the training, he had almost given up this bad habit. Now he was backsliding, which wasn't totally his fault, but must be corrected. He liked to run in front of the sled and was an energetic team member who pulled strongly and well, as long as they were in motion. Now he simply needed a firm reminder to forget about playing enthusiastic games when they stopped.

Part of what Jessie enjoyed most about raising and racing Alaskan huskies was training the young dogs. It was a satisfying pleasure to socialize puppies; teach them obedience and good manners; accustom them to line and harness when they were six to eight months old; then, at almost a year, when they were big enough, gradually to show them what it was all about by adding them to the experienced teams and watch them realize the delight of swift running through the northern wilderness that she loved. The puppies she had brought into the cabin the day before already had individual collars bearing their names and hers, and they were

being trained to leash and picket line. Their minds
were wide open, so the best ones caught on fast; required little correction; and were quick, intelligent, and
good-tempered. But discipline was sometimes necessary, and it had to be applied quickly before the canine
transgressor forgot what behavior had precipitated it.

Believing in positive reinforcement rather than punishment, she very seldom felt a need to discipline a dog
physically. When she did, it was limited to a flat-
handed swat on muzzle or rear, depending on the situation, and was reserved for the most serious offenses,
like fighting or willful disobedience. A sharp "No" was
usually enough. Though puppies were allowed a lot of
leeway as they learned, only a few older dogs pushed
the limit—and that rarely—or they didn't last long in
her kennel or on teams. Most tried their best to please
her and were rewarded with an abundance of petting
and verbal approval.

Now, as she walked back to the sled, she doubted
Jimmy would jump again—at least today. Sweet and
smart, he was quickly outgrowing his grasshopper in-
clinations.

Billy had stopped thirty feet beyond her on the crest
of the hill and was shifting the position of two dogs in
his team. She drove forward and stopped again just behind him.

"Problem?"

"Naw. Tom and Sunny aren't working out like we
thought. Maybe he'll do better by his mom."

"Worth a try. Sadie'll let him know if he's slacking.
Ready?"

"Yup."

Jessie drove her team on past to take the lead for a while. They were soon winding through the trees near one of the small lakes that dotted the flat near Big Lake. The new snow on the trail had already been packed by the runners of other mushers' sleds. Practically everyone who had been trapped by the rain must be out running today, she thought, and she was glad to be one of them. They had passed several teams headed the opposite direction and one taking a break in a clearing a mile or two back.

She wondered what Anne was doing back at the cabin, but resolutely refused to follow that line of thought, glad to be away from her friend's demands and histrionics for the moment. Instead, she began to determine what would need to be done so they could leave in the morning for a quick overnight to the wilderness cabin. A trip to the grocery wouldn't be necessary, since she had plenty of food already on hand, prepared and frozen for training runs. She would have to take a big sled, for Anne must ride in it, but it wouldn't take long to pack enough for an overnight—or possibly two; a couple of expedition-weight sleeping bags, cooking gear for humans and dogs, first-aid kit, and a few other necessities like ax, handgun in case of threatening moose, odds and ends. Only what was necessary, but even that was considerable.

She was mentally sorting her dogs and considering the practicality of taking along two or three of the young ones that were doing well and would benefit from a camp out away from home, when her current team of eight came up over a small rise and was suddenly strung out along the top of a bank that fell off to the left for about ten feet into snow-covered trees and brush below.

All would have been well, had it not been for Smut, a slightly skittish young dog in the second pair on the line, who looked down and misstepped, frightened by the unexpected steep drop. She lost her footing and tumbled over the edge with a panicked yelp. Just in front of her, Pete, the leader, was jerked off his feet and slid over after her before he had any idea what was happening, which took his young running partner Taffy along, too. Behind Smut, experienced Tux dug into the snow with all four feet, but the momentum of the front half of the team yanked him very close to the edge. When everything stopped, three of the team hung in their harnesses, threatening to draw down the rest and the sled with them.

"Whoa. Whoa up," Jessie called, stomping on the brake and jamming in the snow hook, which halted the sled just in time to keep it from hitting Darryl One in his usual wheel position next to the brush bow. He stopped abruptly to keep from crashing into Tux.

"*Back*. Come back, guys. Come on back," Jessie encouraged, not letting go, pulling back with all her weight, while easing off just a little on the brake to see if she could move the sled backward and keep the gang line taut at the same time. Fortunately, Pete was the only experienced dog that had fallen over. Tux, Darryl One, and Lucky all responded by trying to back up, but the two remaining trainees, Shorts and Jimmy, confused by the situation, forgot anything they might have learned about reversing direction and simply stood still or tried to pull forward. The sled stayed where it was, and Jessie couldn't move it an inch.

Vainly looking around for a tree—or anything available to anchor a line—she was about to try to work her way forward to rescue the dogs, afraid they would strangle in their harnesses, though as long as she could still hear them yelping and whining complaints she knew they were merely uncomfortable and afraid, when Billy's team, with Tank in the lead, stopped behind her.

"Good one," Billy called. "Didn't think you'd taught 'em that yet."

"Oh, stuff it. Get up here before the rest of us slide over, too."

He came, grinning, and helped retrieve the dangling dogs, while Jessie held the sled.

In a few minutes, both teams were back on the trail with no injuries, though Pete cast cautious looks back at Smut for a time. Jessie would have sworn he felt insulted and knew exactly who was responsible for the indignity of the accident.

You're not paying enough attention, she told herself. Training required more concentration than she had been giving it today. It was time to forget about Anne and trips into the wild, and focus on what was going on in her team. Trouble would have to wait.

At the end of a long access road near Big Lake, a pickup pulled off into the afternoon shadows of a turn-around space in the trees. Its motor died, and a window was rolled down so the driver could watch and listen intently for a few minutes. Seeing no one, hearing nothing but silence, a figure in dark clothing, with a face-covering ski mask, climbed out and moved quickly down the drive toward a double-wide house trailer, walking only in tire marks on the road and carrying a small canvas bag.

Carefully keeping to the tracks previously left in the snow, the figure tried the door to the double-wide with no success. Still cautiously leaving no new tracks, it moved around to one end of the trailer, where the marks of tires indicated the parking space of a now-absent vehicle. From there it took one long leap across snow empty of any mark to land behind the trailer, where it began to examine the windows. Removing the screen from one that was open a crack, the figure pushed it wide enough to allow entrance, pulled itself up, and crawled through onto a bed, conscientiously removing snow from its boots to avoid leaving telltale damp spots on the floor.

Inside, it went along a hallway to the living room, then directly across to a small television set on a low table near the door. Dropping to its knees, it lifted and turned the set around with gloved hands, careful to leave no marks in the dust on the table. Opening the canvas bag to retrieve several items, the quick hands efficiently used a screwdriver to remove the back and attach a device to the on/off switch. Other wires were linked to a plastic container of explosive accelerant. Replacing the back and turning the set to its original position, the figure rose and checked both television and table for any suggestion of tampering.

Finding none, it went back the way it had come, slipped out the window, closed it to a crack, replaced the screen, and retraced its path around the trailer, once more making the leap to the vehicle parking space, then walked swiftly along the road to the pickup. Climbing into the cab, stripping off the ski mask, the driver started the engine and backed onto the public road.

In minutes, only someone who was knowledgeable and looking for signs of an unwelcome visitor might have determined that a break-in had occurred. No one was.

No one was there to see the unsuspecting owner come home that evening a little later than usual, after a couple of hours in a Wasilla bar. Parking a little crooked in his usual space next to his double-wide trailer, he climbed out and sorted through his keys.

Going in, he tossed his coat on a chair, took a beer from the refrigerator, and reached for the switch on the color television, with nothing particular in mind to watch. For him the talking pictures were company—a voice in the otherwise solitary house.

The result was colorful, but not what he expected. With a deafening explosion the set blew up and, instantly he and everything around him was on fire. Blinded and screaming, he whirled and thrashed in agony, trying to escape the intense heat and fierce pain that clung to his flesh, seared the clothes from his body, consumed his skin. Direction totally lost, he stumbled over the chair that held his burning coat and fell heavily to the floor.

No one was there to hear when he drew a breath that sucked nothing but flame from the carpet into his lungs, and his shrieks abruptly stopped. But the trailer continued to burn, eventually attracting the attention of another resident, who looked out the window of his lakeshore home, caught sight of the blaze, and called the fire department.

6

BY SEVEN O'CLOCK THE NEXT MORNING, JESSIE WAS
loading dogs into the compartments of the dog box on
the back of her pickup. Custom designed for mushers,
the compartments faced outward on each side, two
high and six wide, and were constructed for safe transportation of sled dogs. They had holes in the doors to
let each dog look but not jump out and to allow plenty
of ventilation. Large enough to let the dog stand up, lie
down, turn and move around in safety, they were lined
with straw for individual comfort and warmth. Filled
to capacity, Jessie's dog box would carry twenty-four
dogs at once, a traveling doggie motel of sorts.

Billy, who had come early to the kennel to discuss
the training schedule he would keep while she was
gone, had helped to lift the large empty sled on top of
the box and secure it for travel. In a space between the
two lines of dog compartments, Jessie and Anne had
loaded harness, gang lines, and all the other equipment
and supplies they would need for three days away, with
some extra food and clothing for emergencies.

As Anne came out the cabin door to put the lunch she had been making in the truck's cab, Jessie was selecting dogs for a team of eleven, including three of her most reliable young ones, Lucky, Cola, and Elmer. Skittish Smut would definitely stay at home, but dependable Pete had already been put into a compartment beside the Darryls, One and Two, who would run in their usual wheel position nearest the sled. Tank would lead, of course, and stood near the truck like a supervisor, watching as, two at a time, Billy brought the chosen dogs and helped Jessie lift them into their individual compartments. Already loaded, to fill out the team, were Mitts, Sunny, and Wart, all experienced distance-racing dogs that had gone to Canada with Jessie to run the International Yukon Quest from Whitehorse to Fairbanks a month before.

Billy was crossing the dog lot with the last dog, Bliss, in tow, when the rest of the kennel began to bark. Jessie saw Mike Tatum turn his car into her long driveway. He pulled up behind her truck, effectively blocking it, before getting out.

"Oh, shit," said Anne, realizing who it was and disappearing rapidly up the steps and into the cabin.

"*Hey,*" Tatum yelled after her. "Come *back* here. I've got some questions for *you*."

The door slammed shut, and Jessie, distinctly hearing the deadlock thump into place, knew it was up to her to face his angry scowl.

"Goddammit. Get her back out here," he demanded.

Billy reached the pickup and stopped, holding Bliss by the collar and staring in mute disapproval at Tatum.

Jessie turned away, reached for the dog, then

changed her mind and nodded to the compartment in which Bliss would ride. Ignoring the investigator, she watched Billy lift the dog into the space and close the door. The hole in it was immediately filled with a curious canine muzzle.

"Did you *hear* me? I want to talk to Marty Gifford."

"Well," Jessie told him, calmly moving to Tank, the only dog not yet loaded and giving Tatum a scornful glance, "that's your problem, isn't it? I'm not *Anne Holman's* keeper."

With a furious clenched-fist gesture, he started past her toward the cabin.

"You were *not invited* onto my property, Tatum," Jessie, with no inclination to call him "just Mike," informed him and stepped into his path. "Definitely *not* into my house."

"Get out of my way. You're obstructing an officer in—" he began, but she cut him off sharply.

"You have a warrant?"

"*You* got something to hide?"

They glared at each other, practically nose to nose, Tatum clearly expecting her to back away. She moved an inch closer and folded her arms. "I guess that means you haven't."

Billy came to stand beside her and help to present a silent, united front.

"*Look,*" Tatum all but shouted, "I'm investigating a fire here."

Tank, standing next to Jessie, gave a low warning growl and showed his teeth.

"Restrain that dog, or . . ." The investigator took a step backward.

She laid a hand on Tank's head.

"There hasn't been a fire *here*," she said, deliberately misinterpreting his statement. "If it's about Oscar's, I've already told you what I know."

"Not *that* fire. There was another one set last night and I'm *going* to talk to—"

"Where?"

"None of your—"

"*Make* it my business."

For a long moment, it was a standoff. Then Tatum huffed in annoyed frustration.

"*Ms.* Arnold—" he started, jabbing a finger toward her that elicited another rumble from Tank.

"Don't *threaten* me," she warned, narrowing stormy gray eyes and moving her hand to Tank's collar. "I don't care for that kind of thing—and neither does my dog, if you noticed."

The finger was reluctantly lowered and Tatum took another backward step.

"Look—you don't know who you're harboring."

"I'm not *harboring* anyone. Anne Holman is my guest."

"What she *is,* is a liar, arsonist, and probably a murderer. Where was she yesterday and last night?"

"I told you, I'm not her keeper."

"Dammit—" He hesitated, for the first time realizing that they had been loading dogs into a truck they intended to take somewhere. "Where the hell do you think you're going?"

"Now that's really none of your business. But, since you asked so *very* nicely, I'm taking some of my dogs out for a training run."

"Where?"

"Off the Glenn Highway."

"Looks like more than that to me."

"I don't care what it looks like to you."

"If you leave town, I'll assume that—"

"You can assume anything you damn well please," Jessie told him, finally loosing the leash on her temper. "If you think you can arrest me—or Anne—then do it. Otherwise, get off my property—*now*."

"I'm not arresting you, but I can take you both in for questioning."

"*Try* it. I don't have to talk to you, Tatum."

"Resisting arrest—"

"If you're not arresting me, how can I be resisting?"

He was so angry his face was white and, for a second or two, when she knew he wanted to hit her, a swift image of Greg Holman flashed into her mind. Then, without another word, Tatum spun abruptly and stalked back to his car. Throwing himself into the driver's seat, he furiously overcranked the engine, then backed the length of the drive at top speed, whipping the car into a turn at the end that bounced the vehicle back on the paved road in a spray of snow and gravel, and headed toward town. No one moved until he had disappeared from sight and the whine of his engine faded.

Jessie took a deep breath, let it out, and turned to Billy.

"Whew. Thanks for the backup," she told him, then dropped to her knees in the snow to smile at Tank and give him lots of petting. "You, too, buddy."

"Who the hell was that?"

"An arson investigator with a personal problem."

"Jeez. Hope he doesn't come back while you're gone."

She stood up and shook her head. "I doubt it. But if he does, you call the troopers and ask for Phil Becker. You know Phil. He understands Tatum's attitude—he won't let him bully you. The number's on the list over my desk."

Still concerned, she frowned thoughtfully. "Do you think it would be okay with your folks if you stayed here while I'm gone? I wouldn't mind someone keeping an eye on things."

"Sure—I can do that. Make it easier to feed and run the mutts, anyway, if I don't have to go back and forth."

Twenty minutes later, the dogs riding comfortably in back, Jessie slowed the pickup to cross the railroad tracks as they approached Wasilla. Beside her in the passenger seat, Anne looked back one more time in the side mirror, convinced that Tatum would be following them.

"But I *heard* you tell him that we were going out the Glenn Highway. That's not the way to the cabin."

"So we changed our minds. You *want* him to know where we're going? I don't."

She made a left turn and headed northwest through town on the Parks Highway, away from the area she had mentioned to Tatum.

"Oh. Okay." Anne fell silent, noticing how the small town had changed and grown in her ten-year absence.

Jessie was not unhappy to have her constant chatter and questions cease for a few minutes. She had not been happy to have Anne insist on taking along a day pack stuffed with things she swore she could not leave behind, but had ignored it in order to get going without further argument. The sled, with a passenger, would be heavily loaded and Jessie privately hoped to leave most of whatever the day pack contained locked securely in the back of the truck when they took off on the wilderness trail that would require some hard work at sled handling. One of the reasons she had left the area ten years before was the lack of enough good training trails for her dogs. It was much better to live in an area where many mushers shared trails and kept them well groomed. She did not intend to be overloaded now.

As they neared the edge of Wasilla, where Jessie planned to stop for gas, someone behind them began to honk.

"Oh, God. It's Tatum again, isn't it?" Anne shrieked, trying unsuccessfully to get a look at the driver in the rearview mirror.

Jessie was pulling into a service station on the right.

"Oh—no. Don't stop," Anne wailed. "Oh, Jessie, *please* don't stop."

"Oh, cut it out, Anne. It's just Hank Peterson. I've got to get gas, and I want to ask him about that fire last night. Just stay here. I'll be right back."

She got out and shut the door on Anne. Peterson, who had pulled in behind them, walked forward to where Jessie waited at the pumps, opening the cap on her tank.

"Hey, Jessie. Where you off to?"

"Overnight training run west of Trapper Creek off the Petersville Road. You know anything about another fire last night?"

She inserted the gas hose nozzle and watched the numbers begin to roll over on the pump as the tank filled.

"Not much. Hear it gutted a double-wide out near Big Lake."

The mention of *Big Lake* caught Jessie's attention.

"Was it set?"

"That's what they said on the news this morning."

"Whose place? Anybody we know?"

"I didn't. Guy named Mulligan got toasted—couldn't get out."

"*Cal* Mulligan? You sure?"

"Yeah, that sounds right. You know him?"

"No—just about him. Two of his kids died in a fire ten years ago."

"Sweet Jesus. Bad luck. Did you hear that investigator called Oscar in for more questions?"

"Why? He didn't burn his place."

"Well . . ." Hank kicked at a pebble that skittered away under Jessie's truck, and didn't look up at her. "It looks like he *was* having money troubles. Rumor is that he's behind on his payments, and the bank's been threatening to shut down one or the other of his bars. Nobody saw him in town when the Other Place burned, Jessie."

"Dammit, Hank. He shouldn't have to prove it. We *know* Oscar."

"Yeah? Well—could be we don't. You can't always tell, I guess. Maybe—maybe not."

The gas pump shut off with a snap, and Jessie returned the nozzle to its holder with a sinking feeling, wondering how and why Hank should so easily doubt Oscar's word and actions.

* * *

The idea that Oscar might commit arson to avoid foreclosure on his pub continued to bother Jessie as she drove the seventy miles to the turnoff at Trapper Creek. She couldn't make herself accept it. He had once told her that if he ever had to choose between his two places, he'd take the Other Place—that it was his favorite partly because he'd built it from the ground up and partly because he liked the customers who collected there. If that was true, and if he *had* been tempted beyond reason by a need for cash—which she didn't believe—then wouldn't it make more sense for him to burn the bar in Wasilla that he liked less? Or would being twelve miles out of town be a deciding factor, if he were faced with a choice?

Dammit, I'm beginning to think like Hank, she told herself, refused to examine the idea further, and turned her thoughts to another concern—the fire at Big Lake.

Anne had not asked what Hank wanted, when Jessie climbed back into the pickup and, not wanting to get into another interminable and unconvincing discussion, she hadn't mentioned Cal Mulligan's death in the fire. Tatum's determination this morning to interrogate her friend now made more sense. The two fires involving the same man—ten years apart or not—would obviously seem connected. If nothing else, at least in his obsessed mind, this new fire would link Anne to the old one for the simple reason that she had returned before it occurred and she *had* known Mulligan.

But Anne couldn't have had the time to go to Big Lake, find out where Mulligan was now living, and set fire to his double-wide trailer—could she? Jessie

glanced down at the odometer of her truck. Had there
been any unexplained miles added since she'd driven it
to the airport to pick up Anne? Impossible to tell, because she hadn't checked it then. Had there been less
gas in the tank today? Who knew? She hadn't paid attention or looked at the gauge before filling up today.

You were gone for hours yesterday afternoon.

Anne couldn't know how long I'd be gone. I could
have come back anytime.

But how long would it take for her to drive?

Well—twenty miles from Wasilla to Big Lake, a
generous thirty—thirty-five from my place. Forty-five
minutes? Maybe two hours total turn-around time at
the most.

Plenty to have borrowed your truck, gone out there,
and been back long before you came home.

Not possible. The fire was *last night*. She was at my
place all evening.

And there are no ways for fires to start long after the
person who sets them is gone?

That's crazy.

Okay. If you say so. Still . . .

She glanced at Anne, who was quietly watching the
wilderness rush past on her side of the highway, seemingly in a world of her own, and let it go. The only response Jessie knew she would get from questions was
a resentful and defensive argument. There was no way
to prove anything at this point. Hank's information
might easily be all rumor. She decided to pretend she
hadn't even heard about the Big Lake fire till they had
finished this crazy trip Anne was so set on making and
were home again.

Ahead, she caught sight of the sign that indicated a turnoff for Talkeetna to the right and Trapper Creek to the left. Very soon she could be back on the runners of a sled in the wilderness world she loved best. Might as well enjoy it and forget the rest for the time being. No one's going to die if I forget about it all for now, she thought, and bit her tongue.

7

‒∼oⁿoⁿoⁿ‒

THOUGH SHE WAS TEMPTED TO TURN RIGHT AT THE HIGH-way junction and make a visit to the Talkeetna Road-house for a cup of coffee, Jessie turned left off the Parks Highway, away from the road that led to the well-known community fourteen miles to the east at the confluence of the Susitna, Talkeetna, and Chulitna rivers.

Talkeetna had long been a famous name in moun-tain-climbing circles as the jumping-off point for ex-peditions to Mount McKinley, or Denali, as most Alaskans called it. Most climbers used the West But-tress route, which originated at about seven thousand feet on the Kahitna Glacier, and were flown there in ski-wheel–equipped aircraft by several air services that specialized in the glacier landings necessary to ferry them and their gear to and from the mountain and also provided flight-seeing for tourists. During the summer months the rivers were alive with fish, fishermen, and tourists.

The dry goods and grocery stores, service station,

gift shop, restaurants, bars, hotels, and bed and break-fasts of Talkeetna lined old-fashioned Main Street, the only paved road in the small, thriving, and notably independent community of log cabins and clapboard houses, which dead-ended on the Susitna riverbank. Its residents had a reputation for resisting all outside efforts to infringe upon or change anything about their chosen lifestyle.

Jessie had always enjoyed stopping there, where people were friendly and laid-back, and took care of their own. Even after she had moved closer to Wasilla, almost every year she drove back up the highway to camp at Talkeetna, where hundreds gathered once a summer to indulge in a long weekend of fiddle-fingering, banjo-plucking, foot-tapping bluegrass music. But on this trip, abandoning her thought of coffee and a quick hello, she turned the other way instead, past the big two-story Trapper Creek Inn and General Store, the Trading Post, library, museum, gift shop, and RV park near the junction—most still closed for the season—and drove west on the Petersville Road.

Anne had uncharacteristically said little on the drive north, commenting infrequently on landmarks she recognized. She sat up attentively, however, when they went around a bend in the road and the lower part of Mount McKinley began to flash into view between the trees that lined the highway. The top of the tallest mountain in North America was, as usual, hidden in clouds; but its visible ridges gleamed in sunlight pouring in from the south, each fold a contrast of deep bluish-purple shadows. The color was unique to the northern latitudes, as was the glowing winter light, created by the low angle of the sun reflected from hundreds of miles of snow-covered wilderness. It made the very air seem almost tangible.

The Petersville Road, which soon turned to unpaved snow-covered gravel, ran west and a little north from the junction for fourteen miles to Kroto Creek, beyond which the road was not maintained during the winter. They passed a subdivision or two that had not existed when Jessie had lived in the area and a few tourist cabins, some open for the benefit of cross-country skiers and snowmachiners who drove from Anchorage and the MatSu Valley communities for weekend fun far from town.

As she parked among several trucks with snowmachine trailers by Kroto Creek, Jessie could see a number of tracks that continued west on the unplowed section of the road, and she reminded herself that she would have to be alert. Snowmachines made so much noise that their drivers couldn't hear mushers coming toward them on a trail until it was sometimes too late to avoid them. Unexpected meetings between snowmachines and dog sleds on narrow tracks periodically resulted in disastrous accidents that killed or injured dogs.

In half an hour, she and Anne were ready to go, team hitched to the gang line, sled packed, and both women dressed warmly against the cold, for a chill wind was blowing from the north, bringing more than a hint of glaciers on its breath and adding a significant windchill factor. The soft new powder was blown into the air around them like a mist, and its fine grains scoured their skin when they faced directly into it.

Anne was wearing borrowed winter clothing of Jessie's, having brought none of her own. Through the years Jessie had accumulated a collection of warm wearables, most of which she wore on training runs and in the yard as she cared for her dogs, for they exhibited the prints of dog paws, food stains, and general grime that would not wash out. The somewhat grubby green parka Anne had on was also decorated in several places with duct tape to keep its down from leaking out through holes caused by dog nails and teeth and the sparks from fires Jessie had built on the trail. She had pulled a black ski mask over her head before raising the hood and tying it securely under her chin. Thick down mittens covered her hands, and a pair of heavy winter boots a little too big made walking awkward. Jessie thought it was odd to see her clothes on someone else.

I'd better get a new parka before I begin to resemble a bag lady, she told herself.

"You may not be fashionable," she told Anne with a smile, "but you won't freeze."

"I'll be fine—really. Where do you want me?"

"The sled'll be a little crowded, but there's a sleeping bag for you to sit on if you want in the back. The rest of our stuff is packed in front. Get in and I'll tuck the other bag over you."

"I'll take the padding. I've bruised my butt in sleds before with nothing between me and the flat bottom— don't want to have to eat standing up."

When she was settled securely, the sled bag snapped up far enough to keep out blowing snow, clutching the day pack she had adamantly refused to leave behind,

Jessie checked to be sure the truck and dog box were locked, pulled the snow hook, and let Tank start the eager team west along the road, following the snow-machine tracks.

Pete and Lucky followed Tank, behind them came team dogs Sunny and Wart, Mitts and Elmer, Bliss and Cola, then Darryl One and Darryl Two in wheel position next to the sled. Each of the three young dogs—Elmer, Bliss, and Cola—was paired with an experienced partner and, as Jessie watched, were doing well in pulling their share and keeping in line with no problems. She was glad she had brought them. It made her feel less guilty over disrupting her training schedule and would have been part of her plan for the next week or two anyway. This night or two spent away from their usual boxes in the yard was just happening a little earlier than she had calculated, and on a different trail. As the team trotted quickly forward, the dogs, full of energy and eagerness, soon broke into a lope. For a few minutes, she let them go as fast as they wanted on the straight, flat surface of the snowy road, getting this enthusiasm out of their systems early. After a mile or two, she called Tank to a slower pace. There would be plenty of work for them on the off-road trail ahead.

The Petersville Road, on which they traveled, had been built by gold miners in the 1920s. When home-steading began in 1948, permanent settlers had began to collect in the area, and the population had continued to grow slowly for the next twenty years. With spectacular views of Mount McKinley on clear days, it had remained popular with those who wanted to avoid an urban existence and live close to nature, and who didn't mind driving seventy miles to a shopping center.

Ten years earlier, the idea had appealed to Jessie when a cabin was offered to her for the winter. Though she had had no particular trouble carrying enough supplies to the isolated cabin for a long cold season, the rough trails and distance had finally convinced her she would do better closer to Wasilla, where it was not so far to a doctor, dentist, and, especially, a veterinarian. She had also grown tired of hauling water or melting snow for all her needs and those of her dogs—she had never realized exactly how much water was required of one lone musher, until it came only in five-gallon cans that had to be transported on a sled or melted over a fire built of wood she had to chop.

In five miles, they came to Forks Roadhouse, where the road swung north again toward Petersville and the mining country that lay in the folds of the hills under looming Mount McKinley. Here, rather than continuing to follow it, they swung left onto snow-buried track leading to the Little Peters Hills that lay to the west. This trail was familiar to Jessie, though she had not been over it in years and no longer recalled each rise, drop, and turn as she once had. It ran along the southern exposure of the Peters Hills, crossing creek after frozen creek in the gullies of the rolling landscape.

Peter must have staked a pretty big claim somewhere nearby, Jessie thought, as they crossed what she recognized as Peters Creek. A lot of things were named for him, whoever he had been—some kind of topographer with the USGS at the turn of the century, she thought she vaguely remembered. But dozens of other creeks had been named by the miners who worked them in their search for gold. She remembered the names of some of them as she rode the sled runners into the wilds: Black Creek, Sand Creek, Big Creek, String Creek. Beyond the Peters Hills, in the valley between it and the Dutch Hills, were Coal, Slate, Grant, and Trout creeks, along with Thunder, Dollar, Lucky, and Short creeks, and a place called Nugget Bench. Someone had evidently thought they had staked a winner there; but many gold-rush names, she knew, were deceptively optimistic. Windy Creek and Pickle Creek had piqued her imagination during her time at the borrowed cabin and—even more—Hungryman Creek. Some miner must have had an interesting story about the name for that one, and had obviously survived to tell it and name the creek. There was even a tributary called Creek Creek. Had everyone run out of names?

The trail they traveled had not been used recently, perhaps not for days, and was worse than Jessie remembered—an unmaintained route full of twists and turns now covered with new powder that concealed many hazards. She took it slowly and carefully, afraid some rock or root under the surface would snag a paw and injure one of the dogs that was still anxious to pull, as always at the start of a new run. She also had no intention of battering the sled any more than was absolutely necessary to get them to the Holman cabin. Replacing the sled would take money she needed for many other things.

The team was now breaking trail through new snow but had no trouble, for it wasn't too deep. Somewhere under the fresh powder was a track that had been packed by passing snowmachines earlier in the winter. The dogs had all settled into a steady trot, and even the young ones were minding their manners and doing well. Perhaps eight inches of snow had piled up in the past two days, but it was possible to follow a slight depression that indicated a trail left by snowmachines before the storm. Parts of this dent were filling with drifting snow, but the wind was less severe here than on the more open road.

On either side of the road the country was flat, with scattered stands of thin spruce, alder, and a few birch between swampy areas that were impassable during the summer. Permafrost, a few feet under the surface, refused the questing roots of the spruce, forcing them to remain shallow and the trees above them thin, with stubby branches. Jessie had always thought they looked more like dark pipe cleaners than real trees.

As they traveled onto the flanks of the Peters Hills, the trail began slowly to rise. The few scattered birch disappeared, leaving spruce and alder; and there was lots of brush on the rolling slopes around them. She remembered that this was a prime berry-picking area in the fall.

Jessie stopped the team as they gained one of the first ridges, to look back the way they had come. A faint whine caught her attention, and she watched two drivers pull their snowmachines into the snowy parking lot at the roadhouse. More than half the sky had now cleared, though clouds still shrouded Mount McKinley's summit. The wide Susitna Valley spread itself out for miles, a glory of light in the sunshine that created a million sparkles on the new snow on the ground and in the wind, a blue finger of shadow reaching north from each slender spruce. How, she wondered, could anyone say that winter was boringly colorless? It had a thousand hues, each different, clean, and lovely.

A raven swept onto a nearby tree branch and quarked a ragged call, perhaps alerting others to the passing sled as a potential food source, if they were lucky. He was doomed to disappointment, for Jessie seldom left anything behind on a trail, and a scrap or two wasn't enough to justify their following her for miles. The bird seemed to realize this, for, spreading its wings, it soared off, sliding down the wind toward the roadhouse, where it might find better pickings.

The bulk of the enormous mountain to the north was now hidden by the slopes of the Peters and Dutch hills, but twenty miles across the valley, Jessie could make out a notch in the trees where the road led into Talkeetna.

"Why're we stopping?" Anne asked, squirming around in the sled to look over her shoulder.

"Just looking," Jessie told her cheerfully, impatience erased by the enjoyment of running in such a spectacular setting. When she could have moments like this, it made all the work of raising and training sled dogs worth the expenditure of resources, time, and effort.

"How much longer?"

The question surprised Jessie. "Don't you remember?"

"It's been a long time."

"We're not even halfway yet."

"I don't remember that it seemed so far."

As Anne settled back, Jessie took one last look at the huge valley before calling up the team, bemused at how quickly people forget places they've known. Had Anne ever really seen the glory of the country when she'd lived here? *I never noticed if she did or not, but she wasn't much of an outward-looking person then—and even less now—*Jessie realized a little sadly. *What a loss.*

Most of the dogs had rested, lying down on the snow when she didn't immediately encourage them forward again. While her back was turned, however, young Elmer, a hardworking dog with one floppy ear and a sense of humor, had begun to persistently gnaw at the protective fleece booties she had put on his feet. He disliked wearing them, couldn't seem to learn to leave them alone, and had developed the adroit trick of ripping open the Velcro fastenings with his teeth and pulling them off every chance he got. Jessie turned back just as he had successfully stripped them from both front feet.

"Elmer—*no,*" she admonished and, setting the snow hook, stepped from the sled to replace them. Instantly she was thigh-deep in powdery snow and had to wallow clumsily forward to reach him.

He lay with his front paws and muzzle on the booties he wished to abandon, moving nothing but his eyes as he looked up at her, knowing he had transgressed—again.

"No," Jessie told him. "Booties stay *on your feet.*"

He watched attentively as she replaced them, then he shook one foot to see if the bootie would, perhaps, fall off. When it didn't, he gave up and left them alone for the time being. But Jessie suspected that at the next opportunity he would repeat the removal.

"I'm not climbing back and forth through this powdery stuff every time we stop for a minute," she told him firmly and, wading back to the sled, unsnapped a bag to rummage for the roll of electricians tape she used when she needed something narrower than duct tape. Though she thoroughly searched the bag, she could not find it anywhere.

Gone with my favorite hat, she told herself, shaking her head, and finally, irritated, took the roll of duct tape instead. Tearing off two strips with her teeth, she waded back to Elmer to cover the cuffs of his booties with tape, securing the Velcro fasteners. "There, now you won't be such a sly dog, will you?" He examined the silvery additions, then glanced up at her, head cocked to one side. As she wallowed back to her place on the sled, to start the team moving again, she had to smile—it was evident that he was already mentally at work on this new challenge.

The trail followed the gulch that held Black Creek for about five miles, over another ridge, before dropping down to run along the north edge of a frozen, snowy swamp. Where Sand Creek ran into it, Jessie bore left toward the Little Peters Hills and the cabin she had borrowed for the winter and the one beyond it that Anne Holman had for a while called home. At the far edge of the swamp, next to an alder thicket, she halted the team in a sunny spot and called a lunch break.

"Don't know about you," she told Anne, "but I'm starving and the mutts need water. Let's make a fire and melt some snow for them—and make some coffee for us."

*   *   *

An hour later, they had eaten, fed and watered the dogs, and crested the hill and were looking down on the Kahiltna River, spread out frozen below them.

"It won't be long now," Jessie told her passenger. "At least to the cabin I lived in—then it's only another mile to yours."

It wasn't long. Running along the ridge of the hill, they soon dropped back to the Susitna Valley side and came to a low log cabin sheltered by a small stand of spruce.

"Whoa, guys—whoa," she called to bring the team to a halt. From the runners of the sled, she examined the cabin and considered a quick look around, but quickly changed her mind as she assessed the deep, unbroken snow around it.

Boarded-up windows and front door told her the place was empty. No one lived there now and, from the look of it, hadn't for some time. On the edges of the boards that covered the door, she could see some long scratches from the claws of a bear in its attempt to gain entry, but it had evidently been unsuccessful, for the planks remained in place. It had probably been discouraged by the dozens of six-inch nails that had been driven through those planks, their points facing outward.

Snow had drifted deeply against the north wall, and the roof was piled high. The metal chimney lacked any sign of welcoming smoke; all was very still; and the cabin looked abandoned and sad, not as she had expected, for it had been a happy place for her ten years ago. Like many deserted small cabins in the area, it left her with a feeling that it huddled there, patiently awaiting its own demise—would gradually fall apart, decay, and once again become part of the wilderness around it.

"Hey, let's go," Anne demanded from the sled.

No nostalgia for *her,* Jessie thought. "Yes—okay."

We'll stop on the way back tomorrow, she decided, or the next day—whichever. She clucked the dogs into motion toward the Holman cabin, a mile farther along the trail.

It was growing colder. The sun had followed them over the last hill and now shone on the west side. Though it shed very little warmth this time of year, even the illusion of it disappeared on the east side that they now traveled. The frosty blue-purple shade was darker in the shadows of the few sparse trees. It would be good to reach their goal and get a fire built in the stove to warm the cabin in which they would spend the night. Anne wiggled restlessly on the sled, looking ahead eagerly at each corner they turned in traversing the mile of hillside, headed southwest on the east-facing hill.

They came at last to a sharp bend that Jessie remembered, knowing that, as soon as they rounded it, she would be able to see the Holman cabin ahead through the trees.

They turned, but she could see nothing but trees—dead trees, black and scorched. The cabin was gone.

"Oh, Anne, it's burned down," she said in surprised regret.

Halting the dogs, she stood staring at the spot where the cabin had been, then glanced down at the face of her friend, expecting to find similar consternation there.

What she saw was anything but. Anne was slowly nodding and smiling.

"Yes," she said, "I knew it was. Greg burned it—when we left."

8

IN THE SOFT BLUE OF THE SAME EVENING, JUST AFTER sunset, when the neon signs and street lights of Wasilla appeared brighter than they actually were, a compact rental car swung into the parking lot of Oscar's in-town pub. A large man in jeans, scarred leather work boots, and brown Carhart's jacket, who would have looked and felt more at home in a pickup, pulled himself up out of it, stretched widely to relieve assorted discomforts—the result of confinement in a too-small space—and ambled toward the pub's front door.

A wall of noise hit him inside—happy hour at full volume—the place full of clamorous people who had stopped for a drink or two on their way home from work. Loud conversations combined with the crack of pool balls to make it almost impossible to hear the wail of a Garth Brooks hit on the jukebox. The smell of hot popcorn, slightly scorched, hung in the air.

Oscar Lee, who had fired his incompetent bartender and replaced her with himself, was efficiently working to keep up with the demand for liquid refreshment—proficiently mixing drinks, pulling drafts, and prying the tops from beer bottles to satisfy the thirst of his customers. The grin on his face, however, revealed that he was thoroughly enjoying the press and the relaxed good humor of the crowd, half of whom were regulars from the Knik Road area.

"Hey, Oscar. When're you gonna start work on a new Other Place?" a Budweiser drinker called from a seat halfway down the bar.

"Soon as the ground thaws," he answered, placing a pitcher and four glasses on a barmaid's tray, along with change for a twenty.

"Gonna have a pub-raising?"

"Sounds like a good idea. You gonna wire it for me, Jake?"

"Sure. I'll work for beer."

"Cheap at twice the price."

"Okay—two beers, then."

The man from the rental car took the only empty stool, at the far end of the long bar, and glanced around as he waited for Oscar to deliver a bourbon and water to an already waiting customer, then pause in front of him to lay down a cocktail napkin.

"What's your pleasure?"

"Got Coors?"

"Sure."

The beer and a clean glass quickly appeared, along with a basket of buttery popcorn, but he ignored the glass and sipped slowly from the bottle, examining the faces around him for any he recognized.

On the next bar stool, a petite, lacquered blond in a

green blouse set down her margarita, lit a cigarette, and looked up at him with a friendly smile.

"Nothing small about you, is there?"

He shrugged in response and smiled his agreement.

"New in town or on your way through?"

"Just passing."

"So—welcome to beautiful downtown Wasilla." She offered a hand, cool and damp from the condensation on her glass. "Gloria Sorenson—Glory to my friends."

He shook it briefly. "Greg . . . Holman."

"Where you from, Greg?"

"Colorado."

"Nice country. I went to college in Laramie. We used to drive down to Denver for weekends."

Holman nodded and sampled the popcorn, which needed salt, still searching the room for anyone he knew.

When he didn't respond, Glory gave him a quizzical, half-amused look. "Don't say much, do you?"

He grinned. "Haven't much to say."

"Well . . . that's okay. Who you looking for?"

"Thought I might see somebody I know."

"You been here before?"

"Used to live around here ten years ago."

"This place wasn't Oscar's then."

"The Hangout."

"That's *right*."

Greg Holman gave up searching the crowd and turned back to the bar. "You know Jessie Arnold?" he asked casually.

"Hey, everybody knows Jessie. She's an Iditarod musher."

"That's the one. Still live around here?"

"Has a place out on Knik Road. She a friend of yours?"

"Just like to say hello."

"She's listed—Arnold Kennels."

"Thanks."

He drained the beer bottle in two swallows, left a tip for the bartender, and, before his new wanna-be friend Glory could think of another question, disappeared through the door into the night.

Billy Steward had spent the day on two long training runs with the usual mix of experienced and inexperienced dogs, which several times had resulted in tangles and confusion among the ranks. Late in the afternoon, on the way back to Jessie's cabin from the second run, everything was finally going smoothly when young Smut suddenly decided she didn't want to pull anymore and began to drag against the tug line.

"Smut—let's go, Smut," he called to let her know he had noticed her misbehavior.

When she ignored him, he stopped the team and walked forward to see what was causing the problem. Maybe she had a sore foot, though she hadn't been limping or favoring one. Stripping off her booties, he examined all four feet but found nothing amiss. The rest of her, which he checked carefully with knowledgeable fingers, was fine as well.

"There's nothing the matter with you, girl. You're okay. Let's try it again."

When he started the team, she continued to refuse

and tried to sit down against the forward pull, becoming a burden to the rest of the team.

"Dammit, Smut. Cut it out."

Halting them all, he went forward to stand beside her.

"What the heck's wrong with you?"

The dog lay down in the snow and wouldn't get up, resting her muzzle on her forepaws. It was clear she'd decided that she'd done enough for the day.

This was not acceptable, but Billy, tired from a full day of mushing, feeding, watering, and caring for dogs on the trail and back at the kennel, had no intention of putting a lot of time and energy into babying Smut out of her decision and back into action. Without further effort, he impatiently unhooked her from the gang line and put her in the sled, snapping the bag shut so that nothing but her head stuck out, then called up the rest of the team.

It took them less than an hour to arrive at the cabin, but Smut, always skittish and somewhat reluctant, had now learned that if she grew bored or tired of running, or didn't like the trail, all she had to do was lie down and refuse to pull and she would be carried home by her teammates in warmth and comfort. She was developing an attitude that would be impossible to correct.

Smut would probably never have made a good member of a racing team; some dogs just don't have the heads for it. But it would take weeks of frustrated attention before Jessie would finally give up, drop her from training, and use her space on the line for other, more promising dogs. A good home would be found for Smut with someone who wanted a pet, not a working sled dog. Only the best eventually become the racing dogs that delight in pulling sleds for distance races all

the way to Nome in the Iditarod or over the challenging
trails of gold-rush country in the Yukon Quest. Luckily,
a kennel of over forty, and puppies from several litters
a year, gave Jessie enough choices to fill her teams with
eager, dependable dogs. The others were sold, becoming a cash resource that made it possible to raise and
train those that loved running and would quit only
under the most adverse conditions. Many not even then.

Billy finished his long day by watering and feeding
all the dogs, though he was too tired to socialize with
them. Going up the steps in the glow of the halogen
yard lights that came on in response to a motion sensor
and lit half the dog yard, he noticed a white square of
paper jammed between the door and its frame above the
doorknob. Unlocking the door, he took it inside, turned
on the lights, kicked off his boots, and unfolded it.

Jessie,

> *Mike Tatum has a wild hair up his ass over the*
> *Mulligan fire last night. I'm not sure what's got*
> *him going, but I think we'd better talk about it—*
> *and about your friend, whatever her name is.*
> *Please call me when you get back from wherever*
> *you are.*

> *Thanks,*
> *Becker*

The message had nothing to do with Billy. He laid it
down on the round oak dining table, where Jessie
would see it when she came home, and forgot it.

Hungry, he baked a frozen pizza, ate all of it, then followed it with a large dish of chocolate ice cream, while watching an HBO movie on television. He fell asleep on the sofa before it was over. At ten-thirty, he came to enough to turn off the lights and the television, pulled an afghan over himself, then slept so soundly that he didn't even move at just after one in the morning, when the dogs began to bark in the yard.

The crash of something falling in back of the cabin near the storage shed finally roused him. At first he couldn't figure out where he was, but he knew it wasn't his own bed at home. In the dark of Jessie's living room things looked strangely unfamiliar in silhouette against light from the yard that fell through the window in a pale square on the floor. Yawning and shaking his head, he got up and padded sleepily to look out. In the yard lights, he could see nothing but the dogs that were awake and still barking by their boxes. Tux stood silently staring toward the back of the house.

What the hell?

He walked through the dark cabin to the window in the bedroom and looked out into the night. The woods were black and still. Nothing moved but a few branches, swayed by a light breeze; and, as he watched, a clump of snow fell from the side of a spruce, trailing granules like sugar through the air. Everything not covered with snow showed up dark. As his vision adjusted to the dark, Billy noticed a line of tracks in the snow that seemed to have circled the cabin, coming close to it in a couple of places—below the window and near the back door—then disappearing behind the shed.

On the opposite side of the storage shed was Jessie's puppy pen and a smaller shed that she warmed and used for mothers with new litters. From somewhere there he heard a banging, like the pounding of a hammer on something of a wood-and-metal combination. Someone was trying to break into either the maternity or the storage shed—probably the latter, since the maternity shed was empty and unlocked at the moment.

Suddenly wide awake, his first impulse was to go out to confront the intruder and see what was going on. But he remembered the anger Tatum had displayed in the yard earlier that day and had second thoughts. Jessie had said if the investigator came back he should call Phil Becker. It seemed a much better idea.

Grabbing a flashlight from the pocket of his coat by the front door, he went quickly to the cordless phone on Jessie's desk, found the number on the list pinned to the wall, and called the troopers.

Though Becker was not in the office, they promised to get a message to him. In a few minutes, the phone rang under his hand, and Billy snatched it up before the ring was complete, hoping it wouldn't be heard outside, where the pounding was still going on.

"Billy. What's wrong?"

"Jessie said to call you if the investigator came back. I don't know if it's him, but somebody's trying to break into Jessie's shed."

"Where are you?"

"In the house. Jessie's truck is gone, so maybe he doesn't know I'm here—he's making a lot of noise."

"I'm on my way. Stay where you are. Don't turn on a light and keep quiet."

In less than fifteen minutes Billy watched the patrol car pull into the drive. It would have been silent, had it not been for the cacophony of welcome from the dogs. The pounding had stopped soon after Billy's phone call, and he had heard nothing more from outside. The dogs had settled down and the yard lights had gone off.

They blinked on again when Becker parked by the front steps and got out. Billy cautiously opened the front door, but Becker waved him back and, carrying a large flashlight, went swiftly around the cabin to the shed. From the window Billy watched as he thoroughly examined the shed and the snowy ground around it. He then followed the tracks out of Billy's sight around the cabin.

"You can turn the lights on," he told Billy, when he came in a few minutes later. "Whoever it was is gone—but he'd have known I was here anyway from all the yapping going on."

"Gone? Did he get in? What fell? Something crashed out there and woke me up."

"Yeah, he got in. Jessie needs a better lock on that door. This one was pretty easy to bash open with a chunk of concrete. Get some clothes on so you can come look and see if anything's missing."

"How would I know?"

"Aren't you in and out of there?"

"Yeah, but Jessie's got a lot of stuff in there I don't use."

"Well, you can try."

Billy did try but he couldn't see that anything was gone or had even been moved.

"Looks just like it did when I locked up tonight. Except for the door, I mean."

Becker nodded as they closed the shed and went back to the cabin.

"May have scared him off before he could get what he was looking for. Jessie can check what's supposed to be there. Where is she, by the way? She get that note I left?"

Billy pointed to the note on the table. "She's on an overnight with the dogs—and that friend of hers."

"Where? Mike Tatum was out on the Glenn all morning hunting for them."

"Well . . ." Billy hesitated. "She sort of told him the wrong place," he admitted, with a sidelong glance to assess Becker's reaction.

The young trooper grinned. "Sounds like he gave her a bad time."

"He did. But she was tough—dared him to *arrest* her."

"Yeah, that's Jessie. So where are they, really?"

"Somewhere west of the Forks Roadhouse off Petersville Road."

"Camping out?"

"In a cabin where Jessie used to live, I think."

"Back tomorrow?"

"Or the next day. They didn't know for sure."

"Well, *make sure* she sees that note and has a look at the shed. And tell her to call me as soon as she gets back."

"Will that Tatum guy come back here?" Billy frowned at the idea.

"I don't think so, but whoever pounded on that lock

wasn't Tatum," Becker assured him. "He's law *enforcement.*"

That settled it for Becker. *Law enforcement* didn't break into people's sheds in the middle of the night.

Judging from what he'd seen of Tatum that morning, Billy wasn't so convinced, but he didn't say so.

"You gonna be okay here alone?"

"Yeah. Besides, I've got the phone." He nodded, reassuring himself, as much as Becker.

"Well, use it if you need it. You did the right thing to stay inside and call me."

Becker left, but it was a long time and two more patrol calls before he stopped feeling uneasy, wondering who would break into Jessie's shed and take nothing, and why someone circled her cabin first. The tracks looked remarkably similar to some they had found at the Mulligan fire, which did not ease his mind.

It was a very long time before Billy went back to sleep. The dogs woke him once again with their barking very early the next morning, but he heard and saw nothing unusual. When he was even brave enough to go out and check the shed door, he saw no sign of an intruder.

In the four o'clock silence of the early morning, a shadow slipped very quietly, one step at a time, from the shelter of the woods behind Jessie's cabin. The furtive figure was almost to the back door, when a dog, sensing some unusual sound, began to bark and was soon joined by others. Covered by this racket, the shadowy figure moved very quickly along the back of the building, stepping in the boot prints Billy had seen from the bedroom window, and vanished into the crawl space beneath the cabin through a piece of skirting loosened earlier.

Listening carefully, the figure crouched motionless and listened to the soft sounds of Billy's stocking feet overhead as he walked across the floor of the living room and continued to the bedroom window, where he stopped to look out. Seeing nothing he had not seen before, he went back to the living room.

The dogs were settling down, but the shadow held still and, waiting patiently, heard the front door open and the heavy thuds of Billy's boots on the stairs. The scrunch of careful steps in the snow moved around the cabin to the shed, paused at its doors, then went back the way they had come. The cabin door thumped shut and the solid click of the deadlock was loud enough to be easily identified by the listener. Billy's boots dropped one at a time and he padded back to the middle of the room, where, except for a creaking of the sofa as he lay down, the sounds ended.

For a long time the shadow did not move, but continued to listen. All was quiet. Then, finally, there was a faint, barely audible resonance from the room above. The boy was snoring.

Then, with great care, the shadow moved. By gently, cautiously shaking a heavy plastic bag, wood shavings were almost soundlessly poured out and spread over the ground near one sturdy foundation piling. Opening a large square of light fabric allowed pre-crumpled newspaper to drift onto the shavings with hardly a whisper. From a canvas bag, a bottle of fluid was removed and taped to the piling, connected by wires to a digital timing device.

The plastic bag and fabric were left, intended to burn with the rest, but the folded canvas bag went into the pocket of a jacket before the dark figure carefully checked the timer and pushed a button to set it running. Only seconds had blinked away, when the shadow slipped from under the cabin through the loose skirting, hesitated to listen, then went, carefully following its own earlier boot prints, so silently back into the woods that, though one dog woke enough to prick its ears and growl deep in its throat, it did not bark, and the rest dreamed on undisturbed.

So did Billy, warm and comfortably resting on Jessie's big sofa—sleeping the sleep of ignorant confidence, dreaming the dreams of the safe and secure.

9

PALE LIGHT FILTERED THROUGH CRACKS IN THE BOARDED-
up windows of Jessie's old cabin in the Little Peters
Hills when she woke the next morning, snuggled
warm in the heavy down sleeping bag she had spread
out on the floor over an insulated foam pad the night
before. They had managed to get in through a window with a loose latch and avoided having to make a
cold camp in the snow. Though they had built a roaring fire in the stove to warm the place and cook dinner, it was now once again cold in the room. The
banked coals needed more of the wood they had collected the night before to bring them back to life and
warm the air that was so cold she could see the small,
pale cloud of each exhaled breath. Reluctant to abandon her cozy cocoon, she lay still for a minute or two,
looking around the space she could barely see in the
early shadows.

Heavy spiderwebs clung in the corners of the walls
and windows. Near the stove was a pale, yellowing
square that she knew was a Maxfield Parrish picture of

two stylized chefs. Long ago she had torn it from a magazine and pasted it to the log wall. The furniture was gone—stolen or burned. Only the frame of a built-in bunk without a mattress and the stove remained. It felt strange and a little sad to wake in a place where she had once lived and had not seen for so long—made her feel a part of two time periods.

Anne was only a softly snoring lump, completely swaddled and hidden in the other down sleeping bag. The sight of her form brought Jessie's confused exasperation from the night before back into her mind. It made little sense that Anne had insisted on coming all the way to this isolated place without telling her that the Holman cabin had burned down years before. In fact, a lot of what Anne said was suspect, almost, but not quite accurate—a mixture of fact and fiction. Even more important and senseless were the things she *didn't* say. Why couldn't she just tell the truth—all of it? Why and what was she still keeping to herself? She had refused to answer most of Jessie's questions, making it impossible to know what to believe.

Irritated anew, and distracted by her memories of her earlier life in this cabin, Jessie quietly unzipped the sleeping bag and quickly pulled on her jeans and insulated snow pants. She had slept in her thermal underwear and socks. Now she yanked on both a turtleneck and a sweater, then padded across to gently add wood to the stove, careful not to clang the iron door or lids and wake Anne, for she wanted some time by herself to consider the situation. With the fire beginning to crackle and spit, she poured a mug of hot peppermint tea from a thermos she had filled the night before, put on her parka and boots, and slipped out the door into the gray predawn light.

Tank and Pete raised their heads and Elmer gave one short yelp that she discouraged with the wave of a hand as she walked past them toward a clear space in the few sheltering trees that grew this high along the slope.

It was almost sunrise, the snowy crests of the mountains to the east barely rimmed with bright gilding. The valley below lay still and silent in deep blue shadow, dotted here and there with the dark shapes of spruce and brush. Far across it, west of the Talkeetna junction, she saw quick flashes like Morse code from the lights of a vehicle passing trees as it moved along the Parks Highway heading toward Willow or Wasilla, even Anchorage, but it quickly disappeared around a curve.

It was very quiet; not even a bird called, for most were still far away in warmer places or in the early stages of their annual northward migration. Soon there would be familiar honking from chevrons of geese in the sky and the chatter of squirrels abandoning their warm winter nests to search for food.

A scant half mile below, a hint of motion caught her attention, and she watched a long-legged cow moose meander along the slope, pausing to gather breakfast twigs from the bushes. Behind her trailed a new calf, a miniature edition of its mother, that lunged and stumbled as it attempted to follow in her tracks, having trouble moving through the deep snow.

Jessie remembered standing there on other mornings, with Mount McKinley an immense dark bulk that filled the northern skyline. Though it usually kept its secrets well hidden in mist, infrequently, as on this morning, there were no clouds, nothing but cold clear air between it and this slope in the Little Peters Hills. As Jessie watched, almost holding her breath, the first long ray of the rising sun was caught by the highest of all summits, and McKinley's crest was suddenly tinted with a salmon pink, the sharp ridges brushed delicately with a gold so bright it seemed that it should burn the eye. Gradually, the whole apex of the mountain smoldered to life, ablaze with rosy hues, in stark contrast to everything still dark below it. The light slowly descended until, one by one, the lower peaks were touched and glowed as if they were made of rose quartz. The color faded as it crawled across the landscape, shadows fleeing swiftly before it, until the flat, radiant disk of the sun appeared and Jessie imagined she could feel the slightest bit of warmth on her face.

So intent was her concentration on the miracle of sunrise that she didn't notice the whir of the raven's wings that soared from behind the hills to land in a nearby treetop. When it began a conversational commentary on the morning in deep chirps and gurgles, she turned to search out its perch and watch as it strutted, bobbed, and ruffled its feathers. As she listened to the untranslatable language, it paused, then suddenly began to create an odd bell-like sound that only a raven can make, an improbable thing to come from the throat of a bird. Huddling on the spruce branch, it opened its beak wide and, with a convulsive whole-body movement and a dip of its tail, hurled a tone from its throat every few seconds that reminded her of a large drop of water falling on a flat sheet of tin. Metallic and resonant, it seemed a thing that should belong to the ocean, one strange lovely liquid note after another that was seldom heard, but always stopped Jessie in whatever she was doing to listen to the raven's gift.

"Well, raven," she spoke softly, face uplifted to it, "you've found me, as you found the first men and lured them out with that particular sound. Will you carry me away, too, in a clam shell, small and featherless?"

But, with a flick of its inky iridescent wings, the bird sailed away without her, gliding down toward the valley on the back of the wind, soon lost to sight.

Amused, spirits lifted, Jessie sipped at what was left of her tea, found it almost as cold as her icy fingers, and turned to go back to the cabin with coffee for herself in mind and breakfast for her mutts.

The rattle of a bucket full of snow hitting the top of the stove to melt for dog food brought Anne's reluctant face up from the sleeping bag.

"Wha time izhit?"

"Time to get going, if we want to do—whatever it is you want to do—and make it home tonight."

A thrashing in the bag resulted, as Anne attempted to pull on most of her clothes without getting out. Successful at last, she sat up, buttoning buttons, then was attempting to smooth her hair with her fingers, as Jessie went back outside to brush her teeth in more of the warm peppermint tea, leaving the coffeepot just beginning to emit cheerful burbles.

When she returned, she found Anne had put strips of bacon in a frying pan and was tending them, rubbing sleep from her eyes with the back of one hand.

"Any eggs?"

"In a plastic container in the insulated bag—already broken and salted and peppered for scrambling."

Rinsing out both their mugs with a little of the partially melted snow, Jessie flung it out the door. Bringing both to the stove she was about to fill them with coffee, but Anne beat her to the pot, stretching around the bucket to reach it. She had neglected to button the cuff of her shirt, which fell back almost to her elbow.

Jessie stared in astonished dismay at the exposed skin of Anne's forearm, unable to say a word. It was crisscrossed with narrow ridges of nasty-looking scars—some old and white, some healed, yet pink, others red and tortured looking, still covered with scabs. No wonder she had dressed *before* climbing out of the sleeping bag.

At her gasp, Anne looked up and, seeing what she had revealed, swiftly yanked down the sleeve and buttoned it, her face aflame with embarrassment.

"Anne—what in the world . . . ?"

"Greg," she snapped. "And I don't want to talk about it. Okay?"

"No—not okay. Tell me. You can't just ignore this."

"Yes, I can. It's over—won't happen again."

She turned back to the stove, where the bacon was rapidly growing crisper than she liked, and began to lift it from the pan onto a metal plate with a fork, leaving Jessie hesitant to attempt to make her revisit old sorrows by sharing them.

"Okay," she said finally. "But I'm glad you've left him."

"So am I. Now all I need to do is . . ."

"What?"

"Get what I came for and go away—leave you alone."

"Aw-w, Anne."

"No. I know you've got lots of other things to do besides put up with me. It's okay. Just get me back to Wasilla and I'll take off—somewhere safe." She gave Jessie a long look full of something like apology and appreciation. "Thanks, Jessie. I really—ah, just thanks."

It was the first totally honest or generous thing Anne had said since she'd arrived.

By mid-morning they had eaten, packed their supplies—which they left in the cabin with a small fire in the stove to keep it warm while they were gone—and were headed to the burned-out Holman cabin with Jessie's team, Anne in the sled that was now lighter and easier to handle.

The place looked worse in full daylight, though snow covered most of the blackened logs and the charred shell of what Jessie remembered had once been a tight and tidy place in which to live. The flames of the burning cabin had scorched a few nearby trees, killing some, marring others enough to turn them the rusty brown of injury. A few small spruce were beginning to grow near them, however, and would eventually take the place of those damaged by the fire.

Jessie ran a picket line for her dogs between two healthy trees near the trail and took them out of harness for the time being. Then she walked around the wreck of the cabin in the snow, assessing the damage and figuring out where things had been.

"There was the front door," she said, pointing. "That was your stove and the table was here. Why did he burn it, Anne?"

"Wanted to be sure I understood that we were never, ever, coming back here. Didn't want me to have any choice about leaving."

"Pretty disastrous way to make a point. It was a good cabin—better than mine."

"Yeah, I guess."

"Where do we need to dig?"

"Back there." Anne led the way beyond the ruined cabin to a spot between two trees on the edge of the slope. The branches of the spruce had sheltered it and kept much of the snow from the ground.

"Good, we won't have to shovel so much—just build a fire, and thaw the ground."

They collected as much dry wood as they could find under the burned trees, broke off a few dead limbs, and piled it all on the spot Anne indicated.

"How far down is it?" Jessie questioned.

"Not far. Two fires should do it."

With the small fire crackling as it burned pitch in the dry spruce wood, the ground under it slowly heating and thawing, they sat on a half-burned log and shared the last of the breakfast coffee from the refilled thermos, appreciating the warmth of the sun on their faces and the fire on their hands. In less than an hour, Anne raked off what was left of the coals and began to dig away the thawed dirt with the folding shovel they had brought. At her suggestion, Jessie wandered back down the trail to gather fuel for a second fire.

The world was a clean, colorful, sunny place, and

the temperature had risen enough for her to push back
her hood and half unzip her parka. Spring was definitely coming. She could almost smell it and was more
than ready for it, especially after the rainy days that
had kept her indoors and off the trail. Jessie loved gliding on the sled runners through the snowy wilds of
Alaska behind a team of her dogs almost more than
anything. But at the ragged and unpredictable end of
winter, with its muddy thaws and grime, she sometimes wearied of wearing insulated boots and longed
for the freedom of shoes—to have feet again. She
ached to see a hint of pale green as the birch groves
began to leaf out, discover one tulip blooming on the
south side of her cabin, hear the buzz of one bee still
chilled and bumbling.

Finding the stump of a spruce someone, probably
Greg, had cut to clear its branches from the trail, she
sat down on it, closed her eyes, raised her face to the
sun, took a deep breath of the morning air, and thought
about the scars on Anne's arm. How could anyone do
something like that to another person? She couldn't
imagine. It changed her whole image of Greg and
Anne Holman—of the relationship between them.
Anne might not have told her everything, but who
wouldn't want to keep this kind of thing to themselves?

Jessie was not naive, nor was she ignorant of situations of domestic abuse and violence. She had been
part of one herself before she met Alex Jensen, but it
had been mostly a war of words and attitude, shared
with a man who had propped up his ego by making her
look and feel less than adequate. She also understood

some of the reasons women often clung to the devil
they knew, rather than leave an abusive partner for the
unknown. Until the man she had lived with had destroyed the relationship with abuse, she had cared for
him enough to try very hard to make things work for
them. When he had unexpectedly, without warning,
punched her in the face in the heat of an argument, she
had immediately left him, with her mother's words
echoing in her ears and heart: "Hit me once—shame
on you. Hit me twice—shame on *me!*" *Victim* was not
in her nature, nor her personal vocabulary.

But hitting was one thing. The insidious, cruel cut-
ting that produced Anne's scars, another. The reality of
them made Jessie's skin crawl.

How lucky I've been, she thought, remembering
Jensen's gentle ways and appealing sense of humor.
They had come to a seemingly inevitable parting; but
she had missed him, terribly at first, more poignantly
now. Though she had pushed it firmly from her mind,
the last few weeks had been emotionally empty, and
she had kept herself very busy training the dogs and
going on long runs on the back of her sled that took all
her energy and brought her home tired in the evening.
Still, while it lasted, the relationship had been a good
one—never abusive in any way, not adversarial or
competitive, but honest and worthwhile. Their personal dedications had simply been dissimilar, and the
road they traveled together had reached a definite junction. Both would have been diminished had either of
them elected to follow the other's path. But the parting
had been mutually sad.

She couldn't help being glad that Anne had finally

found the courage to leave her abusive husband and hoped she would soon find a place where Greg Holman wouldn't find her—where she would be safe and could start over with some degree of confidence. She would do what she could to help her and stop demanding answers that Anne was unwilling to provide, ones that understandably embarrassed her. If she wanted to talk, fine, but Jessie decided she would stop probing. It *was* Anne's business, after all, not hers.

Opening her eyes, she took another long look around at the gleaming sun on the snow and spruce, and smiled. Whatever the reason, she was glad to have made this trip. The sunrise on Mount McKinley alone had made it worth coming all the way to the Little Peters Hills, to say nothing of the present warmth on her face and the clear air, lightly scented with wood smoke from the fire they had built.

The *fire*. Anne would probably have finished digging out the thawed dirt and be ready to build another. Time to get back with the wood she had collected. Gathering it up, she headed up the hill.

But when she reached the spot between the two trees, Anne was nowhere to be seen. There was part of a hole where the fire had been, but it looked as if she had stopped digging almost as soon as Jessie had left. She was gone and so was the shovel. Jessie dropped the wood she had brought and stood looking around. Probably taking a bathroom break, she thought, and waited a few minutes, expecting Anne to reappear, adjusting her clothes. When she didn't, Jessie walked a little way up the hill, looking, then called her name, but received no response.

"Anne?" she shouted. "*Anne,* where are you?"

There was no answer.

Then she noticed the tracks in the snow that led away from the spot where they had made the fire, and she followed them through the trees to a small clearing that continued for about ten yards along the slope. Across the middle of it were the unmistakable impressions Anne had made floundering in snow that had come well above her knees. The wallowing trail disappeared between two more narrow spruce. Again, Jessie followed.

As she neared the trees, she began to hear something—a rhythmic sound, like a repeated cough. Stopping to listen, she realized she was hearing sobs. Carefully, she moved past the trees until she could see Anne's back and shaking shoulders. She was on her knees at the base of a large, snow-capped boulder. Days of sun on its dark, sheltering surface had melted a small patch of ground bare of snow next to it, softening the earth a little. As Jessie came up behind her, she could see that Anne had scraped away at this bare spot until she made another shallow hole. She was leaning over, looking into it, rocking back and forth and crying so bitterly she did not hear Jessie's approach.

"Anne. What is it? What's wrong?"

The woman swung around defensively, eyes swollen and streaming tears, wiping at her nose with a parka sleeve, but staying on her knees.

"N-no," she wailed, desperately waving Jessie away.

Ignoring her motion and cry, Jessie stepped up to stand beside her and look into the hole that had been laboriously scratched out of the half-frozen earth.

Her first thought was that the bones were those of an animal—a dog, perhaps, that Anne had loved and buried when it died. Then, she noticed the metal box in which they lay, the stained fabric Anne had carefully folded back, and recognized their shape and size.

Horrified, she realized that she was looking at the bones of a child so small it could only have died at birth or before.

Or been killed.

Oh, no.

No?

10

JESSIE STOOD STARING DOWN AT THE TINY BONES, ANNE
Holman sobbing beside her. This discovery was such a
shock she couldn't seem to gather her thoughts or
know what to feel. Laying a sympathetic hand gently
on her friend's shoulder, she simply stayed where she
was and waited for the tears of grief and regret to end
and some explanation to begin. When the sobbing finally slowed, she pulled a handful of tissues from her
parka pocket and handed them to Anne.

"Here. Leave it. Let's go build another fire and make
some tea."

Anne nodded but, without a word, carefully folded
the fabric back over the small skeleton, replaced the lid
on the metal box, and picked it up. Now that she had
found it, she obviously wasn't going to rebury or leave
it. Clutching it close with one hand, using the other for
balance while wallowing back across the deep snow,
she stumbled half blind through the trees to the place
they had built the first fire, and sat down on the log to
watch as Jessie lit the wood she had collected. Neither

woman said anything until the water boiled under Jessie's camp kettle and they each had a mug of tea in hand.

Anne had laid the metal box beside her on the log in order to take the steaming mug. Jessie sat down with it between them, laid her fingertips on what she could only consider a small coffin, and, remembering her earlier decision not to force facts from Anne, spoke softly.

"Do you want to tell me about this?"

Anne sipped her tea, took a shaky breath, and exhaled a deep sigh in a mist that was visible on the air for a moment. "I guess I'd better. Right?"

"I'd like to know."

"There's a lot you don't understand."

"Um-m-m."

"It's mine. At least it *was* mine."

Jessie waited.

"You see, after the fire that killed Cal's kids, I found out I was pregnant. I panicked—didn't know what to do. There was that whole investigation going on—Tatum so damned obsessed with proving I was responsible. Cal and I weren't even speaking anymore. He was telling Tatum all sorts of things that weren't true. I was terrified that if I told anyone I was *pregnant*, Tatum would find out, tell everyone it was Cal's, and use it to prove I'd had a reason to start the fire."

It could have provided a motive, Jessie thought, but didn't say so—a motive for Anne or Mulligan or his wife. Sandra? Sharon? Shana. She frowned a little, wondering.

"But I'd met Greg," Anne continued. "He liked me—really liked me—said he loved me. When he asked me to get married, I said yes. It solved everything. Do you see?"

"Yes, I guess it would have, wouldn't it? But you didn't love *him*?"

"No, you're right—I didn't, but I didn't have much of a choice, did I? But I got to care about him—later. That's part of why I didn't leave him before."

What had happened to make Anne leave him *now*? Jessie questioned. There must have been something—a reason.

"Did you tell him?"

"About the baby? God, no. I meant to, but then I just couldn't. I was afraid he wouldn't marry me."

"So you let him think it was his?"

"Yeah. I know that was bad, but I was really scared, Jessie. What would you have done? It wasn't my fault."

I wouldn't have been in that situation in the first place, Jessie thought.

"Why didn't you . . . ?" she began, slowly.

"Get an abortion? I thought about it, but I'm Catholic—sort of—used to be anyway. Besides, I wanted it—really *wanted* it."

"Why?"

Anne's expression of disbelief told Jessie that her friend couldn't imagine anyone *not* wanting a child.

"You know. Doesn't everyone *love* children? It would have been someone of my own—someone who would love me. I always wanted that. It would have made everything okay."

Jessie wondered what *everything* was to Anne, mentally winced at the word *own* and the assumption of such requited love. "Did Greg want it?"

"Well—no. That got to be another problem. He didn't want kids at all. Said that with the world the way it is—violent—and no child got the choice to be born—he didn't want to make that choice for it. When he found out I was pregnant—that's when he started hitting me."

"So, you were pregnant when I knew you."

"Yeah, but you left before it showed much. It was winter. I was always in fat clothes anyway—sweaters, parka, that kind of stuff. It was easy to hide."

"So what happened? And what are you going to do with that?" Jessie pointed at the metal box that held the tiny bones.

"I'm going to take it to the police, so I can prove Greg killed it. They must have some way of proving how it was killed. Then they'll put him in jail and I can go where I want and stop worrying about him finding me—hurting me. And they'll know for sure I didn't start that fire at Mulligans. Then I'm going to bury it someplace better than up here—with a stone and everything."

Jessie was momentarily speechless. She stared at Anne and thought hard about this idea. How was she rationalizing all that from a few small bones in a metal box? Was she delusional?

"He *killed* it?"

"Of course. I *wanted* it."

"So you're going to tell them all of it? Even with Tatum still suspicious? He won't believe you."

"Well—I don't like that part of it, but—if I go to the police instead—"

"It'll be the troopers, Anne. This didn't happen in town. It happened out here, right?"

"Yeah, well—whatever. At least it won't be Tatum. It'll get him off of me."

"It won't when he finds this out—and that somebody burned your cabin ten years ago."

"*Greg* burned the cabin. How can that hurt me?"

"Can you prove that?"

Anne thought about it.

"How could I have done it? He's the one who kept burning stuff. You can tell them that."

"I told you, I don't remember that."

"But you could *tell* them that."

"I won't lie, Anne."

They stared at each other, each astonished that they couldn't agree on something so basic.

"It wouldn't really be a lie," Anne said, finally. "It happened. You just don't remember."

Jessie shook her head and stood up. "It *would* be a lie, *because* I don't remember any such thing."

Anne frowned and refused to look up at her.

"Come on." Jessie changed the subject. "Let's put out the fire and finish digging up your money."

"Don't bother," Anne spit the words at her, angry and impatient. "There isn't anything there. This is what I really wanted." She picked up the metal box again and hugged it.

Jessie was suddenly furious, sympathy disappearing like fog in sunlight. Another lie. How many had she been told? Was there truth buried anywhere in any of this?

"Why can't you just be honest with me?" she demanded. "You keep telling one lie after another, then expect me to help with whatever you want—whatever you think you need—to trust you—even *lie* for you. How can I?"

Grabbing up the shovel, she stomped off through the snow, around what remained of the ruin of the Holman cabin, toward her sled and team, ready to harness them together and quickly get away from this place and the whole unsettling situation. Once again, all she wanted was Anne Holman out of her life—to be home in her own, much-loved cabin, in peace and security, with nothing to interrupt what was important to *her*—the spring training of her young dogs.

"I just want to get out of here," Anne called after her, echoing her thoughts.

"You've got *that* right," Jessie replied, without turning. "As fast as I can manage it."

Falling to her knees in the snow to pet Tank and croon indulgent phrases concerning *his* trustworthiness, she didn't see the look of sullen resentment on Anne's face as she watched her go or hear the curses mouthed behind her back.

An hour later, Anne in the sled once again, dogs pulling happily, they were back on the trail, heading toward the Forks Roadhouse, Petersville Road, and the Kroto Creek pull-out, where Jessie's truck waited.

Anne had sulked but had helped to collect their belongings from the cabin. She had put the metal box with its infant bones in her day pack and held it on her lap in the sled. Jessie had noticed that she had no trouble making room in the pack for the box and wondered what Anne had discarded, for it had been full on the trip into Little Peters Hills. Unwilling to initiate another argument with her stubbornly resentful passenger, however, she asked no questions. What could it matter, anyway?

She made no stops on the trip down, but maintained a steady pace and they arrived back at the pickup at a little after noon. Though it was a brilliant sunny day—mild, with no wind—that made for extremely pleasant running, invisible angry thunderclouds had continued to hang over the sled and its riders, so Jessie had simply pretended she was alone and enjoyed the efficient working of her dogs in their spectacular surroundings. The summit of Mount McKinley had continued clear, with only a small cap of cloud that hung above it like a halo. The shining crystal white of its glaciers, ridges, and slopes fell like a robe with deep-blue shadows between the folds, bringing a smile to mind as she envisioned an enormous angel, minus the wings.

Arriving at Kroto Creek, Jessie found two young men loading their heavy snowmachines onto a trailer behind their truck. They greeted her with recognition, friendly smiles, and interest in her team, asking permission to pet the dogs and asking a few questions about distance racing. Anne had silently and immediately climbed into the pickup, leaving Jessie to unharness and load her dogs. It exasperated her that she had to ask the snowmachiners to help her lift the long sled to the top of the dog box and secure it for travel, though they were happy to assist.

As soon as Jessie had driven east on Petersville Road, reached Trapper Creek, and swung her truck back onto the Parks Highway, heading south toward Wasilla, Anne, who had said nothing, curled up facing the passenger window and went to sleep, or pretended to, clutching the day pack with its sad contents. It was a long, unhappy return trip, with no conversation.

Jessie was not displeased to be able to ignore her companion and consider the unsettling events of the last two days that had seemed to happen one after another, without warning or cessation, leaving her off balance and struggling for answers—and peace. Fires, demands, secrets, deceit—now this problem of a more deadly nature, contained in a metal box. It all felt confusingly out of control—as if somehow it had nothing, yet everything, to do with her. Had she had choices? Had she made bad ones? Could she have anticipated and avoided them? She felt exhausted and discouraged, as if she had seen only the middle part of some action-adventure movie, with no way of knowing how it had started or would end.

She flipped on the radio, searching for some upbeat music to take her mind off the problems at hand, and caught the last few bars of a country-western song she almost recognized. Still feeling disheartened, she was listening with only half her attention, when the bright introductory music-box notes of an old Stevie Nicks' song filled the cab, catching her off guard and vulnerable. It was a tune of such an infectious rhythm that she had hardly been able to sit still when it played. Together, she and Alex Jensen had danced to it—and smiled at the words, for some of them held fairly accurate personal meanings. Phrases like "have my own life" and "stronger than you know" had made Alex grin and point a defining finger in her direction. Others, like "lovers forever," had never passed without a hug and a moment of sweetness. Coming now, out of nowhere, it brought sudden tears that blurred the road, as she suddenly missed him with an intensity that closed her throat and turned in her stomach like a shard of glass.

"Dammit." Angrily, she twisted the radio knob and the music disappeared into static. Switching it off, Jessie swiped at her eyes with the back of her hand. Whatever happened to normal people?

Anne shifted position slightly, but did not respond.

No more, Jessie told herself, with an impulsive surge of energy.

So, what can you do?

I can stop letting things just happen. I can take control of what's going on that concerns *me*.

Like?

Like making sure that someone who knows what to do finds out about the remains of her baby.

Tatum?

No. I don't like Tatum or trust him. Becker would be better. I can also make sure that Anne leaves my house. I won't be responsible for her, or her problems, any longer.

That's reasonable, probably best, but . . . It's really not your responsibility. Let her do what she says she wants to. But if she doesn't . . .

No buts. She promised to go. Tomorrow she will.

Why not tonight?

I'm too tired. I don't want to get involved in any more lies—or any long explanations to Becker tonight. It can wait till tomorrow. That's soon enough.

It wouldn't be, but Jessie had no more way of knowing that than she could have predicted what they had found at the cabin site in the Little Peters Hills.

When they arrived at her cabin on Knik Road, Jessie spent two hours with Billy and her dogs, feeding and watering, appreciating them, checking the health and welfare of each. Then she went into the puppy pen and lost herself in their half-grown enthusiasms and clownish behavior for half an hour, which brought back some of her good humor.

Anne had made dinner for them both and packed up all her things in preparation for leaving the next day. They ate with hardly a word, and it was clear she was still bitter with unreasonable resentment.

After dinner, she disappeared for a long shower, leaving Jessie to do the dishes and clean up the kitchen. By the time she came out almost an hour later, Jessie, wanting a shower herself, was gritting her teeth with irritation. This did not lessen when she found that Anne had made a wreck of the small bathroom. Damp towels had been left on the floor; the soap lay dissolving in the bottom of the shower; and the sink was covered with toothpaste, short pieces of hair, a used razor blade, and a streak or two of blood, where Anne had evidently shaved her legs and cut herself. Altogether unacceptable and distasteful, it exasperated Jessie further to have to clean the room before she could comfortably clean herself.

"Do you need a Band-Aid?" she asked Anne a bit sharply, when she returned to the living room, feeling better after her own shower.

"No, thank you," Anne replied stiffly formal, without looking up from the television program she was watching. "I'm just fine."

Jessie went to bed and quickly to sleep. But it wasn't long until Anne turned off the television and the lights and a long, dark, waiting silence fell over the cabin.

11

IN THE DARK TWO O'CLOCK STILLNESS OF JESSIE'S CABIN, the only sounds were tiny hisses and cracklings from the banked fire in the woodstove and a small rustle of blankets and sheets as Jessie turned over in her big brass bed and settled again. Anne was almost hidden under a pile of blankets on the sofa.

The yard was empty, every dog curled up warmly on the straw inside its box. A pickup driving late on Knik Road passed with only a whisper, had anyone been listening inside the log structure. There was no wind, so even the trees in the surrounding forest were silent in the dim light of the faraway stars and the thin rim of a new moon in the western sky.

Under one corner of the cabin, in the crawl space directly beneath the bedroom, there was the sudden tiny click of metal touching metal, as the readout of a digital timer reached zero and closed an electrical circuit, causing a spark along wires piercing a plastic bottle of cigarette lighter fluid. The bottle exploded with a pop that went unnoticed, casting a wide circle of fire that lit the crumpled newspaper and wood shavings that had been spread heavily on the ground and, in a place or two, ignited the exposed wood piling that formed part of the foundation of the cabin. The paper flared quickly, lighting more of the shavings that, encouraged by the flammable liquid, burned hotter and longer, transferring flames, heat, and a plume of rising gases to the joists and subfloor three feet above.

The inverted troughs between the joists were filled with urethane foam insulation, the surface of which immediately caught fire, burning as fast as if not faster than the dry wood around it and releasing a combination of smoke and hot gases. Confined to the space behind the cabin skirt, which was now heating up as well, these gases began to accumulate and flow away from the fire between the joists, along with thick brownish-black smoke.

Slowly the blaze grew, and with paper and wood shavings gone, now ate its way into the insulation, creating pockets of intense heat that seared through to the plywood subfloor. Through small spaces the colorless, odorless gases crept, finally beginning to escape through cracks in the upper floor into the room above, long before the flames themselves would make an appearance.

Outside, all was still in the dog yard. Inside, no one woke or moved; sleeping silence filled the space.

Without warning the carbon monoxide detector between the kitchen and bedroom door went off with a shrill scream, startling Jessie groggily awake in the dark. Living in a log house had made her conscious and wary enough of fire to be sure she had alarms for smoke and for the poisonous gases fire could produce, as well. Religiously, she checked them and replaced their batteries.

Still tired after the trip to Little Peters Hills and the stress of dealing with Anne, she sat up, trying to figure out which alarm was creating the shrieking that assaulted her ears and why. Swinging her feet out of bed on the living room side, she started across the room. Halfway to the door, she realized that the floor under her bare feet was warm.

She flipped the light switch and looked down. There was nothing unusual in the appearance of the smooth finished wood, but it was definitely not its normal temperature. In the rectangle of light that shone out of the bedroom, she could see Anne sitting sleepily on the edge of the sofa in the sweats she had worn to bed, frowning in confusion, her hair a tangle around her head. Her lips moved in a question Jessie could not hear above the howling alarm.

At that moment the fire alarm above the bedroom door also sprang to life with a slightly different but equally disturbing screech, raising the combined noise to an intolerable level. Anne's hands flew to her ears as Jessie hurried to silence the carbon monoxide detector and then turned back to do the same to the bedroom alarm, which was still shrieking its warning.

"What is it?" Anne shouted, as she passed.

Jessie didn't even try to answer, dragging a chair across to climb on to reach the fire alarm. Both alarms quiet, she stepped back into the bedroom and, grabbing her jeans, yanked them up over the extra large T-shirt she had worn to bed. The floor she moved across was warmer now beneath her feet and seemed to give oddly as she crossed the room to the back bedroom window. It was hot enough to make her dance from one foot to the other as she looked out into the backyard. The woods were dark, but a warm glow was reflected from the drifted snow nearest the cabin.

"Get out," she called, turning back and snatching the quilt from the bed as she passed. "Something's burning under the house. Get your clothes, quick. We've got to get out of here."

She could now see a thin haze in the room and, as she left it at a run, she caught a faint whiff of smoke that smelled oddly like a newly mowed lawn or hay field. What the hell was burning, and why?

Anne was in motion throwing on her clothes. Before going to sleep, she had moved her suitcase into the living room. Now she was carrying it, and the rest of her things toward the front door.

"Leave it," Jessie said impatiently. "Just get outside and help me get some water going."

Detouring past the desk she grabbed up the cell phone she carried on training runs and, dialing the emergency number on her way to the door, gave the dispatcher the necessary information while stomping on her boots. Hesitating, she ran back and snatched her Iditarod trophy from its shelf on the wall, then taking her parka, she went out onto the porch. Anne followed, still determinedly carrying everything she owned, including the pack that contained the metal box of tiny bones. She took it all down the porch steps and dropped it just beyond Jessie's truck.

The motion censor had turned on the yard lights on their tall pole, allowing Jessie to see as she ran around the cabin, cramming the phone into a parka pocket and tossing the quilt and trophy at a snowbank. Scanning the back of the cabin, she located the source of the glow she'd seen—a narrow break in the skirting that should have been solid. Racing to it, she grasped the edge. Throwing her adrenaline-aided weight behind the attempt, she ripped it loose. She felt the bite of heat on her palms and fingers and took two steps back as she swung around and tossed the board away into the snow, a motion that saved her from the flames.

Through the narrow break in the skirting, enough oxygen had now reached the fire to replace what it consumed and feed it. But, as it grew within the confined space under the cabin, the temperature of everything—wood, insulation, the very air—had rapidly risen to ignition level of over a thousand degrees. Jessie had no way of knowing that by tearing off a section of skirting in order to see what was burning she had provided a sudden inflow of oxygen to superheated conditions. The fire exploded in the whoosh of a flashover that hurled flames to the farthest reaches of the crawl space, and back at her through the opening she had created in the skirting. It missed setting her clothing on fire by inches, and she felt an almost intolerable heat on her exposed skin.

Between the storage and the puppy pens was an insulated water spigot that provided water for her kennel. A long garden hose, which she carefully drained after use so it would not freeze, was rolled near it. Frantically, Jessie attached the hose, turned the water on as far as it would go, and ran it back to where the flames were now reaching from under the cabin to lick up the walls under the bedroom window.

"Anne," she yelled. "Anne! Help me!"

There was no answer. Jessie turned the water on the fire flowing up the outside logs and, when it died, directed the inadequate flow into the hole in the skirting, where it sizzled and turned to steam but did little good. The whole crawl space was now a glowing hot furnace.

"Anne! An-n-ne," she screamed again, but heard nothing.

"Dammit. Where the hell *is* she?"

Giving up, furious, she focused on getting as much water under the house as she could, also drenching what she could reach of the outside back wall, which steamed and quickly dried. She knew that the wood of the cabin was bone dry. Kept from the damp ground on pilings, warm enough to live comfortably within, the few years since its construction had parched it, like most other Alaskan residences—especially those made of logs. Glancing up at the window, she thought she could see a flickering orange glow on the ceiling of the bedroom. Where were the firefighters? How long would it take them?

All the dogs were frantically barking and howling in the yard, but she had no time to consider them, knowing they were safe. Realizing she was achieving little in dousing the conflagration in the crawl space, she turned to the nearby storage shed. Perhaps water on that would keep it from burning if the whole cabin went. Directing the flow from the hose onto the walls and roof closest to the cabin, she began to soak what she could reach, straining hopefully to hear sirens on the road over the roar of the fire and the rush of water splashing. Looking back, she saw that the fire had once again escaped and was beginning to burn the exterior cabin wall. Quickly she returned the stream of water to it and was still fighting to put it out when she heard the first wail in the distance.

My truck, she realized desperately. It'll be in their way.

"Anne, move my truck."

No response.

She realized the keys were in her parka pocket.

"Damn! *Anne?*"

Dropping the gushing hose, digging for the keys, she dashed back around the cabin with the intention of moving the truck farther into the dog yard and saw the first fire truck swing into her long drive, followed closely by the vehicles of three firefighters, red lights flashing from their dashboards, reminding her of the recent wild ride to the Other Place.

Running toward her truck, Jessie looked around in shocked, incredulous anger, realizing why Anne had not responded to her frantic calls. The place where she had dropped her things was empty. They were gone— Anne and her belongings had vanished into the night.

As she moved the truck out of the way, parking it between the dog yard and the outbuildings, and climbed out, the windows of her cabin exploded and she could hear the bellow of the fire inside in a second flashover. The interior was now as involved as the crawl space.

*   *   *

Hours later, Jessie sat, wrapped in the quilt she had snatched from her bed, slumped and shivering in the passenger seat of Becker's patrol car with the door open, watching the firefighters, some of them still wearing tanks and masks to avoid breathing the poisonous gases and smoke, carefully extinguishing hot spots, kicking and pulling apart still-glowing piles of unidentifiable material, overhauling the collapsed cabin, a ruin of rubble, charred and half-burned logs scattered like pick-up sticks. She felt numb and sick to her stomach, had vomited twice. Everything was gone, burned to ashes, and, beneath the ashes, some of her former life still smoldered.

The yard was full of people; attracted by sirens in their neighborhood for the second time in three nights, they had rushed to help and now stood, as they had at the pub fire, in small regretful groups, shaking their heads, speaking in low voices. Many of them had driven in, bailed out of their vehicles, and gone immediately to work to help fight the blaze. With help from Jessie's hose, they had managed to save the storage and maternity sheds and the puppy pens, and had moved her dogs to the back of the yard, out of harm's way. No dog had been injured or scorched by falling debris, but the vet had showed up in his mobile clinic van, wearing sweatpants and his pajama top, notified by telephone. "Just in case."

Jessie knew she was, and would be, grateful, to them all for their help and concern, but she was still trying to take it in—to realize that the cabin she had built and loved was gone forever. With it had gone all that she owned, except her dogs, racing and kennel equipment, and the trophy that lay beside her on the seat. Somewhere under the smoking debris where the bedroom had been lay her big brass bed, distorted and dull. Her wonderful sofa—found in a yard sale and carted home because of its amazing comfort and length, enough for two people to sprawl—was now nothing but some blackened coils and springs. Her carefully refinished oak dining table—and the bright-colored chairs she had collected one by one and painted herself—cinders. All the paperwork and records for her kennel, the Celtic and country-western music she enjoyed and the system that played it, her much loved books, photographs, keepsakes, other things she hadn't even remembered yet—vanished and buried in the black, steaming, smoking ruin. Though the floor had fallen into the crawl space and the roof after it as the building collapsed, unbelievably, from where she sat, she could see that the living room woodstove had somehow dropped straight down and landed without tipping. It sat in the midst of the wreck, on the charred ground, as if it belonged there. Incredibly, it still supported the cast iron dragon humidifier that had resided, full of water, atop it. Scorched clean of color and boiled dry in the intense heat, the dragon was just visible, but no trail of humidifying steam now rose from its nostrils.

"At least you woke up and got out," Hank Peterson had told her, when he, once again grimy and coughing from smoke, had found her standing helplessly by his truck with no idea what to do next. He gathered her into a huge, sooty hug that in its simple comfort had, finally, made her cry. "It's only walls and *things*, Jessie. You're okay. Be glad for smoke alarms."

Mentally, she knew it was true and that she would be able to appreciate it—later. Right now, she felt paralyzed, anesthetized, exhausted, and desperately sad. The loss was too much to absorb. Other reactions would soon follow, she knew; but, for the moment, she could only stare in disbelief at the place where her cabin had been, slow tears making clean streaks that she couldn't see on her dirty cheeks and dripping from her chin onto her filthy parka, for she had been everywhere, fought as hard as any.

Why? she asked silently now. Why? And somewhere deep inside a spark of anger began to glow through the dark grief and loss. Why? And—*who*?

She was still sitting there, wiping her streaked face and hands with a warm damp towel handed to her by a thoughtful neighbor, when Mike Tatum showed up by the open door of the patrol car.

"Well, *Mizz* Arnold," he said in a self-satisfied tone, "I guess you'll want to talk to me *now* about Marty Gifford."

Jessie was very still for a moment, glanced up without speaking, then slowly swung her feet out onto the ground and turned toward him, expressionless.

"You sorry son of a bitch," she said clearly in a low and level voice, and, directing the total power of her strong, rising body into the effort, buried her fist in his unguarded stomach, remembering that it was better not to break your hand on bony targets like his face.

12

"I *WILL NOT* HAVE TATUM ANYWHERE NEAR THIS FIRE—not one foot set on my place."

Jessie stood by the patrol car, feet apart, hands on hips, stubbornly refusing to give an inch, still so angry her jaw ached from clenching her teeth.

"Jessie, he's the assigned arson investigator. I can't tell him he can't—"

"Becker, you'd damned well better. Get someone else assigned. The .44 I take with me on runs wasn't in the fire. It's in the shed, and I swear to God I'll use it to keep him away from here if you don't."

"*Jessie*. You gotta be reasonable."

"No. Not this time, Phil. There's something not right about that guy—he's got real problems. You let him take over here and I'll figure out some way to make a lot of trouble. I promise you, I'll start by screaming to the media and all the way to the governor's office, and you know I can do it."

Becker scowled at her and shook his head in frustration. "Okay—okay. I'll see what I can do."

"Not good enough."

"Look, he's gone for now . . . you made sure of that."

"*Hank* made sure by escorting him back to his car."

"Yeah, and he may regret it."

"Not if I have anything to say."

"He could make *you* regret *punching* him by pressing charges."

"He had it coming, and I'm not sorry."

"Maybe so, but you don't just punch—"

"Well, I already *did*. So whatever happens, happens."

"Okay. I said I'd try to take care of it. For now, let's get you set up somewhere in town—a motel."

She shook her head emphatically. "I'm not *leaving*."

"You can't stay here."

"Sure I can. My equipment's in the storage shed and that's all I need. My mutts have got to be taken care of."

"I don't think . . ."

"It's okay, Phil—really. I want to be *here*."

"Well, there'll be people around checking on the fire for the next few hours. I guess it'll be all right. You're sure?"

"Yeah. I'd worry about my guys if I was anywhere else. Besides, it's only me. Anne's gone."

"But she got out, right? You got *any* idea where she might have disappeared to?"

"Not a clue. She hauled her stuff out when the fire started and took off while I was out back with the hose. Didn't help—didn't say a word."

He frowned thoughtfully. "You think she set it, Jessie? Somebody did."

"O-oh, Phil. I don't know. I don't think so, but . . . She seemed awfully ready to get out of the cabin with all her stuff—but she was leaving today anyway, so who knows?"

When Becker and the rest had gone, and only a firefighter or two were still poking in the ruins of the cabin, Jessie walked slowly around it, trying to come to some kind of terms with the magnitude of her loss. Half the neighbors and friends who had showed up at the fire had offered her shelter, and she knew some of them would be back in the morning to help any way they could. Several mushers had offered to stay with her, but she had sent them all off, knowing she needed to assess the whole situation by herself.

Many had volunteered to help muck out the remains of the cabin when that was possible, and help build a new one if she decided to do so. Hank Peterson said he would bring his Bobcat for some of the heavy work. "We'll dig a hole and bury a lot of that burned stuff." But it would have to wait until the investigation of arson was complete. As long as Mike Tatum had nothing to do with it, Jessie was content to be patient, not knowing what she wanted to do anyway. It was too much and too soon, though she felt a little better knowing that the cabin had been insured, but the papers had gone up in smoke with the rest of her belongings and records. That was okay—there were other copies somewhere else.

The halogen lights on their tall pole had not been burned and now shed a circle of light over the destruction. She noticed that someone had carefully rolled up her hose and hung it back over the spigot by the shed, ready for use. The bottom two front steps, half charred, stood forlornly leading up into a space that had been porch. Window glass that had blown out crunched under her boots. Stepping closer she looked at what was left of one of the wood pilings on its concrete base; it was now only a few blackened inches high.

"Watch that corner, Jessie. There's still a hot spot over there," one of the firefighters called. They were both so covered with smoke and soot they looked as if they were wearing blackface from an old-time minstrel show—their eyes and teeth very white in contrast. Looking more closely, she saw that the cautioner was a musher she recognized from evenings at Oscar's.

"Thanks, Jimmy. I will."

"You need any help with your dogs?"

"Naw. They're fine. I'm going to water them again."

It was a good idea. The dogs had been up and in motion through the whole event and would be thirsty. Knowing they would be more comfortable and less stressed in their normal places, she moved those that had been shifted away from the fire back to their own boxes. It made her feel a little better to take time with them. They responded to her attention with friendly nuzzling and licks on her face and hands, relished the petting and affection she gave them, slightly diminishing the desperate emptiness she was feeling.

"Oh, you are such good dogs," she told them all. "The very best dogs in the whole world, I bet."

When they were all calmed, settled, and resting, she took Tank with her for company and went to the storage shed where, in the light from the door, she located a couple of sleeping bags that she spread out on a camp cot. Laying an old piece of carpet on the floor for Tank, she folded her filthy parka inside out to use as a pillow, took off her boots, and crawled into the top bag, pulling the quilt that she had rescued over it and up to her chin. It smelled strongly of smoke and bore dirty streaks from being wrapped around her grimy self in the patrol car, but it was nothing that couldn't be cleaned, she thought, glad to have it. Closing her eyes, Jessie lay still and gradually grew warm, but she didn't think she would sleep. That was all right; under the circumstances she hadn't expected to. She simply relaxed and allowed thoughts to drift through her mind, good and bad. Slowly, some of her physical tension melted away.

The question Becker had asked about whether Anne had set the fire had stuck in her mind, and she worried at it a little. *Was* it possible?

She was sure the fire had been set. There was nothing under that particular corner of the cabin to cause a fire. She had helped build it and knew the electrical wiring for that room had all been run through the ceiling, not under the floor. There was nothing to start a fire in either the layers of the wood that formed the floor or the urethane insulation that had been sprayed beneath it. Nothing but some purposely instigated source could have struck the spark that made it burn. How did it get so hot and spread so fast?

The *why* still plagued her. Why would someone start a fire to destroy her cabin? And who? Had it been meant to kill her? Anne? If not, whoever set it clearly hadn't cared if it did. The idea that Anne would take out her anger over Jessie's refusal to lie for her seemed ridiculous—much too extreme. But she supposed it was possible. Anything was possible. How well did she know Anne? Not very. Obviously, she hadn't known her as well as she imagined when they had been neighbors in the Little Peters Hills. If she *was* responsible for this fire, her leaving so abruptly made more sense, and she *could* have gone out in the night and set it without waking Jessie.

She hated to say *arson*, though she could almost taste the shape of the word, and hesitated to accuse without proof. Had Anne run off because she set the fire, or to escape what she might have seen as Tatum's inevitable investigation? And where had she gone and how? It was a long walk to Wasilla. Was she now going to leave the state?

Where could she be? She had said she meant to take the bones of the child she had dug up to the police. Would she? Or was that another falsehood? There was so much Jessie didn't understand or believe, and was too tired to care about now. One way or another, it would eventually clear up and she would have some answers. There weren't enough pieces to figure out the pattern of the frustrating puzzle.

Letting it go, Jessie began to mentally walk through her cabin and lay sad, thoughtful, loving hands on everything she could remember, carefully listing it in memory. So much would have to be replaced. Her cameras, everything in the bathroom. My toothbrush— my hairbrush—dammit. She moved to the kitchen and started her mental inventory with the large things— stove and refrigerator—appliances—toaster, coffeepot. Dreamily opening cupboards, she imagined their contents—assorted plates, wine- and water glasses, the blue bowls she liked for cereal and ice cream . . . the large platter for the Thanksgiving turkey . . . her collection of mismatched mugs . . . a casserole that had been her grandmother's . . .

She woke with a start. Tank had laid his muzzle on the back of her right hand to attract her attention. It was broad daylight and someone was calling her name from the yard.

"Jessie? Are you in there, Jessie?"

"I'm here. Just a minute."

Sitting up and putting her feet into the boots that stood by the cot, she rubbed her eyes, then took Tank's face between her hands and leaned to lay her cheek on the top of his head. He licked her ear.

"Good boy. Come now," she said as she unfolded her parka and stood up.

They walked to the door together, went out, and found Becker in the yard with a large Styrofoam cup of steaming coffee in each hand.

"Give me a minute," she told him, and went to the spigot to splash water on her face. Running her damp fingers through her short, still-sooty curls, she walked to meet him.

"Hey, good morning." He held one of the coffees out to her. "Cream and sugar, right?"

"Thanks, Phil. Yes."

Next to Becker stood a heavyset man she didn't recognize.

"This is MacDonald. The new investigator you asked for."

"Mac," the stranger said, holding out a hand.

Jessie examined his face closely; direct, slightly hooded eyes; dark hair and evenly trimmed beard; a smile that pulled the right corner of his mouth a little crooked; neatly dressed in casual clothes under the open yellow coat of a firefighter; fire boots, well used; dirty gloves sticking out of a pocket.

"Hello, Mac." She gave him her hand and liked the gentle strength of his grip, reassuring and solid. "I'd invite you in, but . . . well . . . I got a little carried away cooking breakfast." She waved a hand at the still faintly smoking rubble that had been her cabin.

He grinned. "That's okay, I've had mine. Glad to see you've survived with some sense of humor intact."

Becker, who had been closely following their exchange, released the breath he was holding in a relieved sigh.

Jessie laid a reassuring hand on his arm. "Thanks, Phil. I owe you one."

He thumbed back the western hat he wore out of uniform. "I'll keep that in mind. Is there *anywhere* we can sit down?"

"Sure," she told him, "if you don't mind camp stools."

Opening the big door to the storage shed to let in the morning light, she led them in and found two of her wood-and-canvas stools, which they set up and perched on. She sat on the camp cot she had slept on and wrapped one arm around a knee, sipping gratefully at the coffee, feeling very much in need of a shower.

"I smell like what's left after a forest fire."

"Yeah, well . . ." Becker grinned.

"Pretty quilt," MacDonald commented.

"The only thing I saved," she told him, stroking the smudged, but still colorful patchwork of northern lights and silver stars.

"The trophy's in my car," Becker assured her.

"You're staying in here?" Mac asked.

"Yeah. I have dogs that need a lot of tender loving care after last night."

"You need some TLC, too, I imagine. Can't live in a shed forever."

"It's okay, for now. A neighbor's bringing me a big canvas tent. Sometime today he'll haul in a platform to lay down for it. We'll set it up, rescue my wood stove from the wreckage, and in a couple of days I'll be fine—back in business. I'm used to camping out on the trail, so this'll be fine until then."

"Just keep in mind that someone started last night's fire for a reason of their own," he said, turning serious. "You—we—don't know what it was—why it was done. They could make another try, if that motive wasn't just to destroy your residence."

"You mean maybe I wasn't supposed to get out," she stated plainly. "I've thought of that." She lifted the edge of a sleeping bag to reveal her Smith & Wesson .44. "My dogs would let me know before anyone got anywhere close to this shed. Same goes for the tent—when I move into that."

He nodded approval. "I've already spent an hour looking at the remains of your cabin. We look for origin and cause. I found both. Phil says you told him it started under the southeast corner. I agree. I took it back to that point and there are definite signs of arson.

Will you tell me what you remember, so I can confirm my findings?"

"I was in the bedroom," she began, "sound asleep when the carbon monoxide detector went off—then the smoke alarm. I shut them down, then went to the bedroom window and could see a glow that came from under the house. The floor was hot and felt weird—sort of soft."

"Spongy."

"Yeah."

"You were lucky it didn't collapse under you at that point. So you got out?"

"And ran around to see what was burning. There was a crack in the skirting that shouldn't have been there and I could see flames through it, so I yanked a big piece off. The fire just exploded—flashover, I think you call it?"

"You've seen *Backdraft*."

She gave him a very small, rueful grin and nodded, swallowing hard at the memory. "It blew out at me, just like in that movie. If I hadn't stepped back to toss that piece into the snow, it would have got me. I kept yelling for Anne."

"Anne?"

"A friend who was staying with me. She's not here now. I got the hose turned on and sprayed water under the cabin, but it didn't help much."

"Too late by that time—too hot—too well involved."

"Then I hosed down this shed, just before the fire truck got here. I was afraid that if the cabin went, the shed would, too, and it has all my racing gear in it—except for what's in or on my truck."

"What do you mean—*on* the truck?"

"One of my big sleds is on top of the dog box. It's still packed, because we'd just come back from an overnight with the dogs and I was too tired to unload it."

"Jessie, did you see, hear or smell anything unusual?" MacDonald asked, getting back to the fire.

"Well, I can't think of anything under that corner of the cabin that could have caused a fire. But . . . Oh, one thing. I smelled something odd as I left the bedroom—a smell sort of like cut grass."

He frowned in concern. "Phosgene, a lethal gas from urethane foam—the insulation under your house."

"You can die from it?"

"You can. It's very nasty stuff. How much did you get?"

"Not much. Enough to make me think it was a weird smell this time of year, but I went straight outside."

"Having any trouble breathing? Any pain or burning in your throat or chest?"

"No."

"Good. If you do, don't mess around. It can show up hours later. Get to the hospital immediately. Anything else unusual?"

"No."

"When you got outside, what color was the fire and the smoke?"

"It was so dark it was hard to tell what color the smoke was—sort of blackish brown, I guess. Not white. The fire was bright orange and yellow, almost white, very hot looking under the house."

"Do you remember any unusual circumstances before or during the fire? Anyone around you didn't know? Any unusual sounds inside or out?"

"No strangers, but, like I said, we'd just come home from an overnight trip and were both tired, so we were really asleep. Billy was here the night before and might have heard something. You should ask him."

Becker straightened and nodded to MacDonald. "There was the prowler Billy heard and called me about."

"What prowler?" Jessie asked, startled.

"Didn't you notice the lock was broken on the storage shed?"

"I thought one of the people last night did it."

"Nope—a prowler. Nothing missing that Billy could see, but you'll have to check. But there were footprints—boot prints—that passed and came close to the place where you tore off that piece of skirting, Jessie. I should have looked under there, but I thought they were headed for the shed. Sorry."

"Is Billy okay?"

"Fine. He thought he heard something later, but checked and didn't find anything."

"Do you have any idea who might have a grudge or a reason to set this fire?" MacDonald asked.

For a second, Jessie's face crumpled, then she sat up straight and determined. "I can't imagine anyone doing this. But we couldn't imagine anyone burning the Other Place, either. Things have been pretty confused around here the last couple of days—the other fires, Anne coming, trying to get in some training . . ."

"How *about* this friend of yours—this Anne? The one who isn't here—right?"

She nodded. "That's another story entirely, but I'm beginning to wonder if it might be related somehow. It all seems connected in my mind. Maybe just because it's all happening to me at the same time."

"Tell me."

Becker leaned forward, elbows on knees, hat in hand, to listen, as Jessie began to relate the details of Anne Holman's unexpected visit and the background of their relationship that had begun at the Little Peters Hills cabins a decade earlier.

MacDonald took careful notes and listened with a keen expression of interest, periodically nodding, and he interrupted only once early in her story.

"And this is the same person that Tatum has a thing about—that got him burned in a fire ten years ago—a Marty Gifford, right? Lot of old, personal history there?"

"Yes," Jessie told him, "but that was all before I knew her. It's been pretty obvious that he's obsessed with proving she's responsible for that fire—any fire. She says she wasn't. I don't know. But he's been a real bastard—unreasonable and way out of line."

"Well, Mike Tatum's a good investigator, but he's got a few problems of his own. He shouldn't be back to bother you again. If you need anything, call *me*, okay? Go ahead, Jessie. I need to hear this and what you think about it."

She told him what Anne had said about the abuse she had suffered from her husband, Greg, and her fear that he would follow her to Alaska, the metal box of bones she had taken from the hill above the Susitna Valley, and that Anne had said she intended to take the box and her accusation to the authorities. Then she told about Anne's sudden disappearance the night before.

It took a long time, but she felt a little better when it had been shared with someone else. It didn't bring answers but at least she wasn't alone with the questions anymore.

13

JUST LOOKING AT THE BLACK RUIN OF HER CABIN MADE Jessie want to cry. Grief lay like a stone in the pit of her stomach, and her chest ached with the refusal to allow tears. Control was too hard to come by to risk losing it. She simply could not imagine anyone who could hate her enough to do this, but the thought kept recurring that Anne's problems could somehow be responsible for the disaster. In no way did she think that Anne had told her the complete or even the most accurate account of the history and rationale behind her sudden unexpected trip to Alaska. The woman had told her only as much as she felt was necessary—not the whole truth. Jessie felt used and angry—both at herself for allowing it, for walking into such a situation—and at Anne, who seemed to feel that everyone in her life should exist to respond to her demands.

More than anything she could think of, Jessie wished it were several days earlier, that none of it had happened, and that she had nothing on her mind but the hard work of spring training. As she began the morning routine of caring for her dogs, she tried to concentrate on their needs and get on with that training, get a team harnessed up, let the rest take care of itself until she had time to accept her losses and decide how she would deal with them.

But, however much she would like to have taken some of her dogs and found solace somewhere on a trail, it was soon clear that it would not be possible to escape the depressing remains of the fire. All through the long day, people kept showing up in her yard—mushers, personal friends, acquaintances, her insurance agent, Iditarod committee members, fans—people Jessie had never even met but who had followed her racing career. She soon lost track of how many. They came to express their support, bringing gifts of food, dishes, pots and pans, a card table and two chairs, a roll-away bed, towels, blankets, sheets and pillows, a small electric stove with an oven. The young son of a neighbor even insisted on loaning her his teddy bear. "You can keep Bumper till you get a new house. Okay?"

Toni Dunbar and Carol Hooker, long-time friends and racing fans, came all the way from Anchorage with a car full of clothes they thought would fit her. "You made the *Daily News* this morning," they said, when she asked how they knew about the fire, and handed her a copy. The picture on the front page showed Jessie working hard with a shovel, light reflected on her exhausted, sooty face from the fire in the background. She vaguely remembered a photographer in the confusion of the night before.

Half the state trooper detachment from Palmer

found one reason or another to stop by with offers of off-duty help—friends and coworkers of Alex Jensen, who had grown to be her friends, too.

Billy Steward's father came with him to help feed and water her dogs, then he and Billy took out two of her teams for training runs. "You can come stay at our house," Billy told her three times, but understood when she refused and thanked him for the invitation. "Anything you need, you just call," his father added, waving as they drove the teams away and left her looking longingly after them from the yard, surrounded by well-wishers and unable to escape to the wilds.

The promised tent was standing on its platform near the driveway before noon, raised with the help of so many hands that Jessie could only stand and watch, overwhelmed with the expression of so much caring, as others outfitted it for living and discussed among themselves what else she would need. It had been placed with the entrance facing away from Knik Road, half of it within the circle of the halogen yard lights, so that any motion in front would cause them to blink on.

Someone went home and came back with an easy chair and a floor lamp that fit into one corner. "You've gotta have a comfortable place to sit down." A small television appeared on an end table near it. "Bet you could even have cable if you wanted it." Blocks-and-boards shelves were set up and filled with cooking equipment. A rug appeared on the wooden platform-floor with a washtub nearby. Clothing went into plastic baskets and onto hangers suspended from a wire. Some generous reader even toted in a box of assorted paperback thrillers and whodunits—*Inferno* prominently displayed on top. "Hey, I couldn't resist—but it has a happy ending." The large tent began to look small with all it contained.

Jake, the electrician, showed up, ran a line to the tent, and installed overhead lights he had brought with him, a space heater donated by someone else, and outlets for other electrical appliances.

"It'll be safer than your woodstove," he cautioned. "You've had enough fire, yes?"

"You got that right."

"When you get ready to rebuild, let me know. I'll be here."

Jessie was swiping at a few grateful tears when Hank Peterson put in an appearance with a half-dozen sacks of groceries and a couple of large ice chests.

"Hey." He grinned over her head, as he gave her another bear hug. "I've never seen you cry—over anything. Now twice in less than twenty-four hours?"

Oscar Lee brought lunch for the whole crew: hot soup in a huge insulated container, several loaves of bread with ingredients for sandwiches, sacks full of apples and oranges, cases of soda and beer.

"We burn-out casualties gotta stick together." He grinned, organizing the food on a temporary table, quickly fashioned of Jessie's sawhorses and a couple of planks brought from the shed. "I'm really sorry about your place, Jessie. But you could have just told us that you were so damned desperate for a party."

"Are you okay, Oscar—with the Other Place arson stuff, I mean?"

"Yeah, it's working itself out. There's nothing for that investigator to find that could hurt me, because I had nothing to do with it. So—I've just had a little bad luck, right? Nothing irreplaceable. He can go take a hike and find out who really burned my place—and maybe yours, too, huh?"

By the time they'd all left, late in the afternoon, she was so full of the warmth of Alaskan goodwill that the sharp stab of grief had receded to something like a dull ache—a bruise rather than an open wound. The day had been a surprising and positive start to her personal recovery. Healing the ugly black scar where her cabin had stood could begin tomorrow—or the next day—when the investigation was finished. As Hank had said, it was really only walls and *things*, nothing to do with her most important resources—this generous crowd of friends and heroes.

She was waving Hank on his way when arson investigator MacDonald turned into the drive, alone this time in his own Jeep Cherokee.

"Hey," she greeted him as he stepped out and stood looking around in amazement, "I can offer you coffee this time—or beer, or soda—even a late lunch, if you're hungry."

"My God," he said. "Look at all this. Do you have a magic wand?"

"No, just terrific, magic friends and neighbors. Can you believe it?"

"Hardly. I'm impressed—with them, sure—but mostly with you for inspiring all of this."

"Aw-w, not true, Mac. Alaskans are great people with huge hearts. We're a pretty tight community out here in the sticks. They'd have done the same for anyone—have in the past."

"*Right*. And if my grandmother had wheels . . ."

He accepted a can of Pepsi and they sat together on a bench someone had set beside the tent's door—an actual wooden, you-can-open-and-close-it, even-lock-it door. There was a mat that looked so odd in front of a tent that Jessie couldn't help laughing. Green, it bore two skinny, black-and-white-striped legs and feet in red shoes. DING-DONG! it read, as if the rest of the witch had been flattened under the tent. Whoever brought it had wanted to give her a smile.

"I've got some interesting but kind of unsettling news," MacDonald said after a minute, "and a few more questions. We did some checking on your house-guest, Anne 'Marty' Gifford Holman. You said you picked her up three days ago at . . . ah—" he flipped through a loose-leaf pad to find his notes "—at nine-twenty in the morning on Alaska Airlines flight number eighty-one from Seattle?"

"I don't remember the number, but the rest sounds right."

"Did you actually see her get off the plane?"

"I *was* going to the gate, but I was running late. Passengers were already coming down the hall, so I decided not to go through security and waited for her in the hallway. There was no other way out, so I knew I couldn't miss her."

"But she came from the direction of that gate?"

"Ye-e-s. Why?"

He frowned and shook his head.

"Flight eighty-one," he said slowly, "was scheduled for arrival at eight-fifty-two, not nine-twenty, and it was on time. But your friend Anne didn't come in on it. There's no record of her on that or any flight on any airline that arrived at Anchorage International that day—or on either the day before or the day before that."

Jessie stared at him in astonishment. "She wasn't on a passenger list? Maybe she didn't use—"

"Holman? Nope. And we checked all the combinations of names we could think of. We even talked with the attendants that were on the flight that morning. No one remembers her at all and, from the way you described her, I don't think she'd be hard to pick out in a crowd, do you?"

"Probably not." Jessie frowned, thinking hard. "She was pulling a dark, wheeled carry-on bag, and we picked up a larger bag that matched it from baggage. She was wearing a blue sweater and jeans that were way too big for her."

"Just the way we described her to anyone who might have remembered. No one did. She may have met you at the airport, Jessie, but I don't think she came off a plane from Seattle. Any ideas?"

"But she called me from Seattle the night before and specifically told me the flight and arrival time. She emphasized nine-twenty. Said it more than once, so I'd have it right."

He looked at her without speaking, waiting for her to figure it out.

"She could have called from anywhere. And she wanted to make sure there was a plane already in so it would look like she'd been on it?"

"Right—probably. You don't even know that call *was* long distance."

"She could have already been in Alaska—gone to the airport from anywhere—sometime before she met me."

"Right again. You can't prove she got off that plane. You didn't see her get off and it looks like she didn't want you to."

He hesitated for a second, then asked another question and watched closely for her answer.

"Did you see anyone else you knew at the airport—anyone who'd remember you?"

Jessie tried to think. "I was really tired. The Other Place burned the night before, and I barely got to bed before I had to get up again. No—I can't remember recognizing anyone. Wait—there was . . . No, I didn't see his face. I know I didn't speak to anyone else."

"I'm sorry, Jessie, but I've got to say this. You can't even prove you picked her up at the airport, can you?"

"Why would I have to prove it?"

"Unfortunately, Mike Tatum's tossing around some pretty wild accusations—that you had it in for him—and her—or the two of you did. He's intimating that you may have had something to do with her disappearance. He's mentioned your name in connection with all three of the arsons that happened in the last week—including this one."

Jessie stared at him, speechless with shock that quickly turned to hot anger.

"You don't *believe* any of that, Mac. He doesn't even know me. Why would he do that? Why would Anne lie to me about arriving that day?"

He laid a restraining hand on her arm.

"I don't know. But belief has nothing to do with it. I

have to investigate every lead, however ridiculous. He's also upset about my being called in, so he's not being cooperative."

"But I—"

The crunch of tires on gravel interrupted what she had been about to say and she turned to see Phil Becker climb out of his patrol car.

"Hey," he called, looking around at what had been accomplished by her visitors. "Somebody *lo-oves* you. This is *great*. You've got a new home already."

She got up to give him a hug.

"It's not quite home, but it'll do for now."

Stepping away, he handed her what looked like a large cellular phone in a protective leather case. "I'm still not completely comfortable with you being out here alone. So here's something I doubt anyone else could give you."

"Oh, Phil, thanks, but I've got one." Jessie pulled her cell phone from a pocket.

"You don't have one of these," he told her with a grin. "It's an iridium phone—a satellite connection that works just about anywhere in the world. We're trying these when we have to go places our radios and cell phones won't reach. I'll feel a lot better knowing you can call us from—anywhere. The dispatch number's already programmed in, so all you have to do is push a couple of buttons. Commander Swift wants you to call him, so he knows it works and if there's anything else you need."

"I'll call to tell him thank you," Jessie said. "These things cost the earth. What if I lose it or break it? Jeez!"

"So? It's just a phone—insured. No worries."

"Thank *you*, Phil," was followed by another hug that knocked his western hat askew, but pleased him into blushing like a teenager.

"You're more than welcome. Now—I guess Mac's told you about the nasty nonsense Tatum's busy spreading?"

He upended a wooden box someone had left near the tent and, sitting on it, raised a questioning eyebrow at MacDonald.

The interruption had given Jessie's astonished anger a little time to cool. Now it surged back with controlled questions.

"I get the general idea. How could he possibly think I burned down my own house—or anybody else's—let alone helped Anne disappear? Why would I?"

"He's got just enough backing up his implications to force us to take another look—just to prove him wrong," MacDonald told her. "And I'm sorry, Jessie, but he isn't saying you *helped* her disappear. Just that she's gone and you were the last one to see her."

"Not true. Billy was here and saw her . . . Oh—and Hank Peterson saw me at the gas station on our way out of town—so he saw her in my truck. At least I think he did."

"Tatum says that Anne may never have made it back here. He's claiming that there may have been foul play on your trip with the sled."

"The bastard. Listen—there were two guys loading snowmachines at the Kroto Creek parking area when we came back. They helped me lift the sled onto the dog box. They'll tell you she came back there and left with me."

"Who were they?"

"Ah, Mark—something, an architect, and a Gary—ah—Jeffers. I recognized him—had met him somewhere else at a race, or something. They were both from Anchorage."

"Good. That's something positive we can check." He pulled a plastic evidence bag from his pocket and held it out to her. "Do you recognize this, Jessie?"

Inside the bag was a blue knit hat.

She stared down at it, frowning. "Can I take it out?"

"Yes. It's already been to the lab."

She took out the hat and turned it inside out. Catching her breath, she looked up and held it out to show.

"It's mine. See this piece of red yarn? I tied it in there, because I kept getting it mixed with other people's. It's been missing for a few days."

The bright red tail of yarn showed plainly from the inner side of the hat.

"Where did you—"

"Tatum says he picked it up behind the burned Mulligan trailer at Big Lake. Any ideas?"

"I've never been there. Don't even know where it is."

It was all coming at her with unbelievable swiftness, an ambush to ragged emotions already stretched to their limits. She knew Becker didn't believe this, was on her side, and that MacDonald was asking his questions as considerately yet insightfully as possible. Still, the implication that she was somehow involved in arson and Anne's disappearance rocked her off balance. Why would Tatum or anyone try to set her up?

"Where were you in the afternoon the day Anne supposedly arrived? Before Mulligan's place burned?"

"She *did* arrive—well, at least she was here," Becker interjected before Jessie could answer. "I saw her myself, remember—when Tatum and I came to interview Jessie about the Other Place fire."

MacDonald nodded and turned back to Jessie, waiting for her answer.

"I was here with Anne, then out on a training run with Billy Steward. We each took out a team of the young dogs."

"Together all the time?"

"No. About half the time we ran together, then he went back. His folks had something special planned for that evening, so he had to get home early. I stayed out for more than an hour more before I started home."

"Time enough to run your team to Big Lake, with no one to prove you didn't."

Heartsick, angry, and confused, Jessie had to agree.

14

BECKER AND MACDONALD HAD GONE, LEAVING JESSIE
incensed and a little afraid because of Tatum's attempt
to make her a suspect and her inability to refute his insinuations. She thought there was more that MacDonald
wasn't telling her, but questioning him had brought her
no further information. To shake off her worries, she determined to keep busy with some of the many things
there were to do to keep the kennel running smoothly,
despite the fire, starting with unpacking the sled, which
she had not done last night. It was growing dark as she
worked, and, as she took items from the sled bag, she
couldn't help wondering where Anne could have gone
and why. How had she disappeared so fast and so completely without transportation? Had someone picked her
up on Knik Road? Was there any way to find out who?

After moving the leftover food from their trip to the
tent, she sorted the other supplies and equipment.
Extra harness went on hooks near the shed door, sleeping bags were spread out to air, dog food and water
containers piled up to be washed.

She was almost finished and in the process of putting the first-aid kit on a shelf on the back wall of the shed, beyond the four-wheel ATV that she used for summer training runs, when she noticed an unfamiliar green gym bag sitting next to a cardboard box on one of the lower shelves. Frowning in an attempt to remember what it was and where it had come from, she pulled it out and unzipped it.

At first she thought it might be some forgotten things of Jensen's, but, as she assessed the contents, that idea grew less likely. What would he want with a digital timer, several batteries, some coils of electrical wire, a roll of black electrician's tape, a plastic bottle of lighter fluid, a few other electrical items? Slowly, the use for these items sank in, and, stomach turning over, she realized that she was probably holding the components for a fire bomb. What could they be doing on a shelf in her shed?

Abandoning the little that was left of the unpacking till later, angry and a little sick at what she had found, she carried the bag into the tent, turned on the overhead lights, set it on the card table, and reached for the Iridium phone Becker had brought her. About to punch in the number for the troopers office, she hesitated. Would they believe that she didn't know where this had come from? Didn't the timing of her finding it seem a little too neat, so soon after their discussion this afternoon— as if she were trying to pretend it didn't belong to her? The knowledge of her having found it—its very existence—could certainly give Tatum another weapon. Still, she thought, I ought to report it right now. It would look worse if they found out later. Besides, there was the unpleasant possibility that whoever had put it there might come back, meaning to make use of it later. Hadn't Mac mentioned the prospect of a second try, if the first one didn't do what it was designed for? But why leave this ugliness in her shed, unless it was meant to cast more suspicion on her?

Unhappy, uncertain, and feeling very much alone, she laid down the phone and stood staring into the open bag. Was it something like this that had started the cabin fire? Had the arsonist put it in her shed? Had the prowler Billy had heard secreted it in order not to be caught with the tools for a possible second try? But the first try *had* worked—devastatingly well—except for the fact that she *hadn't* burned with her cabin. No one would leave this kind of evidence anywhere near the scene of their crime, would they? No, they would carry it away with them—hide it. Someone, for some reason, must have meant this to be found in her storage shed. Who? Why?

Would Tatum go to the extreme of *planting* evidence? She thought he might. This could have been meant to incriminate either her or Anne. He could certainly have broken the lock on her shed door and slipped in with this nasty bag of tricks. She wouldn't put it past him, given his obsession and the behavior she had previously witnessed.

Or had it been Anne? Was she responsible for the fire that reduced the cabin to smoldering rubble? Jessie's anger grew as she contemplated that idea. Why would Anne want to make her seem guilty of starting a fire? To shift Tatum's suspicions away from herself? Resentment over the disagreement they'd had at the

cabin? But Anne wouldn't have had to break into the
shed to do it—the shed key had hung just inside the
cabin's front door and using it would have been less
obvious. Often, when Jessie was busy in the dog yard,
the shed wasn't even locked. Anne could have slipped
in and planted it anytime.

But it could have been anyone. There was no way of
knowing. It was improbable that whoever put it there
had left any fingerprints on its contents. She had not
touched anything but the outside of the bag, but thinking about the roll of electrician's tape, Jessie suddenly
knew without a doubt that it was her own—the one she
had been looking for on the trip to the cabin in the
hills—that it would have her fingerprints all over it.
This new trouble was meant for *her*. But maybe someone else had touched it, too.

God, what do I do now?

Put it back where you found it.

And have someone like Tatum find it or *send* someone to find it, if he was the one who put it there? I don't
think so.

Get rid of it—all of it.

How? Besides, that might not be smart. I might need
these things to show someone later.

And someone might find it very interesting that you
had them and said nothing.

Right, so—what?

Hide it. But not the tape that may have your prints.
Think of somewhere else to put that.

Where?

Living with a state trooper had taught her a few
things. Going out to the shed, she retrieved a box of

Ziploc bags and returned to the tent. Carefully, she used a kitchen fork to lift the black roll of tape from the bag and drop it into one of the Ziplocs without touching it. Separated from the other items in the bag it became innocuous, lost its immediate threat. Though someone might wonder at the plastic bag that held it, no one would give more than a passing thought to her eccentricity in packaging, especially if it were put back where she usually kept it. She put it in the tool bag she carried on her sled, now on a shelf in the shed, then closed and locked the shed door that had been repaired by a neighbor that afternoon.

Now, what to do with the bag and the rest of its extremely offensive contents? Separated, the items were quite ordinary, except the lighter fluid, perhaps. Scattering them in places where they could normally be stored might defuse their damning potential, but for some reason she couldn't identify she felt that it might be wise to keep them together—contents intact and unhandled. Hiding the bag in the woods would leave it vulnerable to discovery by others, but she didn't want it found in her living space or damning her from the storage shed, for that matter. If Tatum had placed it there, he could set the hounds of law enforcement on her, counting on its discovery.

In the back of the dog box on the truck between the dog compartments was the closetlike space that held harness and other equipment for racing. While the box was being made for her, Jessie had asked the builder to install a false back, held closed with magnets, so that all she had to do was press on it sharply and it would spring open. Painted to match the rest of the wooden box and placed in the dark end of the space, it fit securely and looked like a solid panel, with hidden hinges and no handle to reveal its presence. She had screwed hooks onto the visible side of it on which to hang lines and harness. She used the hidden inside for storing guns and camera equipment—anything that might be stolen from a musher's truck that was sometimes left unlocked and unwatched during a training run or a racing event.

Zipping up the gym bag, Jessie took it to the truck, where she deposited it inside the secret compartment. Even if someone searched her truck from top to bottom, it was unlikely they would find it. Only three other people knew of its existence: the builder; Alex Jensen, who had suggested it in the first place; and Billy Steward, who had fallen against it by accident once, but had promised not to tell. Satisfied, she went back to the tent and locked herself in, which seemed a little optimistic considering that it was made of canvas, but made her feel better. She didn't like the idea of the arsonist returning for another try, and felt safer when she had slipped her Smith & Wesson .44 under the roll-away bed, within easy reach.

With the fire bomb kit components as safely hidden as possible, she relaxed a little, switched on the space heater to take the chill from the room, and turned her attention to dinner. With help from Billy and his father, she had fed and watered the dogs before the Stewards left for home, but it had been a long time since she had eaten the lunch Oscar had provided.

There was just enough of Oscar's good soup left for dinner, so she put it on the stove to heat slowly, went out to the puppy pen and brought in Jeep, Daisy, and their two littermates, for a romp on the floor of the tent. The half-grown pups were fascinated by the new environment and immediately set out to explore it and everything in it. Jessie's cabin had been puppy proofed, of course, but now she had to rescue several items that had been set low enough to be reached by these four, who, with more curiosity than discipline, wanted to examine and taste anything within reach.

Sitting on the rug with a handful of chew treats for distraction, she was happily crawled over and accepted as one of the gang. They gnawed at the treats and wrestled each other on and around her, licked her hands and face, and snuggled close to her warmth to be scratched and petted.

All dogs are naturally physical with other dogs, expressing their likes and dislikes in licks, nips, bites, and rubs, tumbling over and around each other in play or in squabbles. It probably starts before they are born and sharing space inside their mother with several other puppies. Nursing from mothers that lick and groom them, sometimes impatiently snap at them, mouth them up bodily when they are small, puppies quickly develop an acceptance of physical relationships, and expect no less of their humans. Though they may figure out that, "Good dog," indicates their behavior is agreeable, the best way a human can express appreciation and affection is with a hands-on approach, in the language they know best, giving them lots of petting, scratching, rubbing, along with words of praise. The best learning environment includes positive reinforcement that is physical, for that is most clearly understood by the dog. Some trainers even nip a dog's ear with their teeth to encourage it to stand still or to correct minor misbehaviors, just as its mother or another older dog would.

Jessie was aware of this, and physical contact with her mutts was very much a part of her training program from the time they were small. The contact was beneficial to her as well. Playing with her puppies and young dogs—as she was doing now on the floor, in the temporary shelter of the tent—calmed her, relieved stress, and gave her a sense of belonging; for humans are also physical animals and susceptible to touch. Still feeling Jensen's absence sharply, physically and otherwise, it was comforting to share the warmth of other live beings.

Scooping young Jeep into her lap, she explored his chest and shoulders with her fingers.

"You're going to be a strong one when you're grown," she informed him. "Good muscles developing here for pulling sleds."

At the sound of her voice, he looked up and cocked his head to listen for a moment, then wriggled his way back onto the floor and padded off to pounce on his littermate Storm.

Jessie leaned back to watch, happy with this energetic bunch, back in her element, cabin fire forgotten for a moment.

When the soup was hot, she left the pups to their own devices momentarily, made a sandwich, then sat at the card table to eat. Her spirits, dampened by the afternoon's revelations of Tatum's accusations and the discovery of the makings for a fire bomb, lightened as she smiled at the antics of the pups. She was thankful that the fire had been confined to *her* living space and had not involved any of her canines, especially these endearing little guys.

"You're not just things and walls, are you?" she asked them, and knew how upset she would have been to lose any of her dogs. Everything else was replaceable. "Maybe it was time I cleaned house anyway."

After an hour, she took the pups back to their pen and turned off the overhead lights. Finding a news broadcast that came in pretty well on the small television, she settled down in the easy chair near the floor lamp to watch it, with a cup of tea and a couple of brownies someone had brought. The corners of the canvas room were dark with shadows, but it felt almost homey in the soft light. The chair was comfortable, though it felt foreign and she missed her large sofa. Halfway through the program, still waiting for the weather prediction, she dozed off, worn out with stress and the overwhelming generosity of the day.

Tomorrow—a last thought drifted through her mind. Tomorrow nothing would stop her from a long training run—*nothing*.

It was fully dark when she woke to full alertness in the chair almost two hours later. The television was showing some sitcom and she reached to turn it off so she could listen.The dogs were barking, the yard lights had blinked on, and a human shadow fell suddenly upon the canvas side of the tent near the door.

"Jessie?" called an unfamiliar voice. "Jessie Arnold. Are you there?"

Slowly, quietly, moving sock-footed across the room, she drew her .44 from the floor under the bed as she assessed the shadow. Apparently male, he stood still, figure completely outlined by the light behind him, and seemed to have nothing in his hands, which were held out to his sides.

"Who is it?" she asked. "What do you want?"

"It's Greg Holman. Can I talk to you, please?"

The answer was completely unexpected. But, she thought, I should have anticipated the possibility that he'd show up sooner or later.

She stood very still for a moment, wondered if she had locked the door, remembered that she had. Considering what to do, she moved closer to the phone on the table.

"What do you want?" she repeated.

"I'm looking for my wife—for Anne. I think maybe you can help me find her."

"I have no idea where she is."

"But she was here, right?"

"She's not here now."

"Where is she?"

"I said I don't know. Go away, or I'll call the troopers."

Considering the evidence of Anne's scars and appearance, and what she had related about Greg Holman's abuse, Jessie had no intention of telling him anything that might help him find her or of letting him come any closer.

"Please, Jessie. I'm really worried about her. Can I come in and talk about it? I've got to know what she told you."

"What I saw and what she told me makes me more comfortable with you outside, Greg—even more if you're not here at all. Why are you sneaking in here after dark anyway? I didn't hear a car."

"I parked out by the road and walked. I went by a couple of times earlier, but there were people here all day and I wanted to talk to you alone."

"Why?"

"I don't want the cops involved. First I've got to find out what the hell's going on." For the first time, impatience found its way into his voice, and a note of pleading. "Jessie, whatever she told you, I didn't do the things she says. I never hurt her."

"Somebody obviously *did*. What about her face— and all those cuts on her arm?"

"Oh, God," Holman groaned. "Is she doing that again?"

"You're kidding, right? No one would do that to themselves."

"No—I'm not kidding. She cuts herself with a razor blade when she's angry or feels insecure. She's done it for years."

Astounded, Jessie knew that she believed him. It made sense, and the discouragement in his voice reinforced it. She remembered the stained tissues and trace of blood on the blade she had found in her bathroom and her assumption that Anne had cut herself shaving her legs. She had briefly wondered why the blade had been taken out of the razor, but had ignored it in her irritation at the other woman's inconsideration.

"Look," she said to Greg, deciding suddenly. "I'm going to let you come in. But I want you to know that

I have a handgun—and a phone that connects directly to the troopers' office. I'll unlock the door, then you wait till I tell you to open it. Got that?"

"Yes—thanks."

"Move away from the tent."

The shadow receded and stopped, waiting.

Jessie went to the door, unlocked it, and retreated halfway across the canvas room. "Okay. Come on in—slowly."

15

GREG HOLMAN CAME CAUTIOUSLY INTO JESSIE'S TEMPO-
rary living space, moving slowly, with both hands
where she could see them. Inside, he closed the door,
stopped, and waited, glancing nervously at the gun in
her hand, while she looked him over.

"I've got no reason to trust you. Take off your jacket,
toss it over here, and turn around—slowly."

Removing the Carhart's jacket, he threw it to the
floor in front of her and turned slowly, so she could
see that he had no weapons, visible or bulging in his
pockets.

"Turn out your pockets."

A rattle of change hit the floor and he stood holding
his wallet, nothing else.

"Raise your pants legs."

Nothing but wool socks. Unless he was a magician,
he was unarmed.

She kept him standing while she went through the
pockets of his jacket, finding only the keys to a rental
car, a roll of butterscotch Life Savers, a round-trip

182

plane ticket from Denver to Seattle and Anchorage with the return half unused, and a book of matches from a motel in Wasilla. She replaced them all.

"Here." She tossed it back and gestured with the barrel of the .44 to one of the folding chairs. "Sit there. And keep in mind that I'm a pretty good shot."

Straddling the other chair, so she could lean her forearms on the back and keep the handgun between them, she sat ten feet away and assessed him more thoroughly.

Though she would have recognized him easily enough, there were significant differences. He looked more than ten years older. Two vertical lines now separated his eyebrows, and several lines wrinkled his once-smooth forehead. The open expression she remembered was gone, and what she saw instead was a guarded watchfulness. Stress had added tension to his face and the way he held himself—tired, worn down, and worried. Though still the strong, fit outdoorsman in his well-worn jeans and battered work boots, there was a new awareness in his attitude that he had lacked before.

"Okay," she said, nodding to Holman, who had been waiting silently while she studied him. "What do you want, and why should I care?"

He sat up a little straighter. "I've got to know where she is, Jessie."

"I told you, I don't know."

"She didn't tell you where she was going?"

"No—didn't even tell me she *was* going, just took off when the fire started this morning—when I really needed her help."

Her irritation at Anne's desertion surfaced again, and she could hear the edge of resentment in her own voice.

Greg sighed deeply and looked at the floor. "Did she start it?" he asked, weary apprehension in his voice.

The question startled Jessie into momentary silence. Uneasy, she frowned as she asked the obvious question, "Why would you think so?"

"It wouldn't be the first time," he told her. She was aware of his watching closely for a reaction, reaching for her belief and trust.

Though he seemed sincere, Anne had also exhibited a twisted sort of credibility. Jessie was learning quickly not to take what she heard or saw at face value, even from Phil and Mac. There was always more—and people had their own agendas, positive or not. She listened as he continued to explain, but she did not let down her guard.

"There's a warrant for her arrest in Colorado, for burning down the house we were renting before she left two weeks ago. That's her solution to problems she can't solve or admit—burn them. I've got to find her. I'm afraid she's going to . . . to hurt somebody again, Jessie."

"*Again?*"

Early the next morning, before anyone could show up with some other bad news to stop her, Jessie was on the trail with a team of nine dogs, three of them young trainees. It was a glorious day. The temperature had risen, snow and ice were melting, and the sun gleamed from every sublimating drift so brightly that it hurt her eyes when a curve in the trail turned the team toward the east. Deep blue shadows defined the slightest unevenness in the trail, and cast long lines from every tree and shrub.

Crossing an open meadow, she saw a moose stretching its neck to strip twigs from the willows along the bank of a partially frozen creek. It turned its head to watch the team and sled pass, but condescendingly ignored the immediate wild yapping of the young dogs, who struggled against their harnesses, itching to give chase. Tank kept the gang line taut. The more experienced dogs ran on, paying little attention, pulling the young ones along with them until the moose was out of sight. *Mind your manners*, they seemed to say in rebuke. *Don't bark at neighbors that are none of your business.* It made Jessie grin and lightened her mood, which was already one of relief and exhilaration in escaping the problems she had purposely left behind her.

The night before, as soon as Greg Holman had gone, she had brought Tank into the tent, locked the door again, and settled into her borrowed bed for the night, knowing she needed sleep to refuel her flagging energy and reduce the emotional overload of the last few days. The sleep she managed was less than ideal. She was disturbed twice by dreams of fire she was unable to quench, from which she woke wide-eyed and breathless. The changing temperature and humidity also made for periods of semiwakefulness. Still, she had felt better when she got up, made breakfast for herself and the dogs, and readied her sled for a day on the runners, determined not to disrupt her training schedule any more than it had been already. House, tent, fires, trouble, or not, the dogs needed her attention.

Now, as the sled glided along the winding trail, heading steadily northwest, she gave herself plenty of time to simply enjoy being part of the sunny day, knowing she would eventually return to a thoughtful examination of what she had learned from Holman the night before.

The dogs were running well and smoothly in the well-broken track they followed. Knowing the capabilities of the experienced dogs in the team, Jessie watched the young ones closely, making sure they were not pushed too fast or asked to do more than they were able. It was important that they learn to work as a team, responding to changing trail conditions as required, following their leader as a single, happy unit. But each dog also had its own individual personality, needs, and abilities that Jessie assessed carefully in deciding where to place it in this team and whether it would be good enough to keep or should be sold to other racing enthusiasts. Some, like Smut, would never make good sled dogs; she found homes for them. It was important that all the dogs she kept enjoyed going out in a team, had fun on the trail, and maintained their desire to run and pull.

She also watched attentively to see which dogs ran well together. Some tended to compete or developed dislikes for each other. These she did not hitch together but paired with a more easygoing partner. Some liked to lead, others to follow. Some did well in the front or middle of the team but were uneasy with a sled running directly behind them. Good wheel dogs were often as hard to find as leaders, for they must be strong enough to shift the direction of a

loaded sled and keep it in line, but not be frightened
that it might slide into them. Figuring out their individual aptitudes and idiosyncrasies was demanding,
but Jessie enjoyed making these discoveries and helping her mutts learn what they could do and how to do
it successfully.

Well-cared-for dogs run best at temperatures well
below freezing that keep them from overheating or becoming dehydrated. This sunny day was pleasant for
Jessie, but warmer than she liked for training her team.
Though her dogs must learn to run in warm or cold
conditions, she planned to stop often to give them extra
water. She soon unzipped her parka and appreciated
the warmth that promised spring, though the sun was
still at a fairly low angle this early in the year.

Snow on south-facing slopes was beginning to melt,
water trickling just a little here and there, and the trail
was punchy and soft. Over the *shush* of the runners on
the snow, as the trail narrowed between some trees, she
could hear the twitter of chickadees. Several skimmed
across ahead of the sled, altering direction with quick
flicks of their wings. Though more elusive, Jessie
often spotted house finches, who also spent the winters
in the north. These were as easily identified as the
brownish sparrows they resembled, though the males
had reddish heads and the females were blush of
breast. Magpies and comical, camp-robbing jays, both
related to ravens, also hung around in the winter. But
soon the migrating flocks would arrive: white snow
geese returning to their summer habitats, followed by
their darker Canadian cousins; swans, cranes, and
many smaller birds would soar in to fill the air with

their songs and calls, a welcome contrast to the silence of the long winter.

With the physical exercise of driving the sled, pumping with one foot on the uphill sections, sometimes trotting along beside it, Jessie felt her whole body loosen up, begin to stretch and move as it should. The stress faded until the only tension she could identify was that of muscles, fit and strong enough to do the job she demanded of them. The breeze created by their motion seemed to sweep away mental cobwebs, mend emotional hurts, and make her problems seem less important and solutions possible. With a new, more positive outlook, she reconsidered last night's late visitor.

What Greg had told her had been eerily similar to what Anne had related earlier, but in his version of the last ten years he was not to blame for their troubles—she was. The facts, according to Greg, had not really helped Jessie clarify the situation or know what to believe. She did not remember him as dishonest, though he was sometimes biased. The night before in the tent, he seemed sincere, but how was she to tell what was truth and what self-serving? Much of Anne's account was also now in question.

According to Greg, he had finally been convinced that Anne had started the fire that killed Cal Mulligan's two children, though he said she had stubbornly continued to deny it.

"I didn't know anything about it until after I married her. Even then, I didn't believe it at first, but there was just too much that didn't fit together any other way. Once, when I was in town, a guy named Tatum told me a lot of stuff about the fire that seemed totally absurd and unfair."

Jessie nodded. "I know Tatum. He's investigating fires officially now."

Her scornful tone caught Holman's attention.

"You don't believe him?"

"I don't like him—or trust him. I don't know *what* to believe. Anne said it wasn't her fault—that he's obsessed with the idea that she set it—is making up proof. I don't know why, except that he was burned in that fire and resented having to quit being a fireman and turn to investigating arson."

"That's what I thought, but I talked to other people. Some of the things Anne claimed didn't jibe with what they said. Tatum may have good reason to suspect her. When she started setting other fires—especially after she burned our cabin—"

"She said *you* did that."

"Not a chance. I built that cabin with my own hands—cut every log, measured and fit every joint. She burned it so we'd have to leave—it was another way for her to run."

"What did she have to run from? It was a year later. They hadn't arrested her. Tatum couldn't prove any of his accusations, could he?"

"No, but he didn't give up—just wasn't around up there. At least we thought he wasn't, but we might have been wrong. A time or two I thought . . . And there were other, unrelated things."

"The baby?" Jessie blurted without thinking.

He looked at her sharply and grew as still as an animal caught suddenly in the glare of headlights.

"What do you know about that?"

"Not much," she backpedaled, damned if she'd help him. "Just that she had one."

"She told you I killed it, didn't she?"

Jessie knew her silence handed him the truth.

"Well, I didn't," he said brusquely, staring at his hands in his lap for a long moment before going on. "I don't really know if it was stillborn, like she said, or if she . . . Look, I came home and she'd had it and buried it somewhere—she wouldn't tell me where. I couldn't find it and didn't have much time to try before she set that fire."

He paused and looked up. "I know that she didn't want it. She hated being pregnant and told me over and over that she wouldn't take care of it when it was born. She refused to see a doctor."

"She said you wouldn't let her go to town."

"That's ridiculous. I stopped her once, early, when she threatened to go and get an abortion. After that she wouldn't go. I had decided to take her in, like it or not—wasn't going to have my kid born without someone who knew what they were doing, if anything went wrong. I wanted that baby—it was mine, too."

"A-ah . . ." Jessie started, but stopped, not knowing if he was aware that the child hadn't been his.

"Yeah, I know now that it *wasn't* mine. But, then, I still thought it was—still believed her—so I thought we had lots of time, but it was two months older than I thought. When she couldn't get out of bed one morning, I made a big mistake—thought something was wrong and went down to use the phone at the roadhouse. When I came back it was over and she said it was born too early and . . . dead."

Jessie caught a gleam of moisture on Greg's face. Tears? For what, exactly? To make her believe him? Was he capable of that much deception?

"I wanted to see how it really died. I looked for a long time, but there's miles of places to hide things up there. Then it snowed that night and I never could find where she'd put it, because right after that she burned the cabin. She wanted to get me away from there before I found it."

"She buried it by a big rock, across an open space on the west side of your cabin," Jessie told him impulsively.

"How could you know that?"

"I found her crying over it up there, Greg. She dug up the remains—the bones—and brought them back with her in a metal box."

He stared at her, astonished. "Why?"

"She said that . . ."

Jessie was jerked suddenly from her remembered conversation with Greg Holman, as the dogs came over a small rise and started down toward a creek bed. It was narrow, not more than four or five feet wide, and perhaps two feet at its deepest. Though the surface was still frozen, the ice looked thin in the sunshine, and water had welled up to run across it in a generous overflow.

Tank did not hesitate but led the team directly into the water on the ice, as he had done many times through the years and crossed creeks quickly, with no particular difficulty. The young dogs in the team, however, were not so casual. The idea of following his confident lead into the icy water did not appeal to them in the least. All three refused, frantically trying to reverse direction and keep their feet out of the water.

Young Taffy, paired with Tux, was dragged onto the creek, much against her will, as Tux steadily followed Tank as usual. Jimmy, who was doing better at not jumping lines, was also dragged onto the ice beside experienced Mitts, followed by Pete and young Shorts. But the opposing pressure of the reluctant, inexperienced dogs on the gang line had slowed the advance of the whole team. As the sled dropped down the bank and onto the creek, the ice began to fracture. Taffy, trying to climb out on the opposite bank, broke through a thin spot, fell back, breaking more, and immediately four struggling dogs were in the water. She tried again at the bank and made it this time, thanks to the help of her partner, Tux.

"Hike, Tank," Jessie called sharply. "Go, guys. Get us out of here."

As her leader threw himself against the harness, Tux and even Taffy followed him in pulling hard on the line. Jimmy and Mitts made it up the bank, and Pete and Shorts were all but across, but Darryl One and Darryl Two, in wheel position, were now forced into the cold water in order to reach the other bank. The sled, coming last, slowly sank several inches with the weight of the sled bag, plus Jessie on the rear runners. Water spilled into her boots, drenching their felt insulation and her feet in their heavy wool socks. By the time the team had pulled her and the sled up the gently sloping bank, her toes were growing numb.

Halting the team, she assessed the situation. The sled bag was designed to keep most of the water from getting inside, so her equipment would at most be damp in spots, but had been bagged in plastic for just such a situation. There were, however, eight wet dogs, all shaking themselves vigorously, and one shivering musher, wet to the knees, to be dried out before they could continue.

"I think," she told the team in general, as she prepared to get a fire going, "that we need some lessons in crossing partially thawed creeks—but not right now."

It was much later before she thought of any problems other than those of training sled dogs.

16

RETURNING HOME LATE THAT AFTERNOON, JESSIE FOUND MacDonald writing a note to leave on the door of her tent. He raised one hand in greeting as he crumpled the note in the other, stuffed it into his pocket, and turned to watch as she pulled the team to a stop near the storage shed.

The snow in the yard had melted thin in spots, and the sound of the runners on a patch of bare ground made her grimace. There wouldn't be many sled runs left if it didn't snow again. She would soon be driving teams from a four-wheeled ATV instead of a sled.

This was effective, and many mushers used them to maintain the training of their dogs after the snow was gone. The dogs pulled them as readily as a sled, and they allowed drivers better control over speed and steered more easily than the carts used by some. The sounds of them warned wildlife that something was coming, allowing them to escape to the woods, and their lights were helpful in providing safety along roads that held traffic. Jessie, however, was much more fond of the silent gliding of her sled, which blended into the soft natural sounds of the wilderness, and was always glad to have the snow come back in the fall.

"I've got to take care of these guys," she told Mac, as he walked up to the sled. "Then we can talk. Okay?"

"Can I help?"

Together, they took the dogs out of harness; and Jessie walked them two by two to their individual boxes, answering his questions about the design as she fastened them to their tethers. The shell of each box was built separately from its floor, so it could be lifted off to clean the interior and change the straw the dog slept on. The wood floor was a few inches off the frozen ground to keep the animal warm. Each door had a raised sill that the dog must step over, which meant that less snow blew or was tracked in.

"Cozy," MacDonald commented. "I guess I never thought much about doghouses—just figured they should have the traditional peaked roof and an opening in front with 'Spot' painted over it, like in cartoons. I've never had a dog."

"Maybe it's time you did," Jessie teased. "Alaskan huskies are great pets. They're generally very bright and affectionate."

She gave him the key to the new lock on the storage shed. She carried it with her now to make sure it didn't fall into the wrong hands. Jessie had thoroughly searched the shed for anything else that did not belong there, but she had found nothing. He straightened the harnesses and hung them just inside the door as she directed, then helped water all the dogs and watched as she examined the feet and legs of those she had taken on the run, carefully making sure they had sustained no damage from the unstable ice and snow.

Finished with kennel work for the moment, Jessie went into the tent and took off her boots and outer gear. She put the kettle on for tea and, turning on the space heater, hung the soggy boot liners and wool socks that she had changed on the trail and brought home in her sled bag near it to dry.

"Looks like you went wading," Mac commented.

"Not by choice, believe me. Some of these younger mutts I'm training need more lessons in coping with spring conditions—specifically the right way to cross half-thawed creeks."

He grinned. "They looked pretty dry now."

"They dry faster and easier than people. I don't have fur to shake."

For a few minutes, until the tea was ready, he asked questions, and she briefly described the physical and mental conditioning and education of young sled dogs.

"It's much more complicated than I imagined," he told her, accepting a mug of tea. "I guess I thought you just put them in harness and it was natural for them to pull sleds."

"A lot of it's natural ability, but it takes much more than that to make real winners of sled dogs. Some of it's quite subtle and even goes against their natural tendencies—like the hunting instinct for chasing moose that I have to discourage aggressively. We saw one today that made them crazy, but the older dogs dragged the younger ones along till they got over it. It takes a long time and a lot of patience and positive reinforcement to help them learn to do things right—a lot like people, I guess. But you didn't come out here for a lesson on mushing, did you?"

She sat down on one of the metal chairs and faced him across the table, mug of tea clutched between both hands, instinct for self-preservation rising.

"No," he admitted. "One of the guys who helped load your sled on Petersville Road is out of state on business—won't be back for a week. I found the other one, Gary Jeffers, but he says they didn't see anyone with you, that the reason they had to help you lift the sled was that you couldn't do it alone."

She thought about it and remembered Anne climbing immediately into the cab of the truck in a sulk. It was possible that they hadn't noticed her. The truck itself had been between them, with the cab farthest away from where they were working with their snowmachines. She explained this to MacDonald, frowning with the frustration of having her proof vanish.

"Dammit, anyway. She *was* there, Mac. She was being a real pain, but she *was* in the cab of the truck."

"Look, Jessie. Is Petersville Road a place you usually use for training?"

"No. It would waste a lot of time—and money for gas—to haul the dogs seventy miles back and forth every time when there are lots of trails right here for day runs. For overnights, I run them out toward Skwentna along the Iditarod Trail, more often than not. I haven't been on the Trapper Creek trails since I lived up there ten years ago."

"You lived there?"

"Yes, for part of a winter. That's how I got to know

the Holmans. But it was too far from town and the trails weren't all that good."

"But, unless you had some reason other than training, you wouldn't have gone out there?"

"That's right."

"What was that reason? Tell me again."

Jessie stared at him. This man was no dummy. He had put his finger on the key question. She frowned and shook her head. What was important to tell him and what not? Should all her feeling of responsibility to maintain a confidence have disappeared with Anne? Exactly why *had* she taken Anne out there? Mostly so she would leave—to stop her begging, demands, and the huge interruption of having her around. She hadn't really cared why Anne wanted so badly to go. But there had also been sympathy for her difficult situation, hadn't there? Again, Jessie felt manipulated and used. If Anne had started the fire that burned my cabin, do I want her to get away with it? Telling MacDonald all she suspected might keep that from happening.

"Listen"—he interrupted her thoughts. "I know you're not telling me all that you know about this whole thing—probably through misguided loyalty. It would be a good idea if you did. We could do better at figuring all this out if we shared information. Besides, she may not have told you the truth."

He could be right and she knew it. But was it wise from her point of view, considering the things that seemed so stacked against her—things she had no way to prove weren't true? The Mulligan fire, for instance, and the fact that she could have been there—couldn't prove she hadn't been. How the hell had her hat gotten there, anyway? Would she be hurting herself by helping him?

"Mac," she said finally, "I'm not opposed to sharing, but some of what I know is other people's business and was told to me in confidence. Besides that, I honestly don't know what'd be helpful to tell you. So much has happened between so many people and at different times that it's a huge confusion. What's related, and what's not? I'm having real trouble sorting it all out, and I don't understand why Tatum's focused on me."

"Why don't you just tell me—whatever—whether it seems related or not, and let me ask questions. If something I don't ask about seems important, tell me that, too. Maybe we can put something together, if you don't try too hard to sort it out by yourself."

He paused and thought for a minute, nodded to himself, and continued. "Some of what *I* know may help. How about if I start by telling you that I've been digging into Tatum's background—the Holmans', too. One interesting thing I found out is that Tatum had a romantic thing for Anne—Marty—*whatever*—back before the Mulligan fire. And she *was* Marty Gifford then—changed her first name when she changed the last to Holman. She evidently flirted with but wasn't really interested in Tatum—strung him along for a while, then put him down pretty hard. One of the firefighters he worked and socialized with then remembered quite a bit about it, because Tatum talked to him. Tatum was angry—resented her rejection, especially when he found out that she was seeing a married man, Cal Mulligan. It may help explain his obsession and the attempt to hang that old arson charge on her—if it was arson. She may have actually been responsible. He kept at it in his spare time after he got out of the hospital. That's how he got into arson investigation—they saw he was good at it."

"You think he'd actually do that out of revenge? Isn't he supposed to be a professional?"

"Sure, but he's human, and he was evidently furious and very convinced he was right—or wouldn't let himself see it any other way. The burns he got probably influenced his fixation. He hated having to give up fire fighting. He was good at that, too, and loved doing it. Not being able to save those two kids did something to him, too. He'd promised their mother he'd get them out, so when he couldn't . . . well. He's not the enthusiastic, happy-go-lucky person he used to be, according to the guy I talked to."

Jessie thought about it and, not for the first time, felt some sympathy for Tatum. But it was combined with her anger at his behavior and insinuations about her.

"You know, there are fires mixed up in all of this," she commented reflectively after a minute.

"Yeah, all three of them happening in such a short time, plus the one ten years ago. I keep thinking they're tied together *somehow* by the people involved."

"But there're more—several more that I guess you don't know about. I don't know much, but more than I did yesterday—maybe. Greg showed up here last night, after everyone had gone. He's looking for Anne."

"Her husband—right? I thought he was somewhere out of state."

"Colorado's where she said she left him. But he's

evidently followed her up here, is trying to find her, and she seemed to be really afraid of him. Their stories are complete opposites. He says *she* burns things—that she burned a place in Colorado before she took off to come here, that *she* burned their cabin in the Little Peters Hills ten years ago."

MacDonald leaned forward in his chair and set down the mug he had half raised to his mouth.

"Make some kind of sense, wouldn't it?"

"But she claims *he burns things*—that it's all *his* doing, that he beat her, terrorized her, even killed her child when it was born."

"And he blames it all on her?"

"Yes. He has a temper and holds grudges. But whoever did what to who, there *was* a child. She dug it up when we were up there. Brought its bones back in the metal box it had been buried in."

"I know you said that, but . . . My dear sweet Jesus. Why?"

"She said she wanted to take the bones to the police to prove he killed it. I don't know how—or what they'd prove—but she seemed convinced. She's got some real problems, Mac. I know firsthand that when she's threatened or angry or insecure, she cuts herself with razor blades. I *saw* the result on her arm. But she told me that it was something *he* was responsible for—like the fires. Each of them accuses the other, but she's the one that's been physically hurt, however it happened. He says she had an affair with a guy in Colorado who beat her up—put her in the hospital."

"What do *you* think?"

"I know it's possible. She was having an affair with

Mulligan, after all, wasn't she—and teasing Tatum at the same time?"

"But which of them do you believe?"

"I don't know. Depends on who's talking and what I'm seeing at the time. Maybe they're both responsible for parts of it. I wish it would all go away. I wish neither of them had ever shown up on my doorstep. I wish I had my house back, dammit. I had nothing to do with any of it, but now I'm right in the middle, and liking it less and less all the time."

"If there *is* a warrant for Anne in Colorado, I can find out pretty fast. She may have run to get away from it."

"She said he promised to follow and kill her, like he killed her baby."

"Pretty convenient, isn't it?"

"Yes, I guess. But he *is* here looking for her."

Jessie got up and walked to the door of the tent. Opening it, she stood for a minute or two, looking out at the ruins of her cabin and at her dogs, many of which were out of their boxes. Tank had jumped to the top of his and lay with supreme dignity, surveying the activity around him.

"The thing I don't like about this tent is not having any windows," Jessie said. "I can't see out and I'm used to keeping an eye on the dog yard."

"Shall I cut you out a couple?" He took a knife from his pocket and waved it at the canvas wall.

She grinned and shook her head. "I don't think the owner would appreciate it." Closing the door, she returned to her chair, once again serious.

"You know, Mac, if I could just figure out how Anne

disappeared and where she's gone, maybe I could find her and get enough information to straighten this thing out somehow. I wonder if she knows Greg is here. If she does, maybe she's hiding from him. Maybe she's gone—back to Seattle or somewhere he wouldn't look. She said she would do that once we'd been up to the hills, but maybe she didn't. She lied about a lot of other stuff. Maybe she's still here—somewhere. I *could* look for her."

MacDonald frowned. "I don't think that's a real good idea. We've been keeping an eye on the airport, and I think you'd better let us do the looking, Jessie. If she's responsible for any or all these fires she could have started yours. If Holman started them, you might put yourself between the two of them, which doesn't sound wise to me. Arson is no game, and it's never reasonable."

She nodded, but didn't let go of the idea. When Mac had gone, promising to keep in touch, she went out to sit on the bench by the door and consider it.

She had absolutely no idea where to begin to look for Anne, but she realized that Greg Holman was another question. Her search of his jacket pockets had told her two things—that he was driving a Budget rental car and that he might be or had been staying at the North by NorthRest Motel in Wasilla.

There were several questions she wished she had asked him. If she could find him, she could ask them now. The motel was at least a place to start looking.

MacDonald could be right about the risk in looking for either Anne or Greg, but she was no longer content to stay home, doing nothing but train her dogs with all this on her mind and a possibly psychotic Tatum making accusations every time she turned around.

In a few minutes, she was on her way to Wasilla in her truck, with her .44 in one pocket of her coat. For Jessie, it was now time to see what she could find out for herself.

17

THE NORTH BY NORTHREST MOTEL, LOCATED JUST WEST
of Wasilla on the Parks Highway, was a small affair,
clearly operated by someone who didn't care much for
his job, for it was conspicuously going to seed, in contrast to other tourist facilities nearby. Two lines of six
ancient units faced each other across an open space
that might have held a pool in some warmer climate.
Instead it was filled with a nightmare collection of
plaster garden gnomes and animals, an odd structure
that couldn't quite decide whether to be a windmill or
a wishing well, a chain-saw carving of a half-size
black bear holding a Welcome sign, and a shabby set
of playground equipment—all slowly emerging from
the melting snow to reveal exotic colors never found in
nature. A faded flock of garish pink plastic flamingos,
heads up or down in one of two poses, seemed to float
on a sublimating drift, wire legs still hidden beneath
the snow. A circular drive looped around this anti-Dis-
ney fantasy and provided a space for parking in front
of each unit.

Jessie stopped her truck in front of the office, a separate building, badly in need of paint. A neon sign in one of its streaked windows faintly glowed VACANCY in the middle of the afternoon, and she wondered if they ever had a reason to turn it off.

Inside, she pushed a button taped to the counter beside a smudged, almost unreadable card that instructed her to PRESS FOR SERVICE, heard a bell ring rustily somewhere in the back of the building, and waited. In a few minutes a door behind the counter opened and a very short man, so bald and pink he looked oddly naked from the neck up, came out and climbed on some kind of hidden step that lifted him high enough to lean his forearms on the countertop.

"Help you?"

"I'm looking for Greg Holman. Is he staying here?"

"Holman? Holman. Let me check."

Having noticed only one car parked in front of the units, Jessie questioned his inability to remember the name, but she waited patiently while he shuffled through a card file as though every room was filled.

"Holman. Right. Unit nine's halfway back on the left, but he's not there."

"How do you know?"

"Car's gone. See?" He waved a hand in the direction of unit nine. "You wanna leave a message?"

Jessie thought for a minute and decided against it. She didn't particularly want Greg Holman to show up at her place on Knik Road again, and if she left a message he probably would.

"I'll come back later," she told the manager.

"Whatever floats your boat. He goes out about nine every morning and usually comes back in the evening, but not always. You might try about seven, but he sometimes goes out again."

"How long has he been here?"

Again he checked the card and counted. "Six—no, seven days."

A week. That meant that Greg had been there even before Anne called, supposedly from Seattle.

"Anyone with him?"

"No. A couple of people've stopped in, but he's alone."

"What's your phone number? I'll call first."

He handed her a book of matches like the one she had seen in Holman's jacket pocket. The motel number was on the back.

"Thanks."

Jessie drove her truck around the driveway loop and across to the far lanes of the highway. As she accelerated, the insulated mug, from which she had been sipping tea as she drove, tipped and fell from the dash to the floor in front of the passenger seat, spilling the two or three swallows of liquid that were left. Pulling off the pavement into the parking lot of a convenience store directly across from the motel, she reached behind the seat for some paper towels to sop up the mess.

Once more ready to roll, she glanced across for a last look at the odd flamingo still life. As she shook her head in wonder at the eccentricities of human taste, a brown pickup swung off the highway into the motel drive, followed closely by a green compact sedan.

Hesitating, she watched the two vehicles stop in front of unit nine. Greg Holman parked nearest to the highway, got out of his car, and walked around it. He stood with his back to Jessie, talking to the driver of the pickup through its open window. She saw him nod his head, wave one hand in invitation, and finally reach to open the pickup door. He seemed to be trying to encourage the driver of the truck to get out. With the door open, the man inside finally did climb out and the two walked together to the door of the motel unit.

Surprised and puzzled, Jessie watched as Holman unlocked the door and went in, but her startled attention was focused on his companion, Hank Peterson, who followed him in and closed the door.

What was he doing with Holman? How did they know each other? And how was she going to be able to find out?

She pulled away and headed back toward Wasilla, afraid they would notice her watching from across the street. Seeing Peterson with Holman had been so completely unexpected that it shook her resolve to talk to Holman again. Though she had defended Peterson to Tatum, she realized that she actually knew very little about him except that he did construction and had been a regular at Oscar's Other Place. Was Peterson somehow involved? Other than playing pool with her, who did he hang with? Could he have known Greg Holman ten years ago? Did it matter? If he had known Greg, it might be helpful to find out more about him. But who could she ask without it getting back to him?

Oscar, of course. If he didn't know Peterson, he would at least know who did.

She headed for Oscar's in-town place.

*   *   *

In the middle of the afternoon the pub was between busy spells. Only a few of the tall stools at the long bar were filled when Jessie walked in and stood blinking as her eyes adjusted to the dim light. Oscar leaned against a cooler, talking to a customer at the far end of the bar. He waved a hand as she took a seat at the bar and walked toward her with a smile.

"Where's your four-legged friend? I've got jerky going to waste here."

"I left him to CEO the kennel while I'm gone."

"Well, I'll give you some to take home to him."

"And make the rest jealous? You're a real pal, Oscar."

He laughed, but handed her the jerky anyway. "What can I get you?"

Jessie stuffed it in her pocket. "The usual, I guess."

"You bet." He fished a Killian's out of a cooler and opened it for her. "What you up to, Jessie?"

"Not much. Just thought I'd stop by and see how things were going with your plans for a new Other Place."

"Hey, that's not a bad name: Oscar's New Other Place. Actually plans're going pretty good. Soon as it warms up a little more and the insurance check comes through, we can break ground—next month, I hope, but it could be early May."

"Great. You should have lots of help. Everybody out our way misses the place."

"Yeah, well—me, too. You going to rebuild your cabin?"

"I'm not sure yet what I'm going to do. Even with the insurance, it would cost a lot."

"You should. That was a nice place and you owned it clear, right? Be deductible as a loss, wouldn't it?"

Jessie had no idea, but thought it was an odd comment and that he had his facts confused in terms of the IRS.

"Maybe, but I'll have to think about it and find out. Have they found out any more about who burned the Other Place?"

"Not that they've told me—but I guess they wouldn't, would they? They found out who the guy was that died, though. Did you hear?"

"A Robert Martin. I didn't know him."

"*Buzz* Martin. They called him Buzz, an airplane mechanic from Talkeetna that—" He stopped short at the startled expression on Jessie's face. "What's the matter? You *do* know him?"

She closed her gaping mouth and shook her head, "No, but . . . Buzz?" How many Buzzes could there be in one small area? Could it really be *the* Buzz? "Did he used to work in a garage for a guy named Cal Mulligan at Big Lake?"

"I think so. Somebody said he switched to planes after—o-oh, I see what you mean—Mulligan's *fire*. Shit, Jessie. Are they related?"

The idea was astonishing. Could this Buzz have really been an intended victim and, therefore, the reason behind the burning of the Other Place? Was it even the same guy? Or, with arson in his background, was he responsible? If he was the pub arsonist, caught in his own handiwork, then the fire at Mulligan's double-wide and Jessie's fire could not have been set by him.

"I don't know," Jessie told Oscar, trying to get her mind around this new insight.

"Well, I guess it would be good to tell somebody

about the connection—but I'm not talking to that Tatum guy again voluntarily. He's a rare bastard."

Jessie had to smile at his vehemence. "You noticed. I'd never have guessed how you *really* felt about him, Oscar."

Then they were both laughing and the tension broke.

"Thank God most of my customers are just regular people with a beer or two on their minds," Oscar said.

"You should have one of those pins Bill Spear designed. You know, 'The night my drink caught fire,' " Jessie told him, still grinning.

"Somebody already thought of it and brought me one," he said, finding it in the cash register drawer and tossing it on the bar—a square enameled pin that showed a glass filled with ice and liquid, with colorful flames blazing from the top. "Seems appropriate."

She agreed, then took the opportunity to lead the subject in the desired direction. "Hank Peterson been around? Thought I might shoot a little pool."

"Nope. Hasn't been in yet today, but he sometimes doesn't show up till after dinner."

"He's a pretty *regular* sort of person."

"Sure worked hard trying to save the Other Place. Hadn't been for him, I'd have had an even ruder shock on my way home that night. Might have found the place burning down all by itself."

"He came to help put out my fire, too. Was he born here, or is he an import, like most of us?"

"Born right here in the MatSu Valley, like me. Lived here all his life."

"You and he must know just about everybody."

"Pretty much, I guess. Except for a lot of new people."

"You ever meet a big guy named Holman? Greg Holman?"

"That mountain man from out the road, who surprised everybody and married Marty Gifford all of a sudden, then moved back to the hills?"

"That's the one."

"Kind of an odd pair, I thought. He was so straight and she was such a party girl. He stopped in here a couple of nights ago—had one beer and left."

"Really. Did Marty ever party with Hank?"

"Not that I knew, but it wouldn't surprise me. She was pretty wild, but that's been years ago."

Ten years to be exact, Jessie thought. "Has Hank always been in construction?"

"Yup. Started working with his dad when he was just a pup. Took over when the old man died—and that was no loss. Old Henry Peterson was another real son of a bitch. He beat that kid black and blue till they finally put him in a foster home. About killed his old lady."

"Any brothers and sisters?"

"An older brother who took off the minute he turned eighteen and never came back. But don't mention it to Hank. He's real sensitive about that brother."

She thought for a minute before asking, "Was Hank ever in any kind of trouble?"

Oscar looked at her and frowned. "Why're you asking, Jessie? Just take him as he is. He's an okay guy. You interested?"

She could see that it might appear so and that any more questions would pigeonhole her interest in Oscar's mental file.

"Naw." She made herself grin. "Just curious. He's a friend—good pool player—that's all." Draining the Killian's, she slid back the bottle and nodded at the questioning raise of his eyebrows. The distraction of opening her another beer wouldn't hurt.

As he set the fresh bottle in front of her, the door opened to let in three young men, who headed for the pool table, drawing Oscar away to take their order for a pitcher of draft. Relieved, Jessie sat nursing her second beer and thinking over what she had learned.

It didn't seem to bring her any closer to locating Anne, but it raised a few more questions in her mind about Hank Peterson without telling her anything that might link him to Greg Holman. Everywhere she turned there seemed to be connections. It was hard to decide what was relevant and what was not. People who lived in small communities for long periods of time *were* connected in numerous ways—everybody seemed to know everybody else and what they did. None of the associations she had found so far might be important—or they all might.

She would particularly like to know what Peterson had been doing with Greg Holman today, but saw no way to find out, short of asking one of them. Maybe it was something to turn over to MacDonald. The connection between Cal Mulligan and Buzz Martin certainly was.

As she considered, the door opened again. She glanced over to find MacDonald coming through it, and felt she had conjured him. Close behind him was Hank Peterson and they were evidently continuing an involved conversation, for neither of them looked around enough to notice her sitting there at the bar but headed for a table toward the back of the room, sat down, and leaned toward each other, still intent on their discussion.

Was there anyone Hank wasn't following through doors this afternoon? What the hell was he talking about so seriously with MacDonald? Holman?

For a few minutes, Jessie watched them in the mirror behind the bar as they gestured, appeared to agree on some things, and disagree on others. As Oscar delivered beer to their table and took a bill back to the cash register to make change, she realized that if they hadn't seen her, they soon would. This meeting puzzled her less than that of Peterson and Holman, for MacDonald was investigating the fires, after all, and might have a reason for wanting to talk with Hank. But, wanting time to think over what she had learned, Jessie decided she'd rather not be noticed.

Leaving the price of her two beers and a tip next to the half-empty Killian's, she quietly slipped out the door and, leaving them to their discussion, headed for home. It was time to feed her dogs anyway, and she could call later and leave a message for MacDonald that she wanted to see him. She couldn't know just then quite how much she'd regret passing up the opportunity to talk to him.

18

<hr style="width:30%">

THE DOG YARD, TENT, AND SHEDS LOOKED JUST AS SHE had left them, when Jessie arrived back at her place on Knik Road. But Tank came to greet her and seemed nervous, moving back and forth between her and as far as he could go toward the storage shed, leaning against the restriction of his tether.

"What's the matter, guy?"

She unclipped his collar from the line and let him loose. Immediately, he trotted to the front of the shed and sniffed the ground. Following, she looked to see what he was examining with such interest.

With everyone who had walked through her yard in the last few days, it was almost impossible to separate footprints from each other in the snow and on the ground, but on the edge of one muddy puddle were two prints that partially covered those she herself had made earlier that morning getting equipment from the shed for the training run. Looking carefully, she saw that they also appeared in the snow around the front of the shed and seemed to come and go from tire tracks of a vehicle that had pulled into the drive and parked. Someone had evidently checked to see if the shed was open and found it locked, but had not broken in this time. Could it have been the same person who left the gym bag with its incriminating contents?

As she rubbed Tank's ears and told him what a good dog he was to let her know that someone had been there in her absence, the sound of a vehicle in the drive caught her attention and she turned to find Phil Becker pulling to a stop beside the tent.

"Hey," he said, coming across to where she stood and bending to drop a friendly hand on Tank's head. "I stopped by earlier. It looked like all your dogs were here, so I figured you weren't out on a training run."

"Did that earlier. I was in town. When you were here, did you walk across to the shed?"

"Yeah—checked to be sure it was secure. How'd you know?"

"You've got big feet, Phil."

He grinned. "That's true. You're keeping a close watch. That's good."

"I had help. Tank led me right to your tracks."

"So much for stealth in a dog yard."

"Well, he's sharper than most. Was there something you needed, Phil, or are you guys just keeping an eye on me?"

"Ah—yeah—little of both, I guess. Have you seen Tatum any time today?"

"No. And I'd better not. Why? Have you lost him?"

"Well, sort of. He was supposed to come in for a briefing at noon, but he didn't show. Mac and I were just wondering where he'd got to—and what he's doing."

"Probably cooking up something else for me, or hunting Anne."

"Maybe. But he doesn't usually just ignore meetings he's set up."

"Well, wherever he is, I haven't seen him. Listen, Phil, I'm puzzled by a couple of things that have nothing to do with Tatum. Come on in and I'll tell you about it."

As soon as they were comfortably seated at the card table, each with a bottle of Killian's, Jessie began her questions.

"How well do you know MacDonald?"

"Oh, come on, Jessie. You're not having trouble with him now, are you?"

"No—no. He's fine. I like him. Just wondered about him, that's all."

"Okay," Becker nodded, plainly relieved. "I know him casually, I guess. We don't have as many fires out here as they do in Anchorage, so I've only worked with him once or twice. He moved up from Juneau five or six years ago. He's a likable sort—seems good at his job. Don't know much more, because we don't socialize much with the fire department people. They stick pretty much together—you know. Why?"

"I just wondered if he was from MatSu."

"You know, I think he *might* be. Seems like I remember someone saying he went to high school here."

"So he would know some of the people involved in this case?"

"Like who?"

"Hank Peterson?"

Becker thought for a minute before answering.

"Yeah, he'd probably know Hank. Everybody knows Hank, don't they?"

"Do they?"

"Well, yeah. He's done a lot of odd jobs around the Palmer-Wasilla area—construction, snow plowing— dug a lot of holes with that backhoe of his."

It reinforced what Jessie had learned earlier from Oscar.

"Does everyone know MacDonald, too?"

"Not so many, because he left—went away to college and didn't come back until he was already working arson investigation. He's in Anchorage now, anyway, not out here."

"How about Greg Holman?"

"You mean does everyone know him, or does he know MacDonald?"

She hesitated, considering. "Both—either."

"He wasn't raised here—didn't live here—so not very many people knew him. But lots of them—at least the ones that spent any time in the local bars—knew his wife, your friend Anne. She was in and out of several of them pretty steady before she married Holman, from what MacDonald says."

"I really need to talk to MacDonald, Phil," she told him, frowning in frustration. "There are things that just don't make sense in all of this. But there are things that keep connecting it together, too."

"What do you mean?"

"Well, for instance, I went looking for Greg Holman this afternoon. When I found where he was staying, I saw him and Hank Peterson together. Then, later, at Oscar's place in town, Hank came in with MacDonald and they seemed to be having a serious conversation about something."

"Maybe Mac was interviewing Peterson about the fire at the Other Place."

"Possibly—but it seemed different than that. They seemed to be discussing something like they were trying to figure it out. I don't know. I'm probably imagining things. But I'd sure like to know what Hank was doing with Greg Holman—and with MacDonald. Will you tell Mac I'd like to see him? I'm taking a team for an early training run and have to make a trip to town, but I'll be here for two or three hours around noon."

"Sure. You're probably imagining a lot, Jessie. Mac has been working a lot of hours on these fires. He's likely to show up with anyone who could be the least bit connected. I wouldn't worry about it, if I were you. He's okay."

But though she knew he believed what he had told her, something about his reassurances didn't sit comfortably in Jessie's mind. Something she couldn't get hold of nagged, and she couldn't seem to let it go. She kept turning over the disjointed situations that seemed related in ways she couldn't understand as she went about her evening kennel work, scrambled some eggs with bacon for dinner, and finally went to bed early, tired with concerns and speculations, determined to try another angle the next day and see if she could learn more about how and where Anne Holman had disappeared. She had to be somewhere and, if Jessie could find her, perhaps she could put a few of the confusing pieces together in a pattern that would make more sense.

Coming home from Oscar's, she had turned into her driveway and stopped to look back along Knik Road, wondering how Anne had disappeared so quickly and completely on such an empty road late at night. She must have somehow found a ride into town with someone who either didn't notice the fire in its early stages or who didn't want to be involved. She couldn't have walked far without being noticed by someone, and none of the people Jessie had asked in a few phone calls remembered passing anyone headed for town on foot rather than toward the cabin fire. Another alternative was that someone expected Anne to show up and was waiting for her in a vehicle, whether she knew it or not. The preplanning this idea indicated did not ease Jessie's mind, for it would have to be someone who knew there was about to be a reason for Anne's leaving, and that meant she could have set the fire with help.

Jessie decided that tomorrow she would try to contact more of the firefighters with the question. Someone *must* have seen something.

She would also tell MacDonald about seeing Greg Holman and Hank Peterson together and see what he would make of it. Did he know that Robert Martin's nickname was Buzz—that he had been a mechanic for Cal Mulligan? The fire at Oscar's Other Place and the one that had killed Mulligan now seemed definitely connected in Jessie's mind. That they had both died must be more than coincidence, but who was responsible, and why should anyone wait ten years to kill them, if it had anything to do with the situation surrounding the old fire in Mulligan's garage? Why kill Martin anyway? What could he possibly have to do with it?

Shana, she thought suddenly. Could Shana Mulligan have waited and now be getting even for the death of her children? Where was she? Still in the area? It was another question for MacDonald—something else to add to her list of things she wanted to know.

But I had nothing to do with any of this, she thought. Why involve me, set me up, and burn my house? Was Tatum manufacturing evidence again? Was Anne?

Sick of worry and loose ends, she gave up and went to sleep, resolved to find some answers tomorrow, one way or another.

It was very dark and silent at three in the morning, when a shadow slipped swiftly from the trees to the back of the large tent in the yard on Knik Road and the dogs began to bark at the presence of an intruder. The yard light blinked on automatically at their movement, and Jessie woke, rose, and padded quietly to open the door and look out, carrying her handgun.

Seeing nothing, she called to the dogs to quiet them, but, as their barking continued for a moment or two before dying, she did not hear the small distinct sound of a razor slicing across the lower part of the canvas wall, opening a long slit, then another, perpendicular to it, which allowed the shadowy figure to slide easily in and freeze into a crouch behind the easy chair—part of the dark.

Satisfied that there was nothing unusual in the noise that had awoken her from a deep sleep—a moose, a scuffle, nothing more—Jessie locked the door and returned, yawning, to her bed, placing the handgun in easy reach. Settling in, she shrugged the blankets around her, wriggled herself comfortable again, and in a few moments had gone back to sleep—with only a passing thought that the room had seemed colder coming back than when she had gone to the door and wondering if she should have turned on the space heater, but sliding into dreams before she could act on the thought.

Silent and unmoving, the shadow waited, listening intently, until everything was still and the small purr of the woman's unconscious breathing was the only sound. Then, with infinite care, it rose, alert and vigilant for any movement or awareness of its presence. Slowly, silently, it removed a small bottle and a folded bandanna from a pocket and unscrewed the lid. A step at a time, it crossed the room until it stood over the bed in which Jessie continued to sleep.

It took only the tiny gurgle of liquid poured from the bottle onto the fabric—a foreign sound that did not belong to the usual night noises—to rouse her again. But before she could move to reach for the gun, a knee, with the weight of a body behind it, pressed her down and the bandanna was applied to her mouth and nose with a strong, forceful gloved hand. A sharp and unpleasant smell was drawn into her lungs with her gasp of surprise and resistance, making her head swim. She tried to hold her breath and move, but was only able to flail with the arm that was not pinned under her. Grasping at the hand that held the bandanna, she attempted to yank it away from her face, but failed, growing steadily weaker as she struggled and drew in more of the consciousness-draining fumes. Her last awareness was of her complete inability to move, or

*even think clearly, that there were sounds and the
weight that was holding her down had gone away, but
the gloved hand remained, holding the fabric to her
mouth and nose. Faintly, far, far away, she could hear
her dogs barking again in the yard. It didn't seem to
matter much. Then there was nothing.*

19

―――∽∾∽―――

THERE WERE LINES OF PALE LIGHT, THIN VERTICAL LINES within a square, and tiny fragments that floated in them like a swarm of infinitesimal insects so small they were almost invisible. It was quiet. Nothing made a sound or moved, except for those bits of whatever they were, hovering like a swarm in the lines of light.

Jessie stared at them through half-open eyes and was perfectly content to do nothing, know nothing, just watch their slow movement in the air. The lines of light seemed familiar somehow, but she couldn't make herself care enough to work out a reason for that feeling. They were simply there, far away and vaguely interesting.

Tired of looking, she closed her eyes and drifted away again, dreamed she was riding her sled behind a team on the frozen surface of the Yukon River. It was too dark to see anything but what was revealed in the narrow beam of her headlamp, and the reflective tape on the harnesses of her dogs caught the slender beam of light and winked back at her as they trotted forward,

pulling the sled toward . . . Where was it she was
going? Dawson? Right—she was headed for Dawson.
So it must be the Yukon Quest she was running. But
how could she be so tired this early in a race? It must
be almost over. But the long run down the Yukon came
after Dawson, didn't it?

A cabin came into view at the top of a bank, with an
old man standing in the doorway, waving something at
her—motioning her in. As she came closer, she could see
that it was a green gym bag, one handle flapping loose.

"Come in for popcorn," he called, waving it wildly.
"It's got your name on it."

Then, suddenly, it was snowing. But it wasn't
snow—wasn't even cold. It *was* popcorn, coming
down all around her. She lifted her face and caught a
fluffy kernel in her mouth—and choked on it. Con-
vulsed with coughing, unable to stop, she opened her
eyes and the dream faded, but the coughing, choking
continued. There *was* something in her mouth and
throat—something uncomfortable and dry that tasted
nastily chemical.

It was still dark, but the lines of light were stronger
now and more familiar. She had seen them before from
this position on the floor. Then Jessie knew where she
was. It was the cabin in the Little Peters Hills, where
she had once lived, where she had brought Anne only
a few short days ago. What was she doing back here?
The lines of light were filtering in from outside the
window through the gaps between boards that had
been nailed up to close the place. And what she had
earlier thought were insects were dust motes floating
in the bars of light.

She tried to spit out what she now recognized as fabric in her dry mouth, couldn't, and knew that something was secured over it, holding it in place. Tape. She could feel its stiffness on her cheeks and lips. Duct tape, probably, from the width of it. Again she coughed, then worked with her tongue until she got the horrid-tasting cloth pushed up to the front of her mouth. It was enough to allow her to stop coughing and gagging.

She started to sit up, to see if she could find out what she was doing in this place, and found that she was immobilized. Both her wrists and ankles were fastened tightly together with something—more tape, she thought. When she tried to raise her head to see, sharp sickening pain flashed through it and dizziness made her almost retch. Afraid she would throw up behind the gag and choke to death, she lay back down and assessed what she could.

She was not only bound but was also inside what felt like a sleeping bag that was secured with tape that had been wrapped tightly and completely around it in three places—at waist, thigh, and shoulder. Some kind of string had been tightened and tied around her neck, enough to keep the bag closed but not enough to strangle her, thank God. Helpless, she could barely roll from side to side, could not even begin to turn over. The wood floor she lay on was hard. The whole cabin was cold. Jessie could see her breath in the air as she exhaled through her nose.

What the hell was going on? Who had brought her here and clearly meant to keep her from moving—let alone leaving?

Thinking hard, she remembered going to bed, resolved to begin a serious search for Anne the next morning and get some questions answered. Something had disturbed her dogs. Someone had been *in the tent*. She recalled a weight holding her down—something strong and bad smelling—struggling—not much else. She had heard nothing but the dogs, seen no one in the dark. Who could it have been?

There was enough light for her to make out the ceiling, its heavy log rafters festooned with spiderwebs that hung in dirty strings and clung stickily in the corners. By tilting her head back, she could see, upside down behind her head by the stove, a pale square that she knew was the Maxfield Parrish picture of two chefs. It was her old cabin all right. How and why had her abductor brought her here? And why had she been left here alone? When would—whoever—come back?

An unexpected and alarming idea slid into her mind, taking her breath with its appalling possibility. What if he or she wasn't coming back? What if he wanted to get rid of her and her questions? What if she had been left here to die? Unable to free herself, she would eventually starve—or freeze, if the temperature fell far enough, as it sometimes did this time of year. Had whoever set the fire at her cabin decided to try again? Would they burn this place as well—*with her in it*?

Suddenly, without warning, she retched again and could taste and feel hot stomach acid rising in her throat. Terrified she would smother, she fought, rigid with effort until the spasm passed and she could swallow and breathe again without panic.

Would she have been left with the sleeping bag to keep her warm, if she was meant to die? Possibly, but probably not. Had they left anything else that could indicate that they intended to return? Jessie raised her head, more slowly and carefully this time, though the room almost immediately began to spin again. She looked quickly around the room, though little light filtered in through the cracks of the boarded-up window.

In one corner, to the left of the door, lay a bag of some kind that had not been here when she left with Anne. Lying back down, she waited for the dizziness to pass, then tried again and, taking another long look, knew what it was—Anne's day pack, the one she had brought here as she rode in the sled, then carried back again, containing the small bones in their makeshift metal box-coffin.

Anne had not been willing to part with it, or anything in it. If it was here, she must be somewhere close. But was her presence voluntary, or had she been abducted, too?

Her panic lessened somewhat with the idea that it was likely that someone would return for the pack, especially if it still contained the bones of Anne's child. She lay like a mummy in the bag, watching the dust motes float in the lines of light between the boards of the window, hoping someone would come to give her a clue to what was going on. Finally, she fell asleep again, wishing she could get rid of the evil-tasting gag, that her head would stop aching—hungry, thirsty, furious, and frightened to the point of tears at her confinement—unwarranted and unfathomable.

*   *   *

Just before noon, MacDonald pulled into Jessie's driveway, stopped by the tent, and got out of his Jeep Cherokee. Noticing that the storage shed door was open, he walked across, laid his hands on either side of its frame and leaned in, expecting to find her there. Blinking, as his vision adjusted to the abrupt shift in illumination, he could just make out a figure moving in the shadows.

"Hi, Jessie, you wanted to see me?"

"She's not here," a young man informed him, turning from the harness he was sorting to walk out into the sunshine that glowed thinly through breaks in a high overcast.

"Oh. And who're you?"

"Billy Steward. I help Jessie with the mutts. Who're you?"

"MacDonald, arson investigator. She said she'd be here for a while around noon, after an early training run. Told Phil Becker she wanted to see me. Any idea where I can find her?"

"Nope. Don't think she was even here this morning— or else she left really early, but she hasn't been back. Her truck's gone, but none of the dogs had been fed or watered, and she didn't take any of them out today."

"Kind of unusual not to feed them, isn't it? I got the impression she was pretty consistent about taking care of her dogs."

"She is, and she didn't call me to do it either. I wasn't supposed to be here today, just found some extra time and decided to see if she needed help— maybe make another run for her, since we missed a couple those two days she was gone."

"So she didn't expect you to show up and take over?"

"Huh-uh. She'd have left me a note saying what to do. Her door's open, but she's not here."

MacDonald frowned. None of this sounded like the Jessie Arnold he had begun to know. The impression he had formed was of a careful, conscientious woman who wouldn't leave her dogs unattended or her living space unlocked. Her unexplained absence seemed out of character and perplexing.

But how well did he really know her? Obviously not well enough, for he had no idea where or why she might have gone. This young man, Billy, did know her well, however, and seemed to agree that her actions were exceptional, curious at best.

"Let's take a look inside," he suggested to Billy. "Maybe she left a note and you missed it."

Billy shook his head, but followed MacDonald across the yard and to the tent, the door of which was, as he had said, unlocked.

"This was open a little," he commented, as Mac opened the door.

"How little?"

"Like this." He closed it to a crack to demonstrate that it had been just short of latching, as if Jessie had gone out in a hurry, shoving it to close behind her but not quite hard enough.

"You closed it?"

"Yeah. Thought the wind might blow it open."

"What time did you get here?"

"Just before nine."

Jessie's lead dog, tethered close to the tent, had been

watching the two men closely. As their conversation paused and MacDonald's attention shifted to him from Billy, the dog paced the length of his tether toward Knik Road, gazed down the driveway, then moved back the other way to the opposite end of his restraint, where he stopped for a moment before repeating the action.

"Does he always do that pacing?"

"Naw, Tank's pretty laid-back. He usually watches from the top of his box—king of the yard, kind of. He's been doing that all morning—like he's waiting for Jessie."

"But he doesn't usually do that when she's gone?"

"Not when I'm here—never seen him do it before."

"Well—by itself it doesn't tell us much."

They went on into the tent. MacDonald flipped on the overhead light and stood just inside the door, examining the space.

"You move anything?"

"Nope, I only came in this far. I saw she wasn't here and there wasn't a note on the table. Didn't really expect one. She usually leaves them in the shed. I've got a key for that."

Slowly MacDonald circled the interior, carefully inspecting everything visible. The bed wasn't made and a blanket hung half off it, partly on the floor. He lifted it, looked under it, and put it back, stopped, and squatted beside the roll-away and reached under the bed to feel around. The Smith & Wesson .44 Jessie had showed him after the fire, when he questioned the possibility of the arsonist returning, was not there. She must have taken it with her.

"You're looking for her moose gun," Billy told him from across the room, where he had waited by the door.

"Yes. She told me she's had it close since the fire. Do you know where she keeps it when she's not out with a team?"

"Locked in the shed or in—ah—her truck. Jeez— she must have been spooked to bring it in here."

MacDonald caught the slight hesitation in Billy's voice. There was something he wasn't saying. He let it go for a moment, considering.

"She any good with it?"

Billy looked relieved at not being questioned about his slip.

"Sure—well, I don't really know, I guess. Never seen her use it. But I know she practices at the range once in a while."

"What did you mean by 'in her truck'?"

The youngster's face fell.

"Ah, you know—in her truck."

"Where?"

"Oh, shit. She made me promise not to tell. Okay?"

"Nope. Not okay. It's important, Billy, and won't go any farther. I'll tell her that I made you tell. Now, where in the truck?"

Billy looked down and kicked at the wooden floor with one boot, clearly unhappy with the situation.

"Aw-w—she's got a secret compartment in the back of the dog box. She keeps it there, so no one will steal it—her camera, too, and other stuff she doesn't want people to find."

"She never leaves it lying around?"

"No—never. She's really careful with stuff like that."

"Well, the truck's gone, so I can't check to be sure it's safe. She probably has it with her. When she comes back, you tell her I was here, okay? And to call me right away."

"Yeah—okay."

There was nothing else that amounted to anything that could tell MacDonald when Jessie had left or where she had gone. There was no sign that she had made coffee or eaten breakfast, but she might have cleaned up afterward. He didn't see the cut in the tent wall that was covered by the easy chair. Nothing seemed out of place or suspicious. She just wasn't where she had said she would be. He left Billy frowning and unhappy at breaking his promise to Jessie about the compartment in her missing truck.

Phil Becker was next on his list of people to contact. Maybe Phil had made a mistake about the time and place. It wouldn't hurt to ask. Aside from that, Mac knew he had a full day ahead of him and could afford to wait until Jessie Arnold found her way home, as he assumed she eventually would.

20

━━━◗◖◗◖◗━━━

THERE WERE NO LINES OF LIGHT WHEN JESSIE WOKE again—nothing but dark—but there were voices. At first she thought it was her imagination playing tricks with the wind she could hear murmuring to the trees outside the cabin. But slowly, the sound of people talking grew louder, came closer, until she knew it was no fantasy. Someone—and more than one someone—was returning to the cabin.

Before she could hear the voices well enough to identify them or hear what they were saying, they stopped talking, and there was only the sound of approaching feet crunching on crusted snow. Someone stomped on the step outside to clear the ice from their boots, the door opened, and two figures stepped in, one aiming a flashlight beam directly into her eyes, resulting in a swift stab of pain that made her wince and close them tightly. For a long minute, she could see red behind her lids, as the light shone on her face. When it finally slid away to one side, she carefully opened her eyes just a little, but the bright beam came immediately back, blinding her. This time it remained.

A whisper—a thump—and someone she could not see because of the light walked across the room and knelt beside her. With a quick, rough gesture, the tape was ripped away from her face, pulling the fabric gag in her mouth with it. All she saw were anonymous hands, mostly in silhouette, bare of mittens or gloves, with no identifying marks. But there was a scent that caught her attention, something familiar and pleasant. Before she could remember what it was or speak, there was a soft gurgle of liquid being poured from a bottle, and the flowery scent was overpowered as a cloth with the sharp smell she remembered from the night before came down over her face. Again Jessie struggled, unable to move her arms but shaking her head back and forth, trying to avoid what she knew was happening, but everything—her captors, the cabin, even the flashlight beam—swam dizzily and faded into black again.

When she came slowly back to consciousness it was still dark. She lay very still on her back as her awareness slowly sharpened; she licked her lips and found the gag had not been replaced and she could breathe without fear of choking. Her head ached with a sickening intensity. She felt nauseous and cold—so cold. Had they taken away the sleeping bag that had kept her warm and left her to freeze after all?

Abruptly she realized that the tape that had constricted her shoulders, waist, and thighs was gone, and her arms and legs were free of restraints. She could move.

Weak, head pulsing pain, she sat up, knowing she

was about to be sick. Assuming she was still on the floor, she rolled over to get up and fell off the edge of whatever she had been lying on to a wood surface below, bumping her head, bruising a shoulder, and hitting a knee in the process. For a stunned moment, she lay still and groaned. Where was she?

At the crash and thump of her fall something moved outside and unexpectedly, abruptly there was light through canvas walls that allowed her to see her surroundings. Shocked and confused, despite her aching head, she sat up, astounded. She was back in the tent—had fallen from her own bed onto the floor and felt her warm quilt which must have slid off sometime earlier—the reason she'd been cold.

A dog barked. Tank, who almost never barked. Something was wrong.

A quick glance around the dimly lit canvas room told her she was alone. She scrambled to her feet and staggered across to a dishpan, into which she retched. Gasping and clinging to a shelf, it seemed that her whole being was one huge ache. She was still dressed in the socks, overlarge T-shirt, and leggings that she had worn to bed. Everything looked the same around her, as it had when she had gone to sleep.

Knocking several things off the shelf onto the floor, she located a bottle of aspirin, gulped down three, and rinsed her mouth with water from a bottle found in one of the ice chests Hank had left her, then splashed some on her face and rubbed her eyes.

Trying to concentrate was hard with the pain in her head, but she knew she had to check on her dogs, so she returned to the bed and took her .44 from under it before walking carefully to the door. It was locked, as she had left it. Stepping into her boots that stood there ready, she released the lock, opened it, and went out onto the welcome mat, into the familiar glow of the yard light.

Most of the dogs were where they should be, curled up and sleeping in their boxes. A few were awake and outside, but they looked normal and okay. Pete woofed softly to her from where he lay, looking out the door of his box. Tank was standing at the end of his tether, as close to the tent as he could get. At the sight of her, his tail began to wag and he strained against the tether.

"Hey, you okay, buddy?"

Jessie knelt beside him, her knees in a patch of cold snow, and wrapped her arms around his neck.

"Did I dream all that? Am I sick with something?"

Laying the handgun on the ground, she clung for a moment to his warmth and felt him lick her ear.

"I don't understand. Did you see anyone? It doesn't make sense."

It didn't. Could she have had a fever in her sleep— nightmare hallucinations? No, dammit. Everything told her it had been real—that someone had taken her from her own bed and out to the cabin in the Little Peters Hills. Who? Why? And, most confusing and unnerving, why had they put her back in her tent, as if she had never been away? Maybe she was mistaken and *had* dreamed it all.

The ache in her head had lessened slightly, but still she felt wobbly and befuddled, unable to remember much but shadows and darkness, or sort it out.

Getting back to her feet, she released Tank and took

him with her back into the tent, locking the door behind them and turning on the lights. Carefully, she looked around again. It all looked familiar and untouched. She gave up and sank into a chair, elbows on knees, holding her head in her hands. Tank sat down next to her, as if on guard.

Emptied, her stomach had settled and she was hungry, starving—as if she hadn't eaten in days. She wanted badly to go back to bed, curl up where it would be warm, and let sleep cure her ills, but knew that hunger was contributing to the ache in her head and would keep her awake. Finding a box of crackers, she ate five or six and washed them down with milk. It wasn't enough.

She tore several slices of bacon from a pound in the ice chest, tossed them into a frying pan on the stove, and heard them start to sizzle as she located three eggs. As soon as the bacon was done, she broke the eggs in as well and scrambled them as they cooked. The smell of the food made her stomach lurch and growl in anticipation, but she forced herself to get out a plate and fork before sitting down at the table to eat what she had cooked, along with some buttered bread she had no patience to toast. Straight from the frying pan, the food was so hot the first bite burned her mouth, but she ignored it and wolfed the meal, sharing one piece of bacon with Tank, who took it politely. He had never left her side and sat watching her closely as she satisfied her hunger.

As soon as she was finished, she put her .44 back under the bed, turned out the lights, crawled in under the quilt, which she pulled up tight around her. She would figure it all out in the morning. It was too much for the middle of this night.

She was almost instantly asleep.

Tank came and lay down by the bed and his sleeping mistress, but, though he rested, muzzle on paws, it was a long time before he slept, and then lightly, aware of all that moved and breathed in the dark of the tent and yard.

Billy arrived next morning, to find Jessie back at home and engaged in the normal process of feeding and caring for her kennel but doing it more slowly than usual, with an air of distraction.

"Hi," he said. Then more hesitantly, "Where've you been?"

"Been?"

"All day yesterday. Lucky I came by to feed the mutts."

Jessie grew very still and turned to look at him questioningly, her face pale, sweat breaking out on her upper lip.

"What day is it?"

He told her.

She didn't answer, but walked off across the yard to slump down on the bench by the tent door so quickly that it looked as if her knees had given out.

Billy followed, concerned at her unusual behavior.

"Hey, you okay?"

She was gasping for air. Without warning, she leaned over and threw up on the ground by the bench.

"Are you sick, Jessie? Shall I call somebody?"

She muttered something he couldn't hear.

"What?"

"Thought I dreamed it," she repeated and paused before going on, trying to catch her breath. "Thought I was sick in the night. But it *was* real, wasn't it?"

"What was real? Did something bad happen? What can I do?"

"Call Becker," she gasped. "Need to call Phil."

"You want me to?"

"No—I will—can you bring me the phone?"

The color was gradually coming back to her face, but she sat as if she'd been struck—limp and drained. Billy, half afraid to leave her, did as he had been asked, and retrieved the phone from inside the tent.

Jessie held it for a minute or two, waiting until she was steadier and could speak without panting. She had just begun to dial the trooper's number when they heard the sound of a vehicle on the drive and she hesitated, waiting to see who was coming, apprehension narrowing her eyes and tightening her mouth.

The now-familiar Jeep Cherokee pulled up beside the tent and MacDonald stepped out, along with Becker. They walked across to her truck, examined the tires and talked for a moment, then, unsmiling, came toward the bench. Jessie could see from their expressions that, whatever the reason for their visit, it wasn't going to be pleasant.

"I was just calling you," she said to Phil Becker, holding up the phone.

"Where the hell have you been, Jessie?" he asked, frowning. "We were about to put out an APB."

"What's wrong? Something's happened, hasn't it? Tell me."

"Inside," MacDonald suggested. "We'll talk in the tent. You take care of what needs to be done out here, Billy."

"Sure."

But he stood and waited till the other three had disappeared through the door before he reluctantly went back to where Jessie had been portioning out food to her dogs.

"What *is it*?" Jessie asked, the minute they were inside.

MacDonald swung a folding chair up to the table and waved her into it. She sat on the edge and watched as he crossed the room to her bed, looked under it, and, carefully, with an evidence bag folded back over his hand like a mitten, removed her Smith & Wesson .44, examining it closely before pulling the bag down, sealing it, and holding it out toward her.

"This gun been used recently?"

"Not for almost a month."

"I'd say it's been fired in the last day or two."

"Not by me."

He pulled the other folding chair up to the table and sat opposite her, laying his notebook on the flat surface, along with the gun he had just retrieved.

"You want to tell us where you've been, Jessie?"

She hesitated, already beginning to see just how the story of her abduction would sound. "I don't know if I do."

"Why not?"

"Because it's going to seem . . . really strange."

"Try us."

"Will you tell me why you want to know?"

He shook his head. "Let's do it my way. Where were you?"

Jessie stared at him, trying to get some hint of what

was going on from the intent, waiting look of the faces of these two men. If she refused to tell them what had happened, they would probably assume the worst, whatever that was. Something serious had clearly brought them here and, for some reason she didn't understand, they thought she was involved. Another fire? A death? What? Had Anne, or Tatum, done something new and horrible now?

So far, she had trusted them—the only people she had felt weren't lying to her in one way or another. Was that still true? It would seem that she had little choice but to follow her usual inclination to speak the truth, however it might appear to someone else. Deciding she had nothing to lose by giving them the facts, she took a deep breath and looked down at her hands in her lap for a moment before beginning her story. They felt like ice and, even by twisting them together, she couldn't stop their shaking.

Slowly, carefully, in a low, level voice that trembled a time or two, she related everything she could remember of the events of the last two nights. She described the dogs waking her, going back to bed, the ineffective struggle with whomever had drugged her, the terror of waking in the dark and her confinement, the dark and the light through the boarded-up window of the cabin, being drugged again, and, finally, waking to find herself back in the tent, cold, sick, and confused.

"I tried to make myself believe it was nothing but a nightmare, but Billy showed up and wanted to know where I'd been all day yesterday. Then I had to admit it wasn't my imagination. I was just calling you. Ask him. How did you know something had happened?"

MacDonald ignored her question and exchanged a long look with Becker, who had stopped pacing during her narrative to listen, and now dragged up an ice chest and sat down. There was a long silence, during which Jessie could hear Billy in the yard, talking to the dogs as he finished feeding and watering them.

"Here, Smut, you slacker, you. Move over, Bliss. Get your foot out of the water pan."

Becker moved restlessly and, finally, with a worried look, joined the conversation.

"Jessie, do you realize how unbelievable that all sounds? You say someone got in here with the door locked but didn't break in—caught you off guard, with a yard full of dogs to wake you up—hauled you seventy miles up the Parks Highway when there're much closer places—held you captive but didn't hurt you—kept you for part of two nights for no evident reason—brought you back and left you where they found you with the door locked again from the inside. And you haven't a clue who or why?"

"All I can tell you is what happened, Phil. I don't know why. You think I don't want to know that? I thought they meant to leave me out there. It still gives me the shakes."

She held out her hands so he could see.

He shrugged, shook his head in frustration, and frowned at her as MacDonald broke in.

"Look, Jessie. Work with us here. Let's go over a few things. You—or somebody—must have driven somewhere. Your truck was gone while you were."

"I didn't drive anywhere, Mac."

The narrowing of his eyes and the way he glanced at

Becker gave away his skepticism. "New tracks were found that seem to match the tread on your tires. We'll have to let the lab work on that, but I can assure you that they weren't found anywhere near the Trapper Creek area."

"Where then?"

"In some mud out near the Mulligan trailer that burned."

"I told you—I've never been there, wherever it is. Is this some more of Tatum's evidence to set me up?"

"That's pretty thin—and cold," Becker told her, a hard tone in his voice. "We *found* Tatum there, too—shot in the head."

"Oh, God. Who would—"

"You tell us. We think you just might *know* who."

She stared at him, astonished, pale as the canvas walls of the tent.

"Phil, you can't believe that I—"

"Dammit, Jessie. I trusted you and—"

"Hey," MacDonald broke in sharply. "Simmer down, Becker. Let's take this one thing at a time—questions first, accusations later . . . maybe. We need some answers, not a fight."

Becker leaned back and stared at the canvas wall. Jessie could see that his outburst had been fueled by disappointment. He thought she had let him down, and it had shaken his confidence, not only in her but in his own judgment of her. His disillusionment came out as exasperated anger, laced with more than a little fear.

"Phil," she said with earnest sadness, "I didn't have anything to do with it. What I just told you really happened."

He refused to respond, and Jessie sat looking at his unhappy face in discouragement. His lack of confidence upset her more than anything they had told her or the questions they had asked. If friends who knew her well didn't believe her, who would?

What else did they have to frame her for Tatum's death? She knew now why she had been abducted—and she thought she might know who was responsible, though the *why* eluded her still.

21

AS IT TURNED OUT, THEY HAD QUITE A LOT STACKED UP to implicate her, or at least to imply that she could have been somehow involved in Mike Tatum's murder. Her dislike of him didn't inspire confidence, for it gave them a motive of sorts. For the next two hours, she and Billy sat on the bench by the door and watched while Becker and MacDonald searched everything Jessie owned.

Her truck was towed off to impound, but not before MacDonald climbed purposefully into the back and worked out how the secret compartment opened. In it, he found the arson kit Jessie had discovered in the shed and so carefully hidden, and, of course, knew immediately what it was and could mean. He did not ask her to explain its presence, just gave her a long, tired look and went to put it in the trunk of his car. He did not say how he had known where to look, but Billy's obvious discomfort communicated the truth to Jessie, who duplicated Mac's disappointed look in his direction.

"I'm sorry, Jessie," Billy said, close to tears and

swallowing hard. "He made me tell. I thought it would be okay."

"Don't worry. It is okay," she told him quietly, but it wasn't—not really, not now—and he knew it.

Her .44, in its evidence bag, also went into Mac-Donald's trunk.

The rest of what worried her most was in what they *didn't* find. There wasn't a scrap of anything to prove that anyone had taken her from her own living space against her will and held her for approximately twenty-four hours.

In a detailed search of the tent, Becker located a three-cornered cut in the canvas, behind the chair, but Jessie knew that there was nothing to show that she hadn't sliced it herself.

There were no footprints outside, for the wooden foundation of the tent had not been laid over bare ground but over grass and weeds that surrounded the dog yard, and anyone could have walked there without leaving a sign. Though they looked for marks in the snow or mud, it was an impossible task, for dozens of firefighters had traipsed back and forth through the yard during the blaze that destroyed her house, and the crowd of visitors had added to the confusion as they came and went the next day, leaving their own tracks. It was the same with tire tracks from a wide assortment of vehicles—even the backhoe shovel of the neighbor who had loaned her the tent and the fire trucks that had pulled into the drive, though it was easy enough to identify the ones that had been made last—those of her truck.

Jessie sat numbly watching, as they efficiently and

professionally went through the little she still owned that hadn't been burned and all that had been given to her after the fire. It would all be covered with the fingerprints of so many people that there would be no use in trying to identify them, for any such attempt would have to include literally hundreds of people—many who had never been to Knik Road but would have touched the items elsewhere.

Had her abductors realized this? She wondered, and also questioned where they could be. Would they have gone, now that they had accomplished what they had evidently set out to do—set her up as responsible for Tatum's death, perhaps for the fires as well, including the one that destroyed her caabin? Or would they, perhaps, still be somewhere close, waiting to see the result? In the midst of her helpless despair over what was happening, a fury was growing, hot and dangerous, that tensed her shoulders, neck, and jaw and clenched her hands into fists.

When they had finally finished the search, Phil Becker left in the tow truck that removed Jessie's pickup with its dog box, taking with him the evidence they had collected for the crime lab to test. But MacDonald came to talk to her before leaving. He told Billy that he could go home, but he would need to answer some questions later. The young man left, giving Jessie an apologetic look and a muttered, "Sorry, Jessie. Call you later."

Inside the tent, they sat again at the table, Jessie, straight and stiff in her chair, to keep from slumping into a position that would look as dejected as she felt. But that glowing spark of hot anger kept her from self-pity, kept her ready to absorb whatever blow came next, to fight, rather than flee.

MacDonald appraised her silently before speaking.

"Stiff upper lip, huh? Relax, Jessie. We need to talk this through. I need your help."

"Seems like you've done just fine so far, with and without my help," she told him sharply.

Another longer pause, as he leaned forward in his chair and considered.

"I guess I have that coming—from your point of view. But it had to be done, you know, as much to help as to hurt you."

"Sure."

"Look. I haven't known you very long. Phil has, and this whole thing has disappointed him pretty badly. He seems to think you just about walk on water. To think you might have wet feet doesn't sit too well with him."

Jessie looked away for a second or two, then back with a lift of her chin and a hint of pride in her voice.

"I'm sorry about that—but he didn't bother to really listen or trust me, did he?"

"Maybe not. But you're asking an awful lot. He's been a staunch supporter of yours—defended you to Tatum— called me in to replace him. It's hard for a homicide investigator to see past his job sometimes, even—maybe especially—for friends. Give him a little slack."

She didn't disagree, just continued to watch him guardedly, wondering what was coming next and how he would approach it.

"Okay," he said, referring to the notes he had taken as he worked. "Let's talk about that gym bag I found in your truck. You want to tell me where it came from?"

"And risk your misinterpretation—incriminate myself? I don't think so, Mac. I think maybe it's time I called an attorney."

"Oh, yeah?" he said. "Then I suppose I should give you a formal Miranda warning—shouldn't I? Well . . ." He took a deep breath and leaned back to stare at the ceiling. "Damn. Guess I just—ah—sort of—forgot, didn't I?"

Jessie stared at him, startled. "You mean . . ."

"Nothing, of course. I just said—*nothing*. This is a *conversation*—an informal interview—not an . . . You understand?"

Not an . . . *interrogation*, she understood and nodded slowly. He meant that he was not going to put any of this on the record but couldn't say so. For some reason, he was giving her a break.

"Now, about that bag."

She told him how she had found it on the shelf in her shed.

"Just sitting there, in plain sight, huh?"

"Yes. And I thought it over a lot. Anyone could have put it there. There've been a lot of people around here the last few days. In fact, there's nothing you found that couldn't be explained if someone else was responsible."

"I know. And doesn't it seem to you that there's almost too much circumstantial stuff floating around here? There's something missing in all this that I can't quite get hold of. It's all connected, but I can't figure out how."

Jessie thought about it and agreed.

"Mac, tell me one thing. Phil thinks I had something

to do with Tatum's murder. Why? It can't be just because of the fact that I wasn't here and some tracks that he *thinks* match my tires."

"It's partly the tire tracks. But it's not simple. You must understand that I can't talk about it, Jessie. Especially not to you."

"When will you know something for sure?"

"Tomorrow, maybe the next day. But let's get back to all this trouble and the people involved in it."

"It all started when Anne showed up, right?"

"No. I think it started a long time before that."

"You mean ten years ago?"

"Yes. It has something to do with what happened back then, but I think the fires and Tatum's death are new pieces to an old puzzle. I'm just not seeing what pattern they'll make when they fit together—the picture on the box. Tell me more about this middle-of-the-night abduction. You think someone's making a concerted effort to make sure you're blamed for Mike's murder—and for the fires, don't you?"

"Yeah, I do."

"Why?"

"Because I know I didn't do any of it. But I can't prove that to you—with everything you've found."

"No, I mean why pin it on you?"

He did have a habit of putting a finger on the primary issues, Jessie thought. It had not occurred to her to wonder just why *she* had been selected as a patsy—just to resent that she had.

"You don't think it was just because I was a handy target?"

"It would make more sense if there was a better reason than that. Also be easier to figure out a less random selection. I think we should assume a motive and work on uncovering it. I think there is one."

"And you believe me—that someone took me out of here?"

"Well, let's say it's a tale I'm not quite convinced you made up. It fits much too well. Stuff that happened earlier bothers me, too. Your hat found conveniently at Mulligan's. Anne Holman's disappearance the night of the fire. That gun of yours was fired recently, Jessie. From what I've seen, you take good care of your equipment. Why would you keep it around in that condition when it would be so easy to clean? And—it wasn't here yesterday when I looked for it."

"You were here while I was gone?"

"You told Becker to tell me when you'd be home, and I found Billy working in your shed. Why would you make an appointment with me and skip it—like Tatum did the meeting that he called and missed? That didn't make sense either, until we found him.

"Why, again, would you keep that gym bag full of the kind of things that started your fire when it would be so easy to get rid of such an incriminating piece of evidence?"

"But I did keep it."

"I know. And it wasn't too smart of you. But you didn't set fire to your cabin, did you?"

"No."

"Who did—or who do you *think* did? You've got a good idea, don't you? Intuition?"

Jessie hesitated, unsure of accusing anyone now.

"Come on, Jessie. Who?"

"All right. Tatum. I've always had an unreasonable suspicion that he started it."

"Interesting. Me, too. Do you know why?"

"No. It's just speculation—his past history and the connection with Anne. That's why I didn't say anything."

"Right again. Now, how do we prove it and get you off the hook?"

Was he being honest? Did he really believe that she had had nothing to do with this unholy tangle? Jessie didn't know. But she also didn't care much as long as he would work on it with that in mind.

She stood in the yard, a little later and watched Mac-Donald drive away, still a little surprised not to be arrested, but feeling better with an ally—any ally. She did not intend, however, to wait around for him to prove she was innocent. There were a couple of things she needed to do on her own, things she hadn't mentioned to him, knowing he wouldn't like what she had in mind. She could tell that, since they'd taken her truck, except for training runs with a team of dogs, he had assumed that she would be at home on Knik Road. She had purposely not disabused him of this notion.

Relatively early in life, Jessie had decided that depending on other people to solve her problems was not only unwise but likely to compound the problem. Though she could be stubborn, she wasn't hardheaded; so this was not a rule she never broke, but she thought it over carefully before she did. Though the suggestion had been made—more than once and by more than one person—that she was, at times, too independent, she had given it serious consideration, disagreed, and continued to take care of things that involved her in ways that satisfied her own standards of self-reliant behavior.

The situation in which she now found herself was no exception, and she meant to take care of parts of it herself, as usual—whether MacDonald liked it or not. That he knew nothing about her plans made no difference. What he didn't know, he couldn't disrupt or hinder. She could only hope he would at least try to understand when, once again, she turned up missing.

22

WHAT JESSIE MEANT TO DO WAS GO BACK TO THE CABIN in the Little Peters Hills.

As she and MacDonald had talked, going over what they knew about the situation, she had come to the conclusion that the cabin somehow played a more significant role in what was going on than it seemed. Her acquaintance with the Holmans had started there; Anne had insisted on returning there; and, finally, it was where Jessie had been taken and held, evidently while Mike Tatum was being killed. More than ever, she wanted to find Anne and get some answers. No one in town had been able to find a clue to her whereabouts. Either she had left the state, as she'd promised—but her promises had not been worth much so far—or she might be at the one other place she had visited since showing up at the airport. MacDonald would soon get around to searching that cabin for evidence, if he really wanted to prove Jessie's innocence, though for the moment he seemed focused on the Tatum murder. Jessie had decided to get there first.

It would have been easier with her own truck and dog box, but that was now out of the question. Whether MacDonald had not realized its significance or dismissed it, Jessie Arnold was a distance racer, used to running long hours at six to eight miles an hour, and so was her racing team. It might be slow going for some people, but in the long run traveling by dog sled covered ground, as every musher knew. The other advantages to this mode of travel were that it was quiet and required no roads. A musher could cut across country that few mechanical vehicles were equipped to cover—only snowmachines could equal an experienced musher with a good sled and team, which was why they were used to break trail for the distance races. They could go faster, but also were dependent on fuel. Dogs carried their own fuel and could go farther, if slower.

It was seventy miles by road to Trapper Creek. Traveling as she would in a race, at an estimated seven miles an hour, Jessie knew she could reach the Little Peters Hills—almost the same distance across back country and a little farther to the west than the road—in ten or eleven hours of running. With two short rest periods for her dogs or one long one she could be there by morning. It was a more than reasonable assumption, considering that her best dogs were in top form from continuous training and had recently completed one of the toughest races anywhere, the Yukon Quest. They had also been resting for more than a day and would be ready and eager to get back out on a trail. All she had to do was pack a sled and go, quickly, before she was intercepted by MacDonald, Becker, or anyone they sent to keep an eye on her, as she half expected them to do.

But first she intended to rearm herself. It would not be smart to go looking where she might run into trouble without some kind of protection. And she knew things about her own living space that no one else did. Her cabin had burned to the ground, but to the ground *only*.

Retrieving heavy gloves and a shovel from the shed, Jessie went to the blackened ruin of what had been the front porch of the structure and began to dig away charred rubble from the north corner. Several times she had to lay the shovel down and lift away the remains of burned planks and their supports, but finally she had worked her way down to scorched dirt and revealed the outline of a narrow horizontal metal door and frame, attached to a concrete foundation. When she had cleaned it off enough to open, a short flight of steps lay revealed below, leading down to what had been a sort of root cellar, a storage space under the house, partly for potatoes and some of the vegetables from her summer garden, kept from freezing until well into the fall before the onset of the real winter cold.

A few other things had also been stored in this space: a large plastic garbage can with a tight lid held flour that she bought in large amounts and used to bake her own bread, some gardening tools put away for the winter, a box or two of old kennel records, other odds and ends that freezing would not damage, and on one back shelf, a rifle that Jessie's father had given her when she'd moved to Alaska from Minnesota to establish her kennel and take up sled dog racing.

It was a reliable Winchester Model 70 Pre 64 that he had used for hunting many years before—a bolt-action rifle, now probably worth more than he had originally paid for it. When she had grown old enough, he had taught Jessie to shoot it. Because of its size, it was unhandy for taking along on races, however, and she did not hunt, so she had kept it around only for sentimental reasons—recognizing it as her father's validation of her abilities. A handgun fit in better with her racing gear and could be carried in a pocket, ready for quick use if she encountered contentious moose on the trail.

Going down the steps, she found that the water used to extinguish the fire had found its way into the cellar, turning the floor into mud and grime. The space smelled wet and unpleasantly of smoke and soot. Her boxes of records were soaked and filthy, but the flour had remained undamaged inside its plastic container, though one side of that had been slightly distorted by the heat. Several empty glass jars she used for canning had fallen and broken when the box that held them disintegrated in the flood. Jessie stepped carefully over them and lifted the Winchester from its place on the shelf, revealing a clean space where it had rested.

In the half light of the open door, she unwrapped the waterproof cover and examined it. No water had found its way inside. The rifle, cleaned and well oiled before she had put it away, was in excellent condition. When Alex Jensen had moved into the cabin with her, his shotgun had replaced the rifle on the wall of the living room, and Jessie had moved the rifle to safety in the cellar. Now she was glad, for it would not have otherwise survived the blaze.

From the shelf, she took a full box of ammunition, which promptly fell apart, scattering the twenty 30.06-caliber cartridges it contained into the mud at her feet. But they'd be usable after she cleaned them, and it took only a minute or two to pick them up and find an unbroken jam jar to contain most of them. The last few she carried in one hand and, taking the rifle and the jar, went back up the steps. In a hurry, she stumbled on the top step and, striving for balance, dropped her handful of shells on the ground outside the door. Hurriedly gathering them up, she put them in the jar with the rest, and took them and the rifle to the tent.

Returning, she closed the metal cellar door and spread dirt and partially burned timbers back over it, disguising the entrance. There was no reason to leave evidence of its existence and she might have a use for such a hidden space in the future, before her cabin was rebuilt.

Rebuilt? Was she going to rebuild it? Jessie smiled to herself. Sometime in the last few days, almost without realizing it, she had come to the conclusion that she wanted to do exactly that. Fine. It was something to look forward to and be optimistic about. Deciding when and how this would be accomplished could wait till later.

It took less than an hour to ready her team for the run back to the Little Peters Hills. Once again selecting the large sled she had used on the trip with Anne, Jessie packed it as if she were starting the Yukon Quest.

There were similarities. Only one sled was allowed for the length of that race—no replacements allowed.

She would have no way of making a replacement in this instance either, so she carefully checked the sled over to be sure it would hold up. There was always the possibility of an accident, however, so she packed materials she might need for repairs and the tool kit she would use if she had to make them.

Plenty of dog food went in, and the cooker she used to melt snow for water, and for thawing and heating dog dinners. The food she packed for herself was the same high-energy edibles she had grown used to carrying on a racing trail. All of it had been previously prepared and kept frozen in the shed for training runs. A change of warm clothing, an extra parka and heavy mittens, several pairs of wool socks and boot liners, the sleeping bag she used during races, her first-aid kit for dogs and humans, an ax—all went into the sled bag. Last, she added the Winchester, once again wrapped securely against weather and within easy reach from the back of her sled. The brass cartridges, now cleaned of mud, went in with it, loose in a heavy plastic Ziploc bag.

When everything was packed, Jessie wrote a note and left it locked in the shed for Billy. In it, she told him that she expected to be away for one night, possibly two, gave him instructions on what he should do at the kennel while she was gone, but didn't reveal her intended destination. What he didn't know, he couldn't tell—even if he didn't mean to.

One or two at a time, she brought the best and most experienced of her dogs and harnessed them to the sled. The Darryls One and Two went into their wheel position nearest the brush bow. Ahead of them, two by two, were team dogs, Digger and Wart, Goofy and

Bliss, Sunny and Mitts, Lucky and Tux, Sadie and Pete. Twelve of the best dogs in the racing business, Jessie thought, as she inspected them carefully to be sure they were all healthy and without injury.

Tank went into harness last, alone at the front of the team, undisputed leader, though Jessie was the real alpha of the pack, for she was the final authority. For a minute, she stood on the back of the sled runners watching them yelp and leap against their harnesses, eager to run as usual, keeping the rest of the kennel in an uproar at being left behind. Then she took her foot off the brake, pulled the snow hook, and allowed the sled to slide forward, gaining momentum as the team pulled it rapidly out of the yard.

"Go, Tank. Get us out of here."

In seconds they had vanished down the trail into the trees and the rest of the dogs quieted, disappointed but resigned to staying at home.

When they had disappeared from sight, Billy Steward stepped out of the trees—where, unseen, he had watched the preparations for this unexpected trip—and stood frowning after her. Contrite and ashamed of his disloyalty in disclosing the secret space in Jessie's truck, he had worried about it and, determined to be there if she needed someone, had not gone home but had returned to wait and watch from the shelter of the forest.

At first, he had thought she was only going for another training run. But, as he noticed what she was packing into the sled and saw her harness up only her best dogs, he began to suspect it was something else entirely. Where was she going? Did this have anything to do with her absence of the day before?

There was no way of finding out, but he did know one thing. It would be a cold day in hell before he told MacDonald—or anyone else—any of Jessie's business again, even if they arrested him. For now, he would stay where he was and work in the yard. There was a lot to be done—dogs to care for, boxes to clean, straw to replace, equipment to repair. Whatever needed doing, he would do. Maybe, if he worked hard enough, she would forgive his betrayal—if she saw how really sorry he was. Resolute, he went to work.

All afternoon and into the night, Jessie ran her team, west to the Susitna River, then north toward Mount McKinley and the Little Peters Hills. The temperature dropped as it grew dark, but the sky remained clear and it did not snow. There was no moon, only stars that shimmered coldly overhead, but what remained of the snow on the ground reflected just enough light to be able to see, and she knew where she was going. For the first part of the run through the dark, she used her headlamp only when absolutely necessary, not wanting to give away her presence to anyone in the houses and cabins she passed. As these grew fewer and farther between, then finally disappeared, she turned on the light and left it on.

About nine o'clock, she stopped and built a fire to feed the dogs and herself. Stretching out in her sleeping bag on top of the sled, she rested for three or four hours, but did not sleep soundly, while the dogs, still in harness, curled into their usual nose-to-tail balls of fur and snoozed, having eaten well and emptied their aluminum pans of water.

Looking up from where she lay, Jessie watched a wisp or two of northern lights drift across the sky in thin ribbons of pale whitish-green, diaphanous and slow moving. It was a sight she had seen many times, though this was late in the year and they were sometimes stronger and more colorful, but it made her feel at home and more self-confident. Somewhere in the dark on a nearby creek she could hear a trickle of water that had melted out during the day and would soon freeze again on top of the ice it overflowed. A breath of breeze rustled through a spruce and quickly died, allowing her to hear the monotonous purr of a far-away generator providing electricity for someone's cabin.

She felt calm and content with her decision, wasted no more time in mental examinations of the confusion of death and fire, guilt and innocence. If there was no one at the cabin, she would rest, then go home. If she found Anne, or anyone else, she would do what she needed to, or could. It seemed simple enough, so she refused to worry about it, though she knew it would probably turn out differently than she imagined. Since she couldn't anticipate anything with accuracy, she allowed herself to expect nothing, and felt better about it than she had in days.

She was almost asleep when she thought she heard a goose somewhere in the distance. Instantly awake, she listened carefully and identified the familiar sound a second time. It was too early for a goose to have arrived, but one was surely honking—and in the dark. Must be a very optimistic bird, she thought. There wouldn't be much for it to eat for quite a while yet. The sound did not repeat itself for a third time, and soon Jessie was as quiet as her dogs, rerunning old trails in her mind.

As soon as the dogs were rested and she was ready to run, they swept steadily north, dark as shadows with one small light to guide them through the unbroken, snow-covered country, and the rest of the night passed like a dream of swift spirits over haunted ground. When the darkness at last began to fade and a pale, predawn gray filtered into the trackless wilderness, they were close under the western slopes of the Little Peters Hills. Jessie could see that the sky would be clear and that it promised another magnificent sunrise on Mount McKinley. It would have been worth stopping to watch, had she not had another, more important goal in mind.

23

"SHE'S GONE AGAIN, PHIL."

MacDonald strode into Becker's office without knocking, banging the door against the wall, and stood looming over his desk with an anxious, frustrated frown. Behind him, Billy Steward had stopped in the doorway and stood glowering at MacDonald's back, head up, chin at an inflexible angle, hair uncombed.

"I found Billy still asleep at her kennel this morning, but he refuses to tell me anything—where she went, when she left, anything."

Billy's lips tightened under Becker's displeased glance, otherwise he did not move.

Becker got up from the paperwork he was attempting to catch up on and came around to confront the young man directly.

"Where is she, Billy?"

"I don't know."

"You've gotta know something. You'd better spill it."

Billy shook his head doggedly. "I don't know."

Becker turned back to MacDonald.

"Too dammed stubborn. Was anything else missing?"

"That sled that was on her truck and I don't know how many dogs."

"She's gone on a training run, then."

"If she has, why won't he tell me?"

Becker huffed angrily and walked back around to drop into the chair behind his desk.

"Well, that tears it, then, doesn't it? I didn't ever expect Jessie to . . ."

"That attitude's as obstinate as Billy's, Phil. You're only seeing what's hurt your feelings."

"You think so?"

"Yes. I don't think she had anything to do with Tatum—or, if she did, it wasn't her idea."

"The lab says he was killed with her gun."

"Which disappeared when she did the first time."

"*Says* she did. Her fingerprints were all over it. That dog won't hunt."

"And the truck?"

"Wiped clean."

"Isn't that a little too much?"

Becker sat staring at him in discomfort, thinking hard.

"Which dogs are gone?"

"What?"

"Which dogs did she take with her?"

"How should I know?"

"Billy?"

No answer.

"I can go out there and find out. Which ones?"

"Find out for yourself." Billy told him grimly.

"Why should that make a difference?" MacDonald questioned. "A dog's a dog."

"No—it's not. If she took some young dogs, she's on a training run. Experienced dogs only would mean she's probably gone somewhere else."

"You're right. Do you know her dogs well enough to tell which are which? I don't."

"Yeah—at least I know most of her racing team from the Quest. I can see if those are gone."

"Well—let's go." He swung around just in time to run into a clerk coming through the door. "Oof, sorry."

They stood for an instant nose to nose, until she stepped back and grinned wickedly, rubbing an arm. "Are you in my way?"

MacDonald apologized again.

"Hank Peterson's here."

"For me or Phil?"

"You—if you don't run him down first."

"Aw, Carol . . . Where is he?"

"Right here," Hank said, stepping around her and Billy into the room. "He's skipped out, Mac."

"Holman?"

"Yeah. Slipped out sometime during the night. Manager says his car was gone when he got up at five."

"That motel manager never got up at five in his life."

"Somebody pounded on his door for a room."

"Well—that *might* do it. Any ideas?"

"Not really, but Holman spent a couple of hours at Oscar's last night. Talked to several people—including Oscar."

"You ask him about it?"

"Nope. Thought I better leave that one alone."

"Good man."

"What's this, Mac?" Becker asked, once more on his feet. "You been having Hank keep an eye on Greg Holman?"

"Thought it might help us locate his wife, since he's spread it around that he's looking for her, too. Hank offered."

"Any leads?"

"Not yet. But, if he's taken off, I'd be willing to bet that—"

"He's found out where she is?"

"Could be."

Jessie was gone. Greg Holman was gone.

"You don't think they're together?" Becker asked MacDonald, when they had searched Jessie's dog yard, sheds, and tent for clues to her intended destination, and found nothing other than the fact that she was gone, along with a considerable amount of her racing gear.

"I doubt it. She doesn't trust him any more than she trusts Anne Holman. Billy says she seems to have given the dogs that are still here in the yard extra food and water, but it wouldn't last more than today, so she must not intend to be gone longer than tomorrow at the latest. She left a note he would have found if she wasn't here then."

Billy, seeing how concerned they were, had finally gone as far as telling MacDonald what he had concluded about the state of the kennel and its dogs. Anything else, however, he still refused to divulge.

"You really don't know where she went, do you, Billy?" the investigator asked, walking the younger man away from the others, toward the ruin of Jessie's house.

"No—I don't."

"And we have discovered for ourselves that she's definitely gone someplace. So you're okay—haven't broken any confidences."

Startled by the man's perception, Billy looked at him and nodded, feeling a little better about the situation and of mending his relationship with Jessie, wherever she was.

"Just give me one thing," MacDonald requested. "Nodding or shaking your head will do. Did she leave on her own? I need to know that no one forced her away from here again."

Billy thought seriously for a moment, then nodded. What could that much hurt?

"Okay. Thanks."

Never content to leave the scene of a fire uninvestigated, as they talked, MacDonald had been kicking at pieces of blackened timbers, turning them over. Now, he suddenly stopped and bent to examine a part of the rubble that he could see had been disturbed. Lying near it, half buried in a boot print that had pressed it into the dirt, lay a 30.06 rifle shell. For all her care, Jessie had not counted those she had dropped and cleaned, or she would have noticed one was missing.

MacDonald now scraped away some dirt and charred remains with his foot to expose the edge of what appeared to be a metal door.

"Billy?"

But Billy Steward was walking quickly away from him toward the storage shed and ignored his question—clearly determined not to tell anything more—if he knew.

Clearing away rubble and lifting the door, the investigator found the short flight of steps that led down into the dark beneath what had been the cabin and soon identified a clean spot on one of the grimy shelves that matched the configuration of a rifle case.

"So, we can guess she was armed," Becker said. "Where the hell has she gone?"

MacDonald had been turning the brass shell over in his fingers while he considered. Now he slipped it into a pocket of his jacket and took his best guess.

"Unless Holman came back and told her where to look for Anne—I think she may have gone back out to that cabin she talked about. The one where she said she was taken and held, west of Trapper Creek. There's some kind of tie-in there."

"Possible, I guess," Becker agreed thoughtfully. "It wouldn't hurt to check, but she could have gone anywhere."

"I think it might be *essential* to check. It makes more sense than anywhere else I can think of. And if the Holmans, or either one of them, is there, and if they are either one or both responsible for all or part of this mess—she could be in real trouble."

"She's no dummy. If she has a rifle, she knows how to use it."

"I expect you're right. Shall we make a run to Trapper Creek?"

"Can't get to where that cabin is in a truck or your Jeep. Only snowmachines will get us off that road and into the hills."

"Oh, hell. I hate those things. But—okay, let's rustle some up and see if we can get out there before dark."

"I've got a couple of Ski-Doos already on a trailer you can use," Hank Peterson offered from where he had been standing with Billy, listening to the exchange. "Another one I can load, if you want me to go along. I've been out there and know where that cabin is."

"Good idea, Hank. How long will it take to get going?"

"Soon as you can, go get into some suits and boots. I could get the machines and meet you in town."

"Let's do it."

Through the night, Jessie had run her team north through the still-frozen and snow-covered swampland and maze of creeks to the west of the Parks Highway and the Susitna River. At Trapper Lake, she had swung northwest and, as the sun rose, she had already crossed both Peters and Bear creeks and arrived at the area between the banks of the Kahiltna River and the Little Peters Hills. Turning east, she directed the team up the slope a little way till she found a flat, sheltered place by a stand of birch, where she stopped, fed and watered the dogs, and settled them to take a long rest while she was gone.

She unharnessed Tank and, leaving him loose to accompany her on his own, began to climb the hill that would eventually lead her to the cabin in which she had long ago spent part of the winter. It was slow going through the deep snow on the more sheltered side of the hills, especially with the rifle she had taken from the sled and a day pack of ammunition, water, and a few supplies, but she took her time and was soon approaching the crest to the west of the cabin.

Stepping out of the cold shadow of the hill into the sunshine made it seem warmer, though the temperature remained almost the same. Pausing for a minute, she looked toward the cabin, but there were too many trees in the way to see it. Without further hesitation, she made her way through the trees along the crest, carefully keeping Tank close and moving as quietly as possible. In about ten minutes she came to the burned remains of the Holman cabin and stopped to look around.

The space near the trees where she and Anne had built the first fire to thaw the frozen ground had been tampered with—the dirt that had been dug out had been put back to fill the hole and flattened. Some snow had been kicked back over it, but without new snow to disguise the work the marks and boot prints were plain to see. Why, she wondered, would anyone go to that much trouble if there was nothing there, as Anne had said?

Nothing else appeared to have been touched, though someone had come and gone on the trail that led toward the other cabin. Anne had left Knik Road still wearing the borrowed boots and work-stained parka, a fact which did not endear her to Jessie, and the familiar prints of the boots were there to be plainly seen on top of the marks of sled runners and the paw prints Jessie's team had left. There was no question that Anne had been here again and, perhaps, still was.

Continuing cautiously along the trail, it wasn't long until Jessie caught the scent of wood smoke. When she drew near enough, she saw that it was coming from the chimney of her old cabin, drifting slowly through the

trees in the still morning air. Stopping on the far side
of a large spruce, where she would not be easily seen,
she stopped and waited, watching for ten or fifteen
minutes, to see if whoever had built that fire would
come out. It might not be Anne. It was, she supposed,
just as possible that Greg had found his way back here,
hoping, like Jessie, to find his wife in this familiar setting. The smoke continued its lazy drift, but all was
silent and still. There was no sign of anyone.

Finally, growing impatient, Jessie slowly circled the
cabin until she could see the front of it. Away from the
cabin, near some trees, a snowmachine was parked.
Again, she watched, but saw and heard nothing from
inside the log building.

At length she decided that, short of spending an in-
determinate amount of time waiting in the cold for
someone to come out, if she wanted answers she would
have to initiate contact with whoever was in the cabin.
If it was Anne, as she suspected, she might still be
sleeping, expecting no one. The later it grew, the more
unlikely it was that she could be surprised, and surprise
would be a definite advantage for Jessie. Thinking
ahead, she very gingerly chambered two shells in the
rifle, muffling the sounds of the bolt action as best she
could.

The sun cast long lines between the shadows of the
dark spruce and bare trunks of the leafless birch as she
slipped through them, taking care how and where she
stepped, for it was not simple to walk silently in
crusted snow. Step by step, she approached, Tank
padding quietly beside her, and finally stood on the
step in front of the door, ready to throw it open.

Closing her eyes for a minute, to allow her eyes to adjust for light that would be dimmer than the brightness of sun on snow, she waited, listening attentively. Hearing nothing, she took a deep breath and holding the rifle ready for use, reached for the handle, slowly turned it, and, shoving the door inward with all her strength, followed it quickly into the room beyond and hesitated just inside to look for an occupant.

The blow that hurled her into darkness came so instantaneously she saw only a hint of motion to her left and had no opportunity to move or defend herself before she was falling against the nail points that protruded from the door to discourage plundering bears. Pain lanced sharply through both sides of her scalp. The pool of sunshine that had accompanied her through the open door onto the wood floor blurred, became murky, and winked out as if a switch had been flipped.

24

MACDONALD WAS HAVING NO TROUBLE AT ALL REMEM-
bering what he disliked about snowmachines. His main
objection had always been the amount of noise they
generated. He liked to be able to hear what was going
on around him and found it impossible over the roar
and whine of the Ski-Doo he was cautiously guiding
along the trail behind Phil Becker. He knew that part of
the guidance problem he was having was the result of
never having ridden a snowmachine enough to learn
how to make it perform the way others seemed to do so
easily. He also knew that it was a skill he would will-
ingly—cheerfully in fact—forgo. Overcompensation
in steering kept him swinging from one side of the trail
to the other, while Becker glided straight ahead and
Hank Peterson kept leaving the trail entirely to run circles around the other two, obviously experienced and
exuberant in his enjoyment of running his machine
through open country.

It had taken over two hours for the three to reach the
pull-out at Kroto Creek on Petersville Road, unload

the three machines, and start for the Little Peters Hills. Enjoying the ride or not, it didn't take MacDonald long to be able to operate his iron dog well enough to speed up a little, so they soon reached the turnoff at the Forks Roadhouse. Though no new snow had fallen since Jessie and Anne had made their trip over the same route, wind had blown snow onto the trail where it left the road, covering all but a snowmachine track that showed plainly in the drift.

"No one's run a sled over this in a couple of days," Peterson observed, stopping to look and let his machine idle, so he could make himself heard by Becker and MacDonald, who did the same. "Jessie didn't come this way. There's snowmachine tracks, but they're everywhere around here."

"Is there any other trail to that cabin?" Becker asked.

"No, but she wouldn't have to follow this with her dog team. It'd be shorter to break her own trail up the valley and come in from the west. That's what I'd do."

"Won't know until we get there, will we? Let's go," MacDonald called, frowning. The farther they went the more concerned he had become about the situation. Feeling remiss that he hadn't anticipated that Jessie, independent and capable, might take off on her own, he was also having second thoughts about several other things. Hank Peterson had seemed just a little too willing to come along on this expedition. Was he leading them off on a wild-goose chase—taking them away from where they should really be paying attention? Could he have had anything to do with either of Jessie's disappearances? It also bothered Mac that, when they had stopped to ask Oscar Lee about his conversation with Greg Holman the night before, they found he had hired a new bartender and taken the day off. He had not answered his telephone either, adding to MacDonald's apprehension.

Though the day was bright and sunny, his thoughts were dark. Mike Tatum's death had been no accident. He had been a threat to whomever silenced him. Like Jessie, MacDonald was beginning to distrust almost everyone that was in any way connected to all this trouble. Committed now to this trip into the bush, he, nevertheless, had an uneasy feeling about it. The farther they went, the more he wanted it over, to investigate the cabin in the hills and get back to town, where he was comfortable with his usual habits of careful planning and efficiency. He did not like following hunches. He knew he was a bit of a plodder, but also knew that his methods got results in the long run. Something about this spur-of-the-moment run to confirm a possibility didn't sit right. That he couldn't decide why it nagged at his sense of caution didn't help either. Becker seemed satisfied with it, but . . .

Phil Becker was not as content as MacDonald assumed. Fully aware of the worried frown on the investigator's face, he was having second thoughts of his own. He felt somewhat responsible for Jessie's disappearance, believed he should have anticipated that she might take it upon herself to investigate her abduction. Whether it had really happened, or she only believed it had, would make no difference to her curiosity and determination. He had ignored what he knew of her independence and hoped that a price would not be exacted from her for his mistake. Drawing his own conclusions from a lot of circumstantial evidence, he had allowed his disappointment to generate distrust. He was sorry for it now—and feeling more than a little guilty.

As they had turned off the road onto the narrower trail, Peterson stopped showing off on his snowmachine and settled down to steadily following the track that led along the gentle slopes between the Peters and Little Peters hills. The pace he set was faster than MacDonald would have chosen, but he managed to keep up, hoping that it wouldn't be too much farther.

Setting Hank to keep a watch on Greg Holman had seemed a good idea to him the evening they met to talk at Oscar's. He had decided that it might accomplish two things: give him an idea what Holman was up to in his supposed search for his missing wife and allow him to keep track of Hank Peterson. Hearing from Jessie later of Peterson's visit to Holman at his motel had made Mac wonder just what connection might exist between the two men. Had he made a mistake? Had Peterson been keeping track of Holman, or an arson investigator? Though he had not mentioned this possibility to Becker, he now thought he should when he had a chance.

"Wake up, Jessie. Come on, wake up."

Without opening her eyes, Jessie knew immediately who was calling her name and shaking her shoulder. She had found Anne Holman, but not as she wished or expected. Her head hurt in two places, a throbbing on the left side, a sharp burning on the right. What had happened? She tried to move.

Anne heard the groan that escaped Jessie's lips, and saw her eyes blink open.

"Oh, good. You're going to be okay. I'm really sorry, but you shouldn't have surprised me like that. How could I know it was you? I thought it was—"

"What did you hit me with?" Jessie interrupted, but tried to move her head as little as possible for the moment. "It hurts—dammit."

"—Greg trying to get in—thought he'd found me. I hit you with a piece of firewood. I'm really sorry."

"Okay. You said that. Why does the other side hurt?"

"I didn't have anything to do with that. You fell against the nails in the door and cut yourself."

Which I wouldn't have done if you hadn't hit me, Jessie thought.

Raising a hand, she felt deep scratches that the nails had made in her scalp—two or three long cuts, still oozing blood. On the opposite side was the lump Anne had raised with the firewood.

"O-oh. Am I going to have headaches for the rest of my life? Where's Tank?" she asked Anne.

"Outside. I was afraid he'd bite me because I hit you."

Jessie listened and could hear him growling outside the door.

"Stop that, Tank," she called. "It's okay. I'm all right; good boy."

His growls subsided, and he was quiet for the time being, knowing she didn't need defending.

Getting slowly to her knees, she waited out the renewed throbbing in her head.

"Have you got any aspirin?"

"Yes. I'll get it for you."

Anne went across and retrieved her day pack from the corner that Jessie remembered it had been in when she was captive, brought back three aspirin and a bottle of water.

"Thanks."

Swallowing them, Jessie looked around for her own pack. It stood across the room under the window, next to the rifle. Anne, seeing where she was looking, stepped between Jessie and these things and stood, eyes narrowed suspiciously.

She said nothing, only shook her head, but Jessie knew that if she tried to go in that direction, Anne could reach the gun first and would. She decided not to make an attempt yet, still feeling a little unsteady. Instead, she sat back down on the floor and waited for the aspirin to alleviate some of her headache while she figured out what to do next—a distraction, maybe, for she was not about to let her personal protection go that easily.

Anne remained where she was, watching distrustfully, while Jessie looked around the cabin. A hint of steam rose from a large kettle and from the spout of an aluminum coffeepot on the stove. Near it, an untidy sleeping bag lay on a pad on the floor. The built-in bunk had been used as a countertop, food spread out over a couple of paper grocery bags—several cans of soup or stew, a large can of apple juice, a loaf of bread, a tub of margarine. The parka that Anne had *borrowed* hung on a shoulder-high post at the end—part of the foot board. It looked like Anne had been here for a day or two since she left Knik.

"What are you doing up here, Anne? Why did you leave my place so suddenly when the fire started?"

"You said it was time to go."

"Did you start it?"

"No-o," Anne told her indignantly. "Of course not."

"Who did?"

"I don't know. But it wasn't me."

"Then why'd you take off when I really needed your help?"

"I was afraid," she whined, and Jessie recognized the familiar it's-not-my-fault tone. "You knew that. I told you Greg was coming after me. Why wouldn't you believe me and help?"

"How did you go? Nobody saw you on the road."

"I don't think I need to justify myself to you. You just wanted me gone, so I went. Never mind how."

Jessie shook her head and instantly wished she had not.

"That's not enough. You're just trying to slip out from under again. I want some answers. Did someone pick you up?"

Anne stared at her belligerently, refusing to say any more.

"Oh, for Lord's sake, Anne. All right. How'd you get up here, then—and why?"

"It's a good place to hide."

"From who?"

"Greg, of course. He followed me from Colorado, like I knew he would. I *told* you. You just didn't care."

Whatever happens to Anne, someone else is always responsible, Jessie thought. Holding both hands to her aching head, she slumped forward in hurt and discouragement, elbows on knees. The fingers of her right hand came away sticky with blood that had run down the side of her face from the cuts in her scalp.

"Have you got something I can use to wash this blood off?" she asked.

Anne gave her another doubting look.

"Hey. Just get me something will you? Please? What's the matter with you?"

Still watching, Anne went to her open suitcase that lay on the floor beside the sleeping bag. Taking out a towel, she dipped one end into the hot water on the stove, wrung it out, and brought it across the room. As she handed it over, Jessie took a deep breath and caught a scent she recognized. Startled, she looked accusingly up at the woman in front of her.

"You took my lotion—my Crabtree & Evelyn freesia lotion. I can smell it on your hands. You didn't have to *steal* it, Anne. If you'd asked, I would have given it to you."

But another memory was surfacing, immediately behind her astonished recognition. She had smelled the same scent just before someone had put a cloth soaked in some sleep-inducing chemical over her mouth and nose to knock her out—when she had been blinded by the light and unable to identify that person—when she had been held captive in this very cabin.

"It was you up here in the dark, wasn't it? You—"

Her indictment was interrupted by a sudden thunderous pounding on the front door followed by Tank's anxious bark.

"Oh, Jesus," Anne said, turning toward it, raising her hands as if to ward off an attack. "It's Greg. It's got to be Greg. He's here."

The pounding continued, steadily, rhythmically, shaking dust into the room from the front walls of the cabin. It hung in the air like the motes Jessie remembered seeing when she'd been lying, bound, on the floor. She could see the heavy planks move with each new blow. Why didn't Greg—if that's who it was—just open the door and come in? For a second or two the noise stopped, then began again, lower on the door this time.

"Anne. Open the door," she shouted.

"No-o. Oh, God, no. It's Greg."

She whirled and grabbed up the rifle from under the window. Pointing it at the reverberating door, she stood facing it, an ugly expression of rage and hatred on her face. The barrel of the rifle caught the light as she raised it, her finger on the trigger.

"No," Jessie yelled above the noise, and the other woman hesitated, glancing around. "You don't *know* that it's Greg, Anne. It could be someone else. Don't shoot without being able to see who it is."

"Who else could it be?" She spat out her contempt, but there was a slight uncertainty in her voice. The rifle wobbled in her hands, and she did not pull the trigger.

"It could be anyone," Jessie told her, standing up and starting to move slowly across the room. "You won't know unless you open the door and find out."

The barrel of the rifle was immediately turned in her direction.

"Sit down," Anne demanded coldly. "You've done enough to screw up my life. Sit back down and shut up. Just shut up."

"What do you mean?"

"You know what I mean, you bitch. You and Greg thought I wouldn't know that . . ."

The pounding paused, then once again resumed, this time on the left side of the door by the hinges.

Jessie sank back to her knees, astonished at the angry outburst and accusation. What was Anne talking about? The rifle barrel was turned back toward the crashes coming from outside.

"Who's there?" Anne called loudly.

There was no answer but the clamorous pounding.

"What the hell do you want? Go away."

No response.

"Just open the door," Jessie suggested again, calmly and just loud enough to make herself heard. "You've got to open the door."

It might *be* Greg Holman. But, if it was, she doubted that he really meant to kill his wife, especially with a witness, unless . . .

"You'd like that, wouldn't you? Both of you? No, I won't open it."

"Then let me," Jessie begged. "You stay there—with the rifle—and I'll open it, see who it is."

The indecision was unmistakable on Anne's face. It was plain that she didn't want to shoot some unknown person, but she was clearly convinced that it *was* her husband. Fear had drawn the blood from her face and tightened her mouth. She stared at the door and the pounding seemed to rattle her thinking along with the wall.

"I don't know . . . all right," she said finally. "But I'm watching, so don't think you can get away with anything this time. Just walk over there and open it, then step back."

Cautiously, Jessie got up and approached the door. As she reached out a hand, wondering why whoever was making such a noise hadn't opened it already, the pounding suddenly stopped. For a long minute everything was utterly silent.

"Who's there?" she called and received no answer.

Then she could hear someone walking from the cabin. Footsteps crunched in the sublimating snow and ice outside, growing fainter as they moved away, but no one spoke. Tank was quiet.

Determined to see who it was, she grasped the handle of the door, thumbed the latch open, and pulled. The door did not move. Again she tugged, then suddenly realized the significance of the pounding.

Whoever it had been had not been knocking—had not wanted to come in. What they had wanted was for no one inside to be able to go out. The door had been nailed solidly closed. She was, again, a prisoner in the cabin she had occupied ten years before, this time with Anne Holman. Why?

Tank barked sharply outside again.

Turning to look at Anne, who had lowered the barrel of the rifle and stood frowning uncertainly, Jessie caught sight of the smoke that was beginning to rise in a small but growing ribbon from between two of the foundation logs in the corner of the room.

25

BELOW THE CABIN, ON THE FLANKS OF THE LITTLE PETERS Hills, the three snowmachiners had followed Black Creek, crossed the ridge, dropped down along the frozen swamp, and turned west at Sand Creek. Mac-Donald, still managing to keep up, was surprised, when Becker suddenly stopped, to hear him swearing over the growl of his idling machine.

"Hey, where's Peterson?"

"Bastard took off," Becker told him, waving a fist in the direction of tracks that MacDonald could see swinging away to the west along the side of a slope and disappearing into a stand of trees. "He just goosed it all of a sudden and took off like a bat out of hell."

"Why?"

"Evidently, he's bailing out as tour guide," Becker snapped angrily. "I'll bet we're not even close to that cabin—that he's got us completely turned around and headed somewhere else."

MacDonald sat for a moment, thinking hard. Was this the answer to his question about Peterson's eagerness to accompany them on this trip? Had he intended to lose them somewhere along the way? It would make sense if he were somehow involved in the confusion of fires and murder, responsible for some part of it, knew more than he had told.

If he had meant to lose them and purposely gone— wherever—without them, where would Peterson be most likely to go?

"Two ideas on where he's gone," he said to Becker. "Either he's planning to leave us here and has gone back to the road, or he's headed for the cabin by himself. If he's involved, he'll probably go to the cabin. You agree?"

Becker nodded. "But why bring us out here at all?"

"Who cares about his reasons? There's nothing we can do now, right? I think we should go ahead and try to reach that cabin by ourselves—not follow his tracks off down the hill but go up there and hunt around till we find it."

"I don't think we'll have to do much hunting," Becker, who had been looking past him toward the top of the Little Peters Hills, said. "Somebody's sending smoke signals."

MacDonald twisted around to look where Becker was pointing. A column of smoke was rising out of the trees just under the crest of the hill to their left.

Later, recalling their wild ride up the hill toward that cloud of smoke that was larger every time they caught sight of it through the trees, he would wonder at his own ability to stay aboard the roaring snowmachine. Following close behind Becker, with periodic glimpses of the frozen Kahiltna River below them on the right, he somehow managed to keep to the tracks the trooper left with little awareness of their speed or the complicated maneuvers they executed in avoiding trees and brush that seemed to fly past. All his concentration was on reaching the source of the smoke and finding out what was burning.

If Jessie Arnold was on that hill, it was clear to him that whoever had started another fire would not hesitate to add another victim to the growing list. She had barely escaped one blaze. Had this one also been lit in her name?

"The cabin's on *fire!*"

Anne Holman, who had still been totally focused on the door, whirled at the word, caught sight of the growing cloud of smoke rising in the corner, and panicked. Dropping the rifle in a clatter on the floor, she ran to the door and began to yank repeatedly with all her strength at its immovable handle.

"Oh, God—oh, God," she shrieked with each yank. "Let me out. I'll be good. Oh, ple-ease, let me out. Oh, God."

Unable to open it, she gave up, ran to the corner farthest from the smoke, flung herself into it, sank to the floor, and curled into a fetal position, face turned away from the sight that terrorized her, eyes tightly shut. There, she began to rock, bang her head against a log, and wail incoherently.

Jessie's first thought at seeing the smoke was more rational—put it out.

"Water."

Grabbing the bottle of water she had used to take the aspirin, she dumped its contents onto the smoke, hoping to reach its source. For a moment, no more, the smoke thinned, but it was soon seeping in between the logs more heavily than before. Listening, she could hear the crackle of flames out of reach on the outside of the wall.

Maybe it would help if she could pour water through from a higher crack. Snatching up a knife that lay on the edge of the countertop-bunk, where Anne had evidently been using it to make sandwiches, she dug at the insulation between two of the logs at waist level above the smoke. When she had extracted enough to open a narrow foot-long crack through which she could see daylight, she took the large kettle of hot water from the stove and carefully poured it through, so the majority of it drained down the outside. There was a sizzle of water hitting fire and a small amount of steam rose, but, when she looked down, the smoke that had been coming in at only one location had spread along the wall to her left and was now rising in three new places.

There was no more water. It was time to get out somehow.

"Anne," she said sharply. "*Anne*. We've got to find a way out of here."

Huddled in the corner, Anne did not respond—didn't even seem to hear.

Crossing the room, Jessie took hold of her shoulder and jerked the woman around.

"Help me, dammit. Do you want to burn?"

The word elicited a moan from Anne, as she struggled to turn back and hide her face.

Raising a hand, Jessie slapped her, hard.

"I said *help me*."

"I can't. I can't. Oh, God, don't let me die."

"You *can*. Grow up. We've *got* to get out, or we'll burn with this place!"

Pushing and shoving, she got Anne to her feet and dragged her toward the window, picking up the rifle from the floor on the way. Once there, she used the stock to knock out the dirty panes.

The glass shattered easily, shards falling back into the room as they hit the boards that had been nailed across outside. When Jessie had broken off most of the sharp fragments that remained, however, and tried pounding at the boards themselves, she encountered not resistance but complete refusal. These boards, too, had been reinforced at some time with heavier, additional boards. The rifle stock was not heavy enough to knock them loose from the nails that held them securely.

The air that now flowed through the broken windowpanes allowed a fresh supply of oxygen to reach and encourage the fire. Jessie could see that flames had followed the smoke and were beginning to finger the logs on the inside. From the loud crackling sound, it was evident that the fire was making headway and had involved most of the outside wall. The smoke grew thicker, billowing into the room, making it hard to breathe without coughing.

Anne whimpered and began to babble again.

Jessie shook her and the gibberish stopped, though she continued to whimper and was now shaking uncontrollably.

"Stop that. What are we going to do?"

She was talking to herself and knew it, but verbalizing helped her think. Coughing that she couldn't control made her headache worse in spite of the aspirin she had taken. At the rate the room was filling they would soon have nothing to breathe but the deadly smoke, would pass out and be unconscious, or dead, long before the flames came anywhere close.

The water was gone, but the towel she had used to wipe her face was half wet. She retrieved it and cut it in half with the knife. Grabbing up the coffeepot, she poured what was left onto the fabric.

"Here. Tie this around your face."

Anne looked at her as if she were mad and dropped it on the floor as she bent double to cough.

"Dammit, Anne. It'll help you breathe," Jessie told her, picking it up and tying it on her before she tied the other half over her own mouth and nose and desperately looked around, assessing everything she could see for some way to get out.

When she had lived here, she had considered digging a small cellar under the floor. Deciding to leave, she had abandoned the idea. Now she wished she had completed it, for she had heard of people surviving fires by crawling into their storage spaces. I'm playing what-if, she thought, and turned her attention elsewhere.

The towel mask smelled of coffee, but seemed to be keeping most of the smoke temporarily at bay. She could feel the temperature rising dramatically in the room. Flames now engaged half the wall and had crept up just under one of the peeled log beams. The builder had planned for heavy amounts of snow. About three feet apart and eight inches in diameter, the solid beams reached across the width of the cabin and supported the posts and struts that braced the rafters and, in turn, the roof.

The *roof*. Could they break out through the roof?

The rising smoke was thickest under the peak of the roof. She knew that you were supposed to get down as close to the floor as possible, where the only breathable air would be found, but there was no possible exit on the floor. The roof just might be worth a try.

"Over here," she yelled to Anne, who did not move but stared at her dumbly, tears streaking what could be seen of her sooty cheeks.

Impatiently grabbing Anne's arm, Jessie dragged and shoved her over to the bunk and pushed the rifle into her hands.

"Stand here and give that to me when I ask for it. Do you understand?"

Anne nodded slowly, hopelessly, and watched as Jessie scrambled quickly onto the foot of the bunk, then, one hand on the wall to give her balance, onto the post at the foot, tossing Anne's parka to the floor. From there she could easily reach the beam over it.

Grasping it with both hands, Jessie swung her legs up and wrapped them around the log that ran straight across to the fiery wall, where, as she watched, a tongue of flame reached up to lick its underside. Hurriedly, but careful not to fall, she pulled herself up and around, until she lay on top and could reach down with one arm.

"Now. Give it to me," she instructed Anne and, for once, the woman complied, holding the rifle up by its stock, so Jessie could grasp the barrel. Settling it securely in the angle of roof and beam, she pulled herself to a crouch, then put one foot on the next beam and stood up enough to use her hands to tear off the plastic vapor barrier, then the insulation. When she had exposed the planks, she turned around and stood, back to the roof, leaning her shoulders against the steep angle. Holding the rifle barrel pointed forward, she began to pound the stock as hard as she could against them, regretting the insult to her father's gift.

These planks had not been reinforced by the person who pounded the door closed but were held in place with nothing more than a single nail holding each plank to each rafter.

At first there was little result, but increasing the length of her swing provided more force, and in a few strikes she felt one plank give slightly. Attacking that spot again and again, she kept up the battering until it splintered at last and broke away from its nail.

Repeating her efforts on the next plank, Jessie soon had it loose as well. Nails still held it to the next rafter and, though now she could use leverage, she was gasping for breath, rapidly running out of air.

"Jessie. Come down, Jessie-e-e," came a shrill wail above the roar of the accelerating fire.

Looking down, Jessie found it was hard to make out Anne's terrified uptilted face through the dense smoke. She could see the burning wall and the flames advancing across the beams on which she stood. The heat was almost intolerable; her exposed skin felt scalded.

"Jessie-e."

Ignoring the panicked wail, bracing her back solidly against the loosened planks, feet on the beams, knees bent, Jessie threw all her weight and strength into applying pressure to the roof.

Escape would have to happen now—or not at all. In a very few minutes it would be impossible to remain where she was.

Years of constant exercise—large amounts of time on the back of a sled, pumping with one leg then the other, or running along beside it and lifting dogs in and out of harness, weighty sleds over uneven trails, and heavy kettles of food and water—had kept Jessie fit and gradually built her a powerful body that she took for granted. The test she had now set for herself, however, required more than her average strength and determination. Had she tried with her arms to lift the weight she had set herself against, she would have failed miserably. By putting her back and legs into the effort and adding to it adrenaline-produced strength, she had a slim chance. The deciding factor was anger.

As she strained against the roof, every muscle tensed and laboring to its limit, she realized she was furiously angry. Unable to waste breath on words, she swore mentally and found herself rhythmically rocking with every curse against the planks that imprisoned her. Come on, you son of a bitch. Dammit to *hell*. I will not *die* in here. Her knees began to ache—her head throbbed. She closed her eyes and pushed till she thought she might pass out and fall from her perch.

Something gave, suddenly, behind her shoulders. One of the planks shrieked a complaint of pulled nails and sprang loose, ripping the exterior roofing paper and shingles with it. She sustained the pressure, and the other plank went as well.

Hanging her head out of the hole she had made, she gulped breaths of fresh air, while smoke poured out past her into the sunshine. The opening was narrow—just two planks wide—but it would serve. They could get out through it.

Looking down, she saw Tank below on the ground and heard him bark.

Over the all-but-overwhelming rage of the fire, a faint cry from inside, "Jessie-e. Don't le-eave me-e. I'll be go-o-od."

And Jessie knew that she must risk going back down into what was becoming an inferno—one that she had fed with the additional oxygen by the escape hatch she had created. The fire bellowed and howled its wrath. Against all her instincts that screamed *get out*, she knew she could not live with herself unless she went into the hell below her feet to try to save a woman who had lied to her, stolen from her, might hate her enough to have set her house on fire, and who had tried to frame her for the murder of Mike Tatum.

26

⚜═══⚜

THE SNOW SHE HAD FALLEN INTO FROM THE ROOF OF THE cabin was cool and soothing on her cheek and blistered hand. Jessie wanted to stay where she was, gasping clean air into her parched lungs, but there was heat, too—growing stronger as the fire finally engulfed the cabin. She heard a wall collapse. Suddenly a shower of sparks and bits of burning ash and cinders were falling all around, hissing as they hit the snow. She knew she must move or be further burned.

Anne Holman spoke from somewhere beyond her sight.

"No. You can't ask me that, dammit. You just tried to burn me to ashes. Why can't you just go away and leave me alone?"

Jessie raised her aching head, got to her knees, and crawled away from the burning building, then sat back into a drift to see who the woman was addressing.

Greg Holman, dressed in a black snowmachine suit, tears running down his face, stood staring at his wife. In his hands was the metal box that held the fragile bones of the child that Anne had dug out of the ground farther up the hill—that she had told Jessie was not his.

"Why?" he said. "Just tell me why. And for once in your life don't lie to me."

In Anne's steady hands, the rifle that Jessie had thrown from the hole in the roof, before going back to help her to safety, was leveled at him, her finger on the trigger. Her expression was as cold and full of hatred as any Jessie had ever seen.

"Because you wanted it so much," she told him contemptuously. "Because you wouldn't let me get rid of it."

"But why tell me now?"

"Because you won't let me go. I want to go, but you keep getting in my way."

"You know I can't let you go—and why."

"I know you *think* you can't. But now you'll have to—won't you?"

As Jessie watched, he stared at her for a long minute without speaking. Then, as if repeating something he had said before, he said, very gently, "No. I can't do that. You *know* why I can't. Give me the gun now, Anne, and let's go home."

"No, you big, dumb bastard. Not now—not *ever*."

The report of the rifle was unexpected. Jessie started to get to her feet, but fell as an ankle she'd injured in her leap from the roof collapsed, tumbling her back into the drift with a yelp. From where she landed, she saw Greg Holman fall facedown, the metal box hitting the frozen ground first, breaking open, and spilling the small white bones it contained into the snow, white on white, sliding, scattering, disappearing against it.

The shot had caught him in the center of the chest. He had fallen silently, and lay silent and unmoving with ash falling on him out of the still air.

Anne stared down at him without a change of expression—as if she had just killed a rabid dog or swatted a fly. Then she turned and caught sight of Jessie sitting in the snow behind her.

"And you," she said in a curiously conversational tone. "What shall I do with you?"

The barrel of the rifle came slowly up to point directly at Jessie's chest.

"You and him." She gave a short jerk of her head toward Greg's still form. "You thought I wouldn't ever know that when you lived here he stopped at your place when he went down the hill—or came back up it. Thought I was really stupid, didn't you?"

"That's not true," Jessie said carefully, knowing she couldn't run or escape. "Greg and I never—"

"Still won't admit it? He wouldn't either. But . . . never mind. It doesn't matter anymore."

Slowly she shook her head and shifted her grip on the rifle.

"I could have left you in there," Jessie told her flatly, "and let you die. But I went back, made you climb—even when you fought me—and dragged you out. When you tried to climb over me to get out and shoved me off the beam, I climbed back again and helped you."

"So you think I owe you? I think it's the other way around. Maybe you should've left me."

"Maybe I should have . . . but—"

The whine of a snowmachine engine grew suddenly

loud enough to be heard over the fire. Jessie and Anne both looked toward the sound and saw Hank Peterson come sailing through the trees and into the open space by the burning cabin. Without hesitation, seeing the rifle turned on Jessie, he increased his speed and drove straight at Anne.

She lowered the barrel and took a few quick steps backward and, as she dodged, Jessie distinctly saw Greg Holman move his arm. Peterson's snowmachine passed almost close enough to knock her down, but missed. He was too close for Anne to shoot, so she turned the rifle quickly and swung the stock at him instead. As it glanced off his left arm she lost her grip on the barrel; the gun flew from her hands over Greg's body, and landed near a spruce.

Immediately she sprang after it, but, as she leaped across Greg, he rolled over and threw an arm into her path, knocking her feet from under her. She landed, rolling clumsily like a rag doll in a wild gyration of arms and legs, tumbled to a stop against Greg's parked snowmachine, hit her face against one of its skis, and flopped over onto her back.

For a moment she lay stunned, a trickle of blood showing up a startling red against the whiteness of her skin.

"No," Greg said sharply, and coughed. His voice was weak but clear enough for Jessie to hear. "No more, Anne. It's got to end now."

Peterson stopped his snowmachine, got off, and removed his goggles.

"What the hell is going on here?" he asked, but got no answer.

Greg was facing Anne as she stared at him white-faced from where she lay. Jessie was watching them both.

Anne pushed herself into a sitting position and swiped at the cut on her cheek, smearing blood across the back of her bare hand. Then she got to her feet, walked over, and stood looking down at Greg in a sort of disdainful amusement. Reaching out, she wiped her blood across his mouth.

"Still in my way?" she asked. Then in a strange, calm, and agreeable tone—with a hint of malicious intent to humiliate and hurt—she said, "Be careful what you wish for."

She whirled and began to walk toward the holocaust the cabin had become.

Hank Peterson raced across the space between them, and attempted to bring her down before she could reach the burning cabin—but failed by inches.

She did not give him a glance or try to avoid the tackle that dropped him just out of reach of her feet, but walked on straight into the roaring inferno. With an odd half smile on her face, like a person going somewhere they have anticipated with pleasure, she disappeared into the flames and never made a sound.

27

ON A WARM DAY THREE WEEKS LATER, JESSIE AND HANK Peterson drove two teams of dogs up the slopes of the Little Peters Hills, left the dogs resting in the sun by the remains of the Holman cabin, and walked west through the trees and across the open space to a large rock to fulfill a promise she had made. He carried a shovel and she, a metal box.

When they had dug the hole and put the box back where Jessie had been asked to leave it—where it belonged—she stood for a minute feeling the rightness of their action. Nothing was said, no prayer or scripture recited, but there were the sounds of small birds in the nearby trees and a gurgle of water melting unseen and running under what was left of the snow on the south side of the hill.

She walked to the edge of the open space, where the slope fell more steeply away to the wide valley far below, and watched a pair of ravens playing tag on the currents of the breeze, their rough cries carrying faintly up the hill to her ears. There always seemed to be ravens—a comforting constant. Beneath them, an almost invisible reddish haze seemed to cling to the bare branches of the birch, a precursor of new green leaves that would soon open to cover them. Grass would spring up when the snow had disappeared, smoothing the sharp lines of rocks and rough ground, and all would be new and seemingly unspoiled again.

Even through the blackened rubble that was left of the two cabins, new life would appear and shove its way up to cover and gradually swallow up the ugly scars. Wishing she could lay her memory down with them for similar treatment, Jessie turned away and walked back through the trees with Peterson to the fire they had built for making tea.

"Greg should be buried there, too," Peterson said, thoughtfully.

"I asked him before he died. He didn't want to be."

"Why?"

"He said—and I quote—'She'll walk up there, you know. I don't think it would be right for us to be so close. She took my son's life—she'll look after him. I took hers—so let her be. It's all she wanted from me.' "

"Je-e-ez. You believe that kind of stuff?"

Jessie noted his shiver and shrugged.

"But she did kill Tatum and start the fires that killed the other two, right?"

"She started all the fires except mine and the last one up here. Greg told MacDonald when he was still in the hospital. Anne held grudges and in her mind nothing was ever her fault. She hated Buzz Martin because he told Tatum about her after the fire ten years ago and aimed the investigation in her direction to keep it away from Cal Mulligan. Mulligan didn't support her when they questioned him—angry—grieving over his kids, maybe. Greg never really knew if she set that fire or not, but he believed she did."

"She didn't start yours? I thought she did."

"No, Greg confirmed that one, too. Tatum is the only person who could have started it, trying to frame Anne—or get me. He was really angry at me for *protecting* her."

"Is that what you were doing?"

"No. But that's how it looked to him." Jessie grinned. "He wasn't too pleased when I hit him either."

"But *Tatum*? He was a fireman—an investigator."

"MacDonald says it's not so big a step from fighting to lighting fires. Both firefighters and arsonists usually have some kind of fascination with it. Tatum's turned into an obsession.

"And, yeah, he set mine. He'd kept track of Anne for the last ten years—always knew where she was. Every once in a while she'd get a newspaper clipping in the mail about an arson in MatSu with a question mark penciled in the margin, and she'd know who'd sent them. He never let her forget. She came back to kill him—to finally get him off her back. Would have done it a long time ago, I guess, but Greg kept such a close watch on her that she couldn't. It's why they left Alaska. She finally got away, but he followed her, knowing where she'd go, and he tried to protect her. Even helped her meet me at the airport and make me think she'd just come in on a plane, so I'd buy her story. He thought she'd be okay with me. When Tatum burned my house it let her get away from both of us."

"He knew what she was capable of—had done—and stuck around all that time?"

"He loved her, Hank. Even when she tried her best to make him leave her—got beat up by other guys she was sleeping with and telling him about it—he cared."

"So she killed Tatum."

Jessie shook her head and was quiet for a moment. "No. Greg did that. He was afraid she'd get caught, so he did it for her. But he knew he couldn't live with it, so he set up the cabin fire. He meant them to die together. Then I came along and got in the way. He was sorry for that, too, but it had gone too far, so he just nailed up the door and would have taken his own life when he was sure it was over for Anne—and me. But we got out."

"What a mess. How'd Anne get so hung up on fire?"

Again, Jessie shrugged. "Who knows?"

But she was remembering what Greg Holman had told her before he died.

"She was haunted by fire—terrified but fascinated, too. When she set fires, *she* was in control of what terrified her. She had nightmares that woke her up screaming. I think she cut herself as sort of a prevention as well as a punishment—thought that, if she hurt *herself*, maybe the thing she was so afraid of wouldn't hurt her." Jessie sighed. Another memory she wouldn't mind not having.

"We're all afraid of something, Hank. Let's go home, before it gets dark."

He got up and looked around. "So—she'll *walk* up here, huh?"

She ignored him, except for a tolerant glance.

"You coming to Oscar's tomorrow for the ground breaking?"

"Of course. Did he tell you he's decided to call it 'The Night My Drink Caught Fire'? He even got permission from Bill Spear, the designer, who thought it was a hoot."

Peterson dumped a shovelful of snow on the coals that were left, carefully extinguishing every spark and stirring them to be sure the fire was out.

"I heard that," he said, with a mischievous grin. "But it'll be 'The Other Place' again in a couple of months."

"Yeah—I know."

Acknowledgments

With sincere thanks to:

Greg MacDonald, fire investigator for the Fire Prevention Division of Anchorage Fire Department, for generous information and assistance on the technical details of arson.

Bridget Bushue, for the loan of her fire boots.

Susan Desinger, at the Forks Roadhouse, Mile 18.7 Petersville Road, Trapper Creek, for information on the Peters Creek area of the Susitna Valley.

Marcia Colson, at the Loussac Public Library, for help in my attempt to identify the Peters for which Peters Creek, Petersville, Peters Hills, Little Peters Hills, Peters Dome, Peters Glacier, Peters Pass, and Peters Bench were named. William John Peters was a topographer and explorer in charge of USGS exploration in Alaska from 1898 to 1901. At least Peters Glacier, north of Mount McKinley, was named for him in 1902 by Alfred Hulfe Brooks (for whom the Brooks Range is named). There is an indication, however, that Peters Creek, which lies on the south side of the mountain, may have been named in 1906 for an otherwise nameless prospector.

Mark Pfeffer, for sharing Susitna Valley snowmachine tales, sublime to hair-raising. More *powder* to you, Mark.

Jeff Baldwin, supervisor of technical services, MTA Solutions, for information about Iridium Satellite telephones and their use.

Barbara Hedges, for information on the wonderful birds of the Alaskan winter.

Bear Claw, at Great Northern Guns, for information on the Winchester Model 70 Pre 64 rifle, its 30.06-caliber ammunition, and the sentimental value it might hold.

And Sue Hilton for being such a great friend.

Turn the page for a chilling excerpt from
Sue Henry's next Alaska Mystery

DEAD NORTH

Available now wherever books are sold

Craig Severson was soaked to the skin, cold, and thoroughly tired of riding in the rain by the time he let his loaded bicycle and trailer coast down the access road from the highway to the Kiskatinaw Provincial Park and found an empty space in which to set up his one-man tent, eat yet another cold sandwich, and crawl into his sleeping bag for the night. Maybe starting off to travel the Alaska Highway this early in the year hadn't been such a good idea after all. If it didn't stop pouring water over him soon, by the time he reached Fort Nelson to meet up with his cycling partner, he would be ready to pack it in and go home to Prince George, preferably not on two wheels.

In three days of peddling, he had worked hard for mileage on narrow roads with many hills, crossed the Rockies at Pine Pass on the second day, and camped twice, the last time at East Pine Provincial Park near Chetwynd. But most of it had been done in some amount of rain and even when it wasn't raining it had been so overcast and damp that nothing ever quite dried out. His sleeping bag was only slightly clammy, wrapped carefully in plastic, but he did not relish the idea of getting back into it. Rain—he hated rain. And, worst of all, today there had been a head wind that drove it constantly into his face. His back ached and he could feel the tension in his neck, shoulders, and arms from leaning forward, trying to keep from being blinded by the water, but forced to raise his head enough to see where he was going.

Waterproof rain gear kept sweat in as effectively as it kept rain out, and clothing worn under it while riding was soon soaked. Instead he wore partially waterproof shells without the slicker and let them get wet. Usually peddling kept him warm enough as long as he kept moving. He kept clean clothes in large plastic bags, zipped tight to keep them dry, but he had now worn everything but a single cotton T-shirt. Should have stopped in Dawson Creek, he thought regretfully, but hadn't wanted to take the time to find a laundromat, then wait for his few clothes to wash and dry. Stripping off his skin tight poly-shirt, he hurriedly pulled on the dry T-shirt and a rain slicker over it.

Dragging the tent, wet from last night, from the trailer, he began to work with cold hands to set it up. Everything was heavier when wet and the tent was no different. It stuck together as he opened it and sagged slightly on its supports when he finally had it secured. Into it he tossed a self-inflating air mattress and the sleeping bag. Slightly damp or not, it was all he had and would be warmer than nothing, if not particularly comfortable.

Weighing in one hand the sandwich he had made

and put into a plastic bag at noon, a can of vegetable soup in the other, he considered the difficulties of heating soup on his Whisperlight stove in the confines of the tent. He longed for something hot to help warm him up and wished he had heated it and filled his metal thermos at lunch time. But getting out the stove, putting it together, pumping to pressurize, then lighting it, was suddenly more than his tired mind and body would accept.

In the space just across the campground road from him was a motor home with its coach lights still on. Though the curtains were drawn and the blinds closed, he had seen a woman looking out in his direction a few minutes earlier. Closing the trailer cover and saddlebags, he took the soup and sandwich, reticence overcome by the idea of something hot to eat, and walked quickly across the road to knock on the door before he could change his mind.

Jessie, startled from her reading by the knock, got up to answer it, Tank by her side. Turning on the exterior light and peering out, she saw the cyclist from across the road and opened the door to see what he wanted. He was wearing a yellow slicker and was tall enough so that, though he stood below her on the ground, he didn't have to look up very far to meet her questioning assessment. With his can of soup and sandwich, he reminded her of a small boy with an empty bowl, out of some Dickinsonian orphanage.

"Hi," she said and couldn't help smiling.

He was shivering slightly without the exertion of peddling to keep him warm. "I was just wondering if I could beg the use of your stove long enough to heat this soup and some water to wash in. I know it's an im-position, but . . ."

He looked harmless enough and clearly in need of warmth of some kind. Jessie made a quick decision and interrupted. "Why not? Come on in." She moved back to give him room to come up the two steps, closing the door behind him.

"Hey, I really appreciate this." He set the can of soup on the table and held out a cold, wet hand. "I'm Craig Severson."

Jessie introduced herself and Tank, wiped her damp hand on her jeans, and picked up the soup. "I'll have this hot in a minute or two."

"I can do it. Just loan me a can opener and a pan."

"Already got it covered. There's hot water, soap, and a towel in the bathroom. Go ahead and wash. You'll feel better—and warmer."

"Thanks," he sighed gratefully, stripped off the rain slicker, and went to do as instructed.

When he returned, combing his wet hair back with his fingers, scrubbed face glowing, Jessie had already poured the steaming vegetable soup into a bowl on the table, set a hot cup of tea next to it, and was in the process of making a toasted cheese sandwich. Some of the grapes from the Jasper market and an apple lay close by in a bowl.

"Help yourself," she told him. "This's almost done."

Carefully laying the dry side of the slicker over the bench cushion, Severson sat down and started hungrily on the soup.

By the time he had finished eating everything but the apple, thanking her more than once, and was working on a second cup of tea, Jessie knew all about his planned trip. But she wasn't surprised when the hot food and warmth of the motor home began to make him sleepy.

"Sorry," he said after a particularly large yawn. "It's been a long day."

"Come for some hot coffee in the morning," she invited him, as he pulled the slicker back on and stepped out the door.

"Thanks again," he told her. "I won't say no to that, if you're sure you don't mind."

"Not at all."

Back in the tent, Severson shed his clothes, wriggled into the clammy bag with a shiver as its chill came in contact with his skin, and turned off the flashlight. His body heat slowly warmed the bag as he drowsily considered tomorrow's ride, which would, with a little luck, take him to Wonowon, maybe farther. In three days he would be in Fort Nelson, where he and his partner Leo would reconsider the wisdom of such an early trip to Alaska. Yes, they certainly would.

Rolling onto one side, he rubbed at his aching neck, moved his feet into the warmer corner of the bag, and gradually slid off into sleep.

The rain had all but stopped again when a thunderous pounding on the door of the Winnebago woke Jessie from a dream of desert country. Zipping jeans on under the oversized T-shirt she wore to bed, she turned on the galley light, and padded barefoot to join an already alert Tank and answer it.

"Who is it?" she asked, cautiously, considering the pepper spray.

"Severson," his familiar voice called in a decidedly desperate tone. "Do you have a cell phone? There's a guy badly hurt under the bridge."

Flipping on the exterior light, Jessie opened the door to find the cyclist, once again in his yellow slicker, eyes were full of anxiety. She motioned him in.

"What's wrong?"

"Somebody fell off the bridge and he's on the rocks down there—hurt real bad. Do you have a cell phone? There's an RCMP detachment in Dawson Creek and they *gotta* get somebody out here."

Astonished and horrified at the thought of anyone taking such a fall, Jessie shook her head. She had considered bringing her cell phone, but knew that for most of the wilderness parts of the trip it would be out of range and unusable. Close to any town it was doubtful that she'd need it anyway.

"Even if I had one, it wouldn't work down here in the gorge, would it?" she asked. "The campground people should have a phone—you know that cabin up nearer the bridge?"

"*Where?* It was dark when I came in." So agitated and upset he could hardly stand still, he started back out the door. "Where it is? *Tell me.*"

"It's easier to show you." Grabbing her raincoat and stuffing her feet into running shoes, Jessie tied them quickly, jumped outside, leaving Tank behind, and headed off at a run, Severson trotting at her side.

"What happened? How could someone fall off in the middle of the night?" she asked him between deep breaths of cool, damp air.

"Don't know. Might have been drunk, I guess. But . . ."

"What was he doing up there?"

"Don't know. I was going to the head when I heard a car on the bridge and then he fell—or jumped. I guess he could have jumped. I didn't see it—just heard . . . Dammit, I heard him hit—the rocks. I saw . . ." Severson stammered, shuddering as he remembered.

"You went down to look?"

"Yeah—kept hoping it might be garbage someone had tossed off—but I knew it wasn't. He made a sound on the way down. Garbage doesn't scream. Oh, God." Without warning, Severson turned aside, stopped and bent over to vomit into the brush by the road. "He's dead," he managed to get out, between convulsions. "I saw."

He was—very. If he had hit the water of the river, shallow, but running fairly high from late thaw and rain, the man might have had a chance. But the body lay on the rocky bank under the northern end of the bridge and there was no doubt at all that he had died instantly, his head horribly crushed, face first, against one of the large, rounded boulders that lay half buried in the muddy bank. Jessie's stomach contracted in nausea, but she swallowed hard at the taste of acid in her throat and managed to keep from losing it by walking a few steps away, while she, Severson, and the couple that were caretakers for the campground waited for the authorities to arrive.

What gave her the sick shakes was finding that there was no chance this person had made a suicidal leap, or fallen accidentally. His wrists and ankles were tightly bound with duct tape. Someone had intentionally dropped him over the bridge railing, for he could not have climbed it himself.

After cursorily checking the body for any sign of life, the caretakers went back up to the road to await and direct the police, but Jessie and the cyclist stayed nearby the body in an unspoken agreement that, whoever he was, he shouldn't be left alone, even—perhaps, especially—in death. Jessie stayed partly because she didn't want Severson, distressed and shivering, to be alone either.

Neither of them said much as they waited. He didn't seem to want to talk and the details of what he had heard, then found, could wait for the police. Jessie sat near him on a log, a dozen feet from the body, backs turned to death, keeping silent company while he nervously, and uncharacteristically for a cyclist, smoked cigarette after cigarette, carefully depositing the scorched filters in his slicker pocket, shivered, and stared out blindly across the dark waters of the river.

The image of what she had seen would not leave her mind. After awhile, she got up and walked back to shine her flashlight on the still form spread-eagled on the rocks, to make sure of what she thought she had seen and to prove, or disprove, a horrible suspicion that was slowly growing. In the beam of light she could see that the dead man was wearing jeans, hiking boots, and a black windbreaker jacket. The hood of the jacket had flopped forward over the uncrushed back of the head. Heart pounding, she hunkered down next to the body, cautiously reached and, slowly, holding her breath with anxiety and dread, lifted the edge of the hood just enough to see the color of the hair it covered.

Brown. Oh, thank God, it was brown—not the red she had been terrified she would find. It was *not* Patrick Cutler. A gasp of relief escaped her and tears flooded her eyes till everything blurred as she released the fabric and stumbled back to her feet.

"What?" Severson asked without turning.

"Nothing." She started to turn and walk back to where he sat, but something new caught her eye.

Separate from all the bright blood that had run down over the wet rock and soaked into the damp sandy ground, on the collar of the black windbreaker was another bit of brilliant red—a tiny maple leaf pin. Hand to her throat as it contracted, she stared at it.

This person wasn't Patrick, was it? But he was not just clad in similar clothes—the jacket on the body *was* Patrick's. The realization was so appalling that she couldn't mentally process it, could do nothing but gape down at the pin in confusion and disbelief. When she couldn't look anymore, she sat back down next to Severson and tried her best to think rationally.

It didn't make sense. How could Patrick's windbreaker be on some stranger and why? He was supposedly traveling alone. Could this be one of the men who had been looking for him? Would they have switched jackets? No, not only jackets—weren't the boots also similar to Patrick's? The combination too unique to be a coincidence, wasn't it, and the pin was the clincher? She could not imagine a circumstance that would explained it, but there were a lot of things she didn't understand, that she was beginning to question.

Had Patrick really been who he said he was? A driver's license could be fake, or stolen. What was she going to do with the disjointed pieces of information that were churning out more questions than answers? None of it sounded credible, even to her. How could Patrick Cutler be involved with this death—this *murder*? She made herself call it what it was. Could this cyclist, Craig Severson, who said he had *found* the body, be involved somehow? She really didn't think so, but if the dead man had screamed loud enough to be heard on the campground road, why hadn't the caretakers heard it, too? Had they been asleep, as she had been, and not heard it? That was possible, of course—especially since their house was higher on the hill and thickly surrounded by trees. Or could they be involved? Suddenly everyone was suspect. It all went round in a confusing mix of thoughts that made her stomach turn over again.

Jessie put her head into her hands, elbows on her knees, and gave up, trying not to think about any of it, but not being able to get rid of any of it. For a long time she and Severson sat, still and silent, until, at least she heard the faint wail of a siren and raised her head to listen, thankfully.

It was beginning to grow light in the east, and that hint of dawn was just enough to reflect from the ripples and eddies and make the river visible, when the Royal Canadian Mounted Police arrived, with an ambulance close behind. Five men came clambering hurriedly from the dark shadows between the trees of the campground and down to the river's edge, two of them bearing a stretcher and medical cases, which Jessie knew they wouldn't need.

While the two RCMP constables with flashlights examined the body, the area around it, and the top of the bridge, for clues, Jessie sat listening, while the inspector in charge, one William Webster, wearing a dark raincoat, a small, clear eyed and watchful man with large hands, took Severson through an account of what he had witnessed and made brief jottings in a small notebook that the growing daylight just allowed him to make out.

"You didn't *see* anyone—just heard them?"

Severson nodded numbly. "Right. I was going to the head, when I heard the car . . ."

"How do you know it was a car?"

"Well, an engine, then. From where I was hearing it—down on the campground road—it might have been a pickup, but it wasn't a heavy engine. I can tell, because I hear a lot of different kinds on the road as they pass me on my bike."

Inspector Webster scribbled in his notebook, then looked up and asked attentively. "Then what happened?"

"I could hear the rumble of the tires on the planks go part of the way across the bridge—then it stopped, but the motor was still running. There was nothing for a minute or two, then I heard . . ." His voice thickened and he sat up straighter as if to brace himself for the rest. "I heard him scream as he fell. It was awful. It startled me so much I stopped walking to listen, and then—then I heard him hit the rocks."

"Did you hear the vehicle leave?"

"Yeah—it went on across the bridge and up the north access road till I couldn't hear it anymore. I went down to the river under the bridge. You know—to see if I could do anything, but . . ." He waved a hand toward the body in mute explanation.

There was a moment of silence, while Webster jotted in the notebook.

"You didn't touch or move him?"

"No. It was obvious there wouldn't be—ah—a pulse. His head was all—broken. I went back up—for help—to find a phone."

"Did you know this man? Had you ever seen him before?"

"No—I don't think so. You can't—really tell, can you?"

"But you didn't recognize anything about him?"

"No."

"How about you, miss? Did you recognize him?" Webster turned to Jessie, who was glad to be able to honestly also say, "No," as well. Just answer what he asks you, she told herself, remembering past advice. Don't volunteer. Still, not telling him that she had recognized the coat bothered her. She would have told an Alaska state trooper, but this wasn't a trooper, or Alaska. However close to Alaska, or the Lower Forty-eight, it was a foreign country and she didn't know this man—or whether she could trust him.

"Did you hear him fall?"

"No," again. "I was asleep."

She told him about waking up to Severson's frantic pounding on her door, their trip to the caretaker's cabin, and from there to the river bank. Still conflicted, she hesitated about the coat and the pin—then it seemed too late. She knew she would have trouble trying to explain what she knew and how she knew it—that it would complicate everything and might not help—so she kept her knowledge to herself, wondering if she would regret it.

"Did you two know each other before this?"

They shook their heads and Severson explained that they were camping in spaces across from each other.

"So neither of you has any idea who this might be?"

They shook their heads.

"Anything else you can tell me?" He gave each of them a level, searching look, one that lingered a second or two on Jessie.

"No? Well, then . . ."

The inspector took both their names, checked their identification, and asked detailed questions about where they were going and how long they would be in Canada, before sending them back to the campground. Letting them know that he could locate them by notifying the RCMP on up the highway, he said he would not delay their travel, then asked them both to check with a post in a day or two, in case he needed more information.

But when Jessie glanced back, as she left the rocky part of the river bank and went into the trees, she saw Inspector William Webster still sitting on a rock next to the log, staring after them, thoughtfully, with his notebook on his knee.

At the Winnebago, she found she had neglected to lock the door, but hadn't the mental energy to be concerned, knowing that Tank, who met everyone at the door, would have repelled any intruder with barks and growls. He had never bitten anyone in his life, but no stranger would know that.

At her suggestion, Craig Severson followed her inside and sat slumped, staring, wordless, at the table, while she turned on the furnace to warm the place up and quickly made a pot of coffee. Filling two mugs, she sugared them liberally, and poured a stiff slug of brandy into each one before sitting down across from him.

They drank the first mug in silence. Jessie was beginning to be concerned about him when, accepting a refill, he finally looked up with an inquisitive expression.

"You saw something you recognized down there, didn't you? What?"

"Nothing," Jessie told him. "For a minute, I thought it might have been someone I knew—but it wasn't."

"Why did you think it was?"

"Just a mistake in the dark." If she hadn't told the inspector what she knew, she certainly wasn't going to tell anyone else, especially a stranger.

Inspector William Webster remained sitting on the rock by the river for a long time after he sent the two witnesses back to the Kiskatinaw campground, writing once or twice in his notebook, mentally organizing his impressions of the interviews. Focused on his own deliberation, he scarcely noticed the flashlight beams of his men, on the bridge and around the body below it, as they grew paler and less distinct in the increasing dawn light, though, as usual, he was aware of everything around him and recording it separately for later reference. The watery rush of the river beside him covered any sounds his men made and left him alone with his thoughts.

His efficient second in command eventually came down from the bridge to report scuff marks on the railing that could have come from the boot soles of the victim. Placed as they were, they indicated that a struggle had probably taken place—resistance that could prove he had been alive when he was lifted over and dropped. These marks would have to be retrieved and held as evidence, and Webster assigned him the responsibility.

"Tire marks?"

"Nothing identifiable."

"Anything to identify the vic?"